Th...

SUMMA
ELVETICA:

A Casuistry
— of the —
Elvish
Controversy

MARCHER
LORD
PRESS

SUMMA ELVETICA: A CASUISTRY OF THE ELVISH CONTROVERSY by Theodore
Beale
Published by Marcher Lord Press
8345 Pepperridge Drive
Colorado Springs, CO 80920
www.marcherlordpress.com

MARCHER LORD PRESS and the MARCHER LORD PRESS logo are trade-
marks of Marcher Lord Press. Absence of ™ in connection with marks of Marcher
Lord Press or other parties does not indicate an absence of trademark protection
of those marks.

Cover Designer: Kirk DouPonce, Dog-Eared Design, www.dogeareddesign.com

Cover Illustrator: Kirk DouPonce
Creative Team: Jeff Gerke, Pat Reinheimer

Library of Congress Cataloging-in-Publication Data
An application to register this book for cataloging has been filed with the Library
of Congress.
International Standard Book Number: 978-0-9821049-2-7

To the young author and the pretty princesses

PROOEMIUM

Quaeritur de Aelvi per comparationem ad homines. Primo, utrum Aelvi habeant anima naturaliter sibi unita. Secundo, utrum assumant gloria. Tertio, utrum in gloribus assumptis occupant opera vita aeterna.

MARCUS VALERIUS LOOKED up from the faded Numidican manuscript in irritation.

The light from the study window was growing dim. Already he'd been forced to light a candle in order to make out the obscure scratchings of the historian Quintus the Elder, whose colorful accounts of his encounters with the pagan desert tribes were as dubious as they were vivid. The imperative knocking at the door threatened a lengthy interruption, one that might cost Marcus what little daylight remained.

"Come in," he called, resigned.

The latch creaked, and a familiar, sun-bronzed face peered around the corner of the door. It belonged to his cousin Sextus, whose brown eyes were dancing with mischief.

"This better be good," Marcus warned him. "I was just getting to the part where the tribal chief is about to sacrifice the centurion to his devil-gods."

Sextus nodded absently. "Oh, yes, you said you were going to read up on old Quintus, didn't you? Well, if it'll save you some time, I'll tell you how it ends. The legions march in, the heathen see the error of their ways, and the great city-state of Amorr triumphs over all. Hallelujah and amen!"

Marcus stared at him and, with some difficulty, rejected the first three responses that leaped to mind. "Thank you, Sexto. Your help is . . . beyond words. Now, go away, please."

His cousin grinned back at him. Maddeningly, he did not leave, but rather folded his arms and leaned against the edge of the entryway.

Sexto was half a hand shorter than Marcus, but with a slim build that made him appear taller than he was. Like Marcus and the rest of their family, his eyes were dark brown, but he was no scholar, and his skin was deeply bronzed by the sun. He wore a plain white *tunica* devoid of any equestrian stripes. He was barefoot, and his belt was an unadorned strip of worn leather. Besides the intrinsic arrogance that radiated from him like heat from a fire, only the finely carved silver buckle clasping the belt showed any sign that he was a senator's son, let alone a Valerian.

"Don't you want to know why I'm here?"

"To plague me?" Marcus guessed. "To keep me from my learning?"

Sextus steepled his hands and did his best to appear pious. The effect would have worked better if he had stopped smirking first. "I'm here in my priestly capacity, believe it or not. The Father Superior sent me with a message for you. You're to go before the Sanctiff."

"What?" Marcus was sure he hadn't heard correctly. "I'm supposed to go where?"

"To the Sanctiff," Sextus repeated. "Yes, you, and right away too. Father Aurelius is already on his way here—he's to escort you to the palace." He grinned and arched his eyebrows. "Now tell me what you did to get in that kind of trouble, Marco! Did I miss out on something?"

Marcus swallowed hard. This wasn't just impossible, it was beyond imagining. The Holy Sanctiff was the highest ranking official in the land since Amorr had no king. Officially, the Lord God Himself ruled over the Republic. However, as the earthly head of the Amorran Church, the Sanctiff was God's voice and viceroy from the banks of the Tiburon to the shores of the Rialthan Sea.

Marcus had no idea why the viceroy of God Almighty wanted to see him. No idea at all.

The Holy Palace was the greatest structure in Amorr, as was only fitting. It boasted twelve spires ringing one massive cupola, a representation in marble of mankind's Savior and His twelve disciples. Marcus, with Father Aurelius by his side, was being escorted into it by the palace's hard-faced soldiers with their red cloaks.

To Marcus's relief they did not march him into the Hall of Judgment. That place was dreaded by every sane and sober Amorran. He had first feared they were taking him there to stand before some inquest. Instead, the guards conducted them to what appeared to be a small, private antechamber just off one of the palace's central corridors.

The room was dark, lit only by seven guttering rushlights. It was cool, but not cold, and two of the stucco walls were obscured with wooden shelves that held fat scrolls of various lengths. Marcus couldn't see the back wall behind the lights, but he stopped looking about the room when his eyes alighted upon an elderly man sitting alone in its center.

His Holiness was reclining on an unimposing, leather-wrapped chair that looked as comfortable as it was worn with age. He wore none of the trappings of his awesome office, only the simple blue robe of a Jamite brother. The robe was darker than his cerulean eyes, which were encased by thin folds of sagging flesh and surmounted by a pair of bushy white eyebrows. But he smiled warmly at his visitors, and Marcus could easily have thought of him as someone's good-humored *paterfamilias* were it not for the gem-encrusted ring of office adorning his left hand.

"Thank you for coming, Father Aurelius." The Sanctiff's voice was deep, but to hear it up close in this small room instead of echoing off the marble of the palace steps made it seem more friendly than intimidating. "I have received excellent reports of your work with the junior scholastics. And welcome, Marcus Valerius. I wished to see with my own eyes the latest prodigy of the Valerian House. Perhaps you shall do for the Church what your illustrious forebears have done for Amorr's legions, hmmm?"

Marcus blushed before the Sanctiff's praise. It was as if the old man had seen into his mind and read his deepest, most hidden desires. "Thank you, your Holiness. I seek only to serve God and Amorr, to the best of my small abilities."

The Sanctiff's aged lips wrinkled in a wry smile, and he glanced toward the shadowy corner of the room. "Admirably courteous, is he not? I should think any concerns regarding his comportment are groundless. Don't you agree, Caecilus Cassius?"

Marcus drew in a sharp breath as a thin-faced man in a black robe emerged from the darkness, accompanied by a cheerful-looking Jamite priest in the blue robe of his order.

Marcus knew the man whom His Holiness addressed so familiarly. Or rather, he knew of him. Caecilus Cassius Claudo was the Bishop of Avienne and one of the Church's leading intellectuals. His famous treatise, the *Summa Spiritus,* written on all the diverse races of Selenoth and their distinct places in the Will of God, had sparked a raging flame of debate that still roared through every scholastic circle in the Republic. Marcus himself had written a short commentary on the *Summa* less than a year ago.

"That remains to be seen, your Holiness." Claudo's arid voice was acerbic and high-pitched. "Certainly, a number of his expressed opinions are impudent in the extreme."

"Oh, come now, Claudo," the Jamite broke in, laughing. His round face was ruddy, and Marcus liked him immediately. "A refusal to abase himself before your lofty eminence does not indicate an inclination toward boorish behavior. Why, it's nothing more than a sign of sheer good sense!"

He smiled broadly, making it clear that he was only teasing his proud colleague, then graciously inclined his head toward Marcus and Father Aurelius. "Since His Holiness does not see fit to introduce us, I shall take the matter in hand myself. I am Quintus Servilius Aestus, a humble priest in service to the Lord Immanuel and, of course, His Holiness. My distinguished colleague is none other than His Excellency, the Bishop of Avienne, whose work I believe you know quite well."

Father Aestus shook their hands warmly, first Father Aurelius's, then Marcus's own. Marcus was in awe, for he was truly in the presence of greatness—not once, not twice, but three times over. Father Aestus was one of the few intellectuals who dared to publicly cross wits with the famed bishop, and he was rumored to be working on his own magnum opus in opposition to Cassius Claudo's masterpiece.

The Sanctiff cleared his throat, and Father Aestus smoothly effaced himself, but not before directing a disconcerting wink at Marcus.

"Father Aurelius, you know why I have summoned you," the Sanctiff stated, "and your presence here answers the question I posed to you earlier. However, Bishop Claudo and Father Aestus have their own questions for your young scholar, and with your permission, I would allow them to inquire of him."

"Of course, your Holiness," Father Aurelius replied obediently. He was an astute man and did not need to be told when his presence was not required. "May I have your permission to withdraw, your Holiness?"

"Go with God, Father," the Sanctiff said, extending his left hand. "And the grace of our living Lord be upon you."

Father Aurelius bent over and kissed the sacerdotal ring of office, then gave Marcus a reassuring pat on the shoulder as he left the room. Marcus suddenly felt alone and intimidated, surrounded as he was by three of the republic's most formidable minds.

Bishop Claudo's dry voice broke in on his thoughts. "Marcus Valerius, I have read your commentary on the *Summa Spiritus*. It is . . . not without merit. But when you say that one does not know, indeed, that one is not even capable of knowing, whether a particular form or being possesses an immortal soul, are you not treading perilously near a concept that could easily be construed as heresy? Or is this passage nothing more than the sophomoric pedantry of a young scholar who has manufactured a reason to doubt the immutable fact of his own existence?"

Marcus gulped. Claudo was cutting straight to the point. Are you a heretic or a fool, boy? That was the real question being posed to him now. The Church didn't burn heretics at the stake anymore, but nevertheless he knew he had to be very careful about what he said next. He closed his eyes and thought quickly before answering.

"Only a philosopher or a fool doubts his own existence, Excellency," he said. "It is true, however, that the two all too often prove to be one and the same. I assert that I am neither. The verb 'to know' contains a number of interpretations, and in the sentence of which I believe you are speaking, I made use of the concept in its most concrete sense, the sense in which a thing is proven beyond any reasonable possibility of doubt. As in the case, for example, of a mathematical equation."

Marcus paused. Was that a frown clouding over the Sanctiff's face? He shook his head, took a deep breath, and tried to clarify his meaning.

"Your Excellency, as you know, where there is surety, there is no faith, no belief, per se. And therefore, knowledge of the soul rightly belongs in the realm of faith, not mathematics." He placed his right hand over his heart. "Do I have a soul? Yes, I believe so, with all my heart. But regardless of my faith, it is either so or it is not, as the Castrate wrote so wisely. My personal belief does not have the capacity to dictate the truth. Indeed, before the eternal truth of the almighty God, my own humble opinion is of no account."

Into the silence that followed, Claudo finally snorted and his eyes narrowed, but he did not speak. Father Aestus looked as if he were about to burst out laughing.

The Sanctiff smiled. "He has you there, Claudo. Unless you did not apprise me of a divine revelation, all your wonderfully conclusive eloquence remain just that—eloquence."

Claudo shrugged. "It is so. And yet decisions must be made, though the decision makers be fallible." He regarded Marcus coldly and stepped back into the shadows.

Marcus stared at the carpeted floor, chagrined. He wondered what was wrong with his answer and hoped he hadn't greatly offended the acerbic ecclesiastic.

"I too have a question for the young scholar," Father Aestus announced. His green eyes danced impishly. "Do you ride?"

"Do I . . . Horses?" Marcus asked, taken aback.

"I wasn't thinking of cows," the priest replied tartly.

"Yes, oh, yes. Of course."

Every Amorran nobleman rode, especially those of the Valerian house. Marcus wondered what kind of trap was being laid for him now. It just didn't make any sense.

"I have no further questions, your Eminence."

Father Aestus bowed theatrically to the Sanctiff and joined Bishop Claudo behind the makeshift Sanctal throne.

Marcus was thoroughly confused now. At this point he wouldn't have been surprised if the Sanctiff suddenly leaped out of his chair and demanded that he demonstrate an ability to juggle apples.

"I anticipate no objections, then?" the Sanctiff asked the two Churchmen.

"None at all," Father Aestus said cheerfully. Bishop Claudo slowly shook his head in silence.

"Very well." A smile creased the Sanctiff's lined face, and he leaned toward Marcus. "I realize this has been a little unusual for you, my son. But I have a problem, you see, and you, Marcus Valerius, are going to help me solve it."

"Me?" Marcus shook his head. "How could I help you, your Holiness?"

"Let me tell you about my problem first. You see, these illustrious jewels in the crown of the Church," he nodded toward Claudo and Aestus, "have each penned a marvelous work on man and his place in this world. The *Summa Spiritus* you have read. The *Ordo Selenus Sapiens* you have not, though Father Aestus will no doubt be interested in what you might have to say about it. In many points they are in agreement, but on one very important point they are at variance. It is that particular point which I would like you to help me settle."

Marcus nodded. "I am yours to command, your Holiness. But what is this point of contention, and how could I ever help you settle it?"

The Sanctiff sighed wearily. "I am an old man, Marcus Valerius, and my days of seeing through this glass darkly will soon come to an end. I am sending a party to Elebrion, you see, but I fear I would not survive the trip. Therefore you, my son, shall accompany Bishop Claudo and the good Father in my stead."

Marcus put his hand over his mouth. Now he understood what the Sanctiff had in mind, and the sobering realization of terrible responsibility hit him like a blow to the stomach.

"By the blood of the martyrs," he cried despite himself. "You're going to decide if the elves have souls!"

Iᴬ Q. VII A. I ARG. I

Videtur quod aelvi habeant animae naturaliter sibi unita. Dicitur enim Gen. II, Deus hominem de limo terrae, et inspiravit in faciem eius spiraculum vitae, et factus est homo in animam viventem. Sed ille qui spirat, aliquid a se emittit. Ergo anima qua homo vivit, est aliquid de substantia Dei. Subsistentes cum aelvi, et diversi homini, non acciperunt substantiam Dei ab Deo. Ergo aelvi habent animae naturaliter sibi unita.

T HE LAST VESTIGES of the setting sun had long since disappeared by the time the small troop of crimson-cloaked Redeemed escorted Marcus past the gate of his uncle's domus.

By day, Amorr belonged to God. But its night was claimed by the worst of His creations. Peril lurked in far too many shadows of the narrow, high-walled, circuitous streets called *vici*. Even a mounted nobleman born to horse and sword could find himself beaten, stripped, and, if fortunate, merely robbed by the cruel gangs of half-human breeds and bandits who ravaged the city by night.

Still, even the most lawless of brigands feared crossing the path of the Redeemed, the most fanatical of the Church's militias. The Redeemed were former gladiators, now rehabilitated—hardened men of violence who had chosen to leave the bloodstained sands of the Coliseum behind them. Slaves they had been and slaves they were still, but they served a different Master now.

Marcus was not entirely comfortable in their hulking, creaking, red-cloaked presence, but he appreciated their company in the darkness of the Amorran night. As they neared the estate, slaves from the household swarmed around Marcus's horse.

He inclined his head politely toward the troop's commander. "My thanks, Captain. A good evening to you and your men."

The captain saluted grimly, bringing his fist to his chest, without a hint of personality crossing his scarred, sun-weathered face. He showed no sign of interest in either Marcus or his House. He'd done his duty, nothing more. "Glory to God, sir."

Without another word, the ex-gladiator turned his mount around in a swirl of crimson and horsestink. The five Redeemed riders followed him, torches held high, returning confidently into the noisome shadows of the city.

Marcus watched them go, fascinated. He wondered what it would be like to be such a man. To be so sure, so secure in one's faith—surely that was a wonderful thing! And yet, what was a man's mind for, if not to use it?

It was another question to ponder, but far less pressing than the one that looked to have him departing on the morning following the morrow. Marcus sighed and dismounted, waving aside the proffered hands of a tall slave offering him assistance. He affectionately patted the soft, fleshy nose of his big grey, a magnificent steed named Barat, before handing the reins over to another slave, this one young, olive-skinned, and thin. But human.

Like most patrician families, it was beneath the dignity of House Valerius to own half-breeds or inhumans. This slave looked familiar. He wore the blue badge of the stables, but for the life of him Marcus couldn't remember his name.

"What are you called?" he asked the young slave.

"Deccus, Maester Maercuss," the boy replied in heavily accented Amorran, not meeting Marcus's eyes as he carefully stroked Barat's ears.

Marcus nodded. Now he remembered. The boy was a Bethnian, one of the lot purchased by his uncle's head steward at the spring auction. Erasto had bought twenty-five or thirty. Bethnians were absurdly inexpensive now, thanks to Pontius Balbus's crushing of a rebellion in that province the year before. But they knew their horses well. Barat would be in good hands with this boy.

"Then please take good care of him tonight, Deccus, and tomorrow as well," Marcus instructed. "It seems I've a journey ahead of me, and he must be fit for the riding."

The slave nodded, and a faint smile crossed his lips at the sound of his name. The Valerian slaves were treated no worse than most and better than some, but the stables were a rough place for a youngster to serve. Marcus knew it could have easily been months since Deccus was last addressed by anything but a curse. The use of the boy's name might be a small enough kindness, but it counted for something. At least, Marcus hoped that it did.

• • •

Rumor spread faster than sickness in the slaves' quarters, so by the time Marcus entered the atrium Marcipor was already there waiting for him.

Marcipor, Marcus's bodyslave, was a handsome, broad-shouldered man of Savondese descent. He was the illegitimate offspring of an officer captured twenty-four years ago by his uncle. He and Marcus were of the same age, almost to the day.

It was obvious that Sextus had not kept the news of the Sanctiff's summons to himself, because Marcipor's blue eyes were alight with curiosity even as they carefully avoided meeting his own. His demeanor was proper today—far too proper, in fact—and Marcus stifled a smile as Marcipor gave an uncharacteristically elaborate bow as he offered Marcus a fresh tunic of light muslin to replace his dusty day-clothes.

"Why don't you just come right out and ask me?" Marcus wondered aloud as he held out his arms and let Marcipor assist him out of the sweat-stained tunic.

"This slave would not dream of such presumption, Master."

Marcus snorted. "Save it for the girls, pretty boy. My uncle should have sold you to the theater long ago. It's a pity Pylades didn't have you for a protégé."

Marcipor grinned and abandoned the servile pretense. He puffed his chest out and struck a dramatic stance. He was a striking young man, with a strong jaw and a close-cropped, golden beard. More than one slave girl living in the vicinity of the Valerian house had given birth to a fair-haired, blue-eyed baby after Marcipor had passed his sixteenth year.

"Indeed," he said, "I daresay I would have outshined Hylos. But you must tell me about this mysterious summons. Is it true you saw the Sanctiff himself? The whole domus has been utterly agog with rumor ever since you left with Father Aurelius! Sextus says they're going to ordain you early and make you a cardinal!"

"What?" Marcus burst out laughing as he donned a clean tunic. He knew a bishopric would soon be his for the taking. No noble, not even one with plebian blood, would expect anything less. And it was even possible that an archbishopric might be in the cards. But not even a scion of House Severus could hope to be crowned prince of the church before reaching thirty. "Sextus, as you so often inform me, is an idiot."

Marcus folded his arms, enjoying the feel of the fresh muslin against his skin A pity he hadn't the time to visit the baths before vesperna. "So, what's the bet?"

He was sure there was a stake involved somehow, for both his cousin and his slave were inveterate gamblers. Marcipor's coin-hoard far exceeded his own. In fact, more often than not he was in debt to his slave. Marcipor's rates were usurious, but paying them was easier than trying to extract money from his uncle's iron fists.

"The archbishopric, of course. Even your lily-white hands aren't clean enough for the lazulate. Which is a good thing, seeing how you're barely even a man yet and you've too much living to do before you seal yourself up in that white mausoleum for the rest of your life."

"You're lying, Marce. And if the bet is which one of you I'll tell first, well, you both lose. I can't tell you anything. In fact, I don't even know if I'll be free to talk to anyone when I return."

"Return . . . ? So you're going somewhere!" Marcipor's face grew calculating for a moment, but then his eyes widened with surprise. "Wait a minute, you can't go anywhere without me! Unattended? Your uncle would never hear of it! And if you think you're going to take that irresponsible lunatic of a cousin—"

Marcus held up a hand. "Peace, Marce." He yawned and shook his head. "Of course you're going with me. Assuming I go anywhere, that is, for I must ask Magnus's permission first. But you should probably start getting things together for a six-month journey tonight, because if we do leave, my understanding is that the Sanctiff intends we shall begin the day after tomorrow, and I can't imagine even Magnus would deny him. Now, leave me to attend him. It seems everyone in that 'white mausoleum' is too holy to bother with food anymore. I'm hungry enough to eat a boar."

Marcus found Magnus reclining in the triclinium, accompanied in his evening meal only by his three favorites.

The room was large, but stark, with no decorations on the white stuccoed walls to detract from the only furniture, a low, tiled table that filled the center of the room and couches on three sides. The colorful tiles told the story of Valerius, the founder of the house, and showed the wounded hero lying in a grove being tended by the wolf who licked his wounds and succored him until his triumphant and vengeful return to Amorr. Magnus often entertained a score or more of Amorr's great citizens here, senators and equestrians, but fortunately tonight he was as near to alone as Marcus was ever likely to find him.

Lucipor, a grey-bearded slave old enough to be Magnus's father, lay on the couch to his left. Dompor and Lazapor, the household's resident scholars, shared the couch on the right.

Marcus stood at the entrance while a young girl washed his feet. He could hear Lazapor raising his voice as he took issue with something his uncle had said.

"You underestimate them, Magnus," Lazapor said. "The villagemen seek no justice. They only slaver after power in the city! What you consider to be an open hand extended in a spirit of generosity, they see only as weakness. Make the mistake of allowing one snake into the Senate, and I assure you a thousand will soon squirm in behind him!"

Marcus entered barefoot. At the sound of his entrance, his uncle turned to him with what appeared to be relief. There was a rancorous tone to Lazapor's voice that indicated this evening's debate was not an entirely civil one. Marcus wondered at his uncle's habit of engaging in disputation while dining, and yet the custom had clearly not affected the great man's appetite. Lucius Valerius Magnus, ex-consul and senator, was great in many particulars. Not least among them was the impressive size of his paunch.

"I shall, as always, take your words under advisement," his uncle said to Lazapor. Marcus noted that he had gracefully evaded disclosing his own position on the matter. "Marcus, my dear lad, do come in and rescue me from these disagreeable scholars. Now, is it true that you were summoned to the Sanctorum, or has my son reverted to his childhood custom of telling fanciful tales?"

"Yes," Dompor said, "we have long expected miracles from you, Marcus, but you seem to have outdone yourself this time. Our darling Sextus is fond of saying that your piety is surpassed only by the *Mater Dei*. Are we correct in assuming that His Holiness has asked you to serve as his father confessor?"

Marcus usually enjoyed the humor to be found in Dompor's acerbic tongue, even when he was its target, but this was no time for such indulgences. He smiled faintly at the slave, then met his uncle's eyes. "I need to speak with you, uncle. Alone."

Magnus's greying eyebrows rose with surprise, and he raised his hand. Without a word, his three companions rose from the couches and departed. Lazapor seemed a little annoyed at the interruption, but Lucipor's face was marked with concern. Dompor, never one given to worry, appeared amused as he surreptitiously slipped a small bell from his tunic and placed it on the table. For it was not only unusual for the great man to banish all three of them from his domestic conclaves, it was almost unprecedented.

But Marcus's strange request did not seem to concern Magnus. He rose with an audible grunt of effort. "I don't recall any recent vacancies," he mused, stroking his chin. "Did Quintus Fulvius die already? I'd heard his see was likely to open soon."

"It's not a see, uncle. I haven't even decided to take the cloth yet."

"You haven't?"

"No, I haven't, truly," Marcus insisted, vaguely irritated that everyone else seemed so sure of his future when he himself had not come to a decision yet.

The heat of his denial seemed to amuse his uncle, but his amusement vanished as Marcus told him of the Sanctiff's intentions.

"You're going to Elebrion? *Sphincterus!* That blasted Ahenobarbus bids fair to open up a vat of worms with this notion. I can't imagine what possesses him to meddle with something that could threaten our northern border while we're already engaged to the east. Soak my foot, but he always did have a tendency to stick that wretched red beard of his wherever it's not wanted!"

Marcus blinked. He was unaccustomed to hearing His Holiness, the Sanctified Charity IV, forty-fourth Sanctiff of Amorr, described in such familiar and unflattering terms. Furthermore, the Sanctiff was not only clean-shaven, but his hair had been white as long as Marcus could remember. Red beard?

Marcus reached over and took a pair of figs from the bowl on the low table and popped one into his mouth, then took a deep breath and attempted to contradict his uncle. "I shouldn't think he's intending to do anything but learn more—"

"You're a scholar, Marcus, not a fool. Stop for a moment and think the matter through. Do you think the High King of the elves is so easily hoodwinked? I've fought with elves and I've fought against them, and I can tell you that if there's one thing they're not, it's fools, my boy. They're pretty enough, but there's steel underneath, lad—never forget it! And their blasted wizards have lived ten times longer than our oldest greybeard. Take it from me, Marcus—no one survives that long without learning something, no matter how stupid he might be to start.

"So, they'll know very well why you're there, and they'll know what's going to happen if those tonsured imbeciles in the Sanctorum completely lose what little remains of their common sense and decide that elves are nothing more than talking beasts."

The great man shook his head in dismay. "Considering what I always heard of King Caerwyn's court, I imagine he would've considered an infestation of monks preaching celibacy and the Church to be an act of war. Tarquin's tarnation! I suppose we can hope this new High King is cut from a different cloth."

Marcus waited patiently as his uncle glared at him as if he were a proxy for God's own viceroy. Despite this unexpected outburst, he still did not believe Magnus would bar him from the journey. There were too many potential advantages to be gained by his participation.

If Marcus took the cloth and was ordained, he would be permanently banned from holding a seat in the Senate. But political power was not the only one in Amorr worth wielding. Marcus's older brother was the politician of the family, having won election as one of the city's fifteen tribunes earlier this year. And his two older sisters had already provided his father with four members of the following generation, including three potential heirs.

Sexto, Marcus's mischievous cousin and Magnus's son, had two older brothers who were junior officers in the field serving under Marcus's father. A third brother had already successfully stood for tribune. So it was not as if the family were in dire need of another soldier or politician.

When Magnus finally spoke, he laid an avuncular hand on the boy's shoulder. "You're a good lad, Marcus. Even if Ahenobarbus is sticking his head in a hornet's nest, the opportunities that will likely present themselves to our house are promising. But be careful! There's more going on here than you can possibly imagine. Keep your eyes open, keep your wits about you, and don't let yourself get overly caught up in all that priestly disputation. Try to think about the world you're in before worrying too much about the one to come."

"Yes, Magnus."

"Now, go say good-bye to your mother, but don't tell her where you are going. Leave that to me. It will be hard on her, with Corvus gone."

"Yes, Magnus. Although I doubt she'll even notice I'm not here, not with Tertia's twins."

"There is that. I'll write to your father, lad. He must be apprised of these developments too. I don't know if he'll be terribly pleased, unfortunately, but I'll knock some sense into him. He expects you to follow in his footsteps, you know. But you were born to think, not brawl or bawl out legionnaires. Oh, and Marcus, you will tell Sextus that he is not to even think of tagging along after you. If he does so much as ride to the Pontus Rossus I'll have him lashed and halve his allowance for the next three moons."

Marcus grinned as he bowed respectfully, then reached for the bowl of fruit before departing. Sexto would brave a lashing if need be, but he'd never risk the coin.

"I'll tell him, Magnus. And thank you, sir. I shall not forget your advice."

Magnus pursed his lips as he watched his young nephew exit the triclinium, an apple in either hand. This news of Elebrion was an unforeseen and unwelcome development.

Should he have braved Ahenobarbus's displeasure and forbidden the old charlatan his nephew? He'd made much harder decisions than this before, given orders that had cost thousands of men their lives without hesitation or regret, and yet something about this one bothered him. Marcus was his brother's youngest son. In Corvus's absence, was there not something he could do to safeguard the lad?

The boy was trained, but he was no warrior. His bodyslave was no better: a lover, not a fighter. Perhaps Magnus could send a soldier along to safeguard Marcus. Able soldiers were easy to find, but with them it was discipline that counted most, not skill, and besides, they were taught to fight as a unit. One alone would be no help.

Perhaps a gladiator?

But gladiators were but men, and Magnus knew all too well the price of a man. What can be bought can always be bought once more by a more generous purse. And it wouldn't be only elves that would be interested in the buying.

Once word of the prospect of a Church-sanctioned holy war against the elves got out, every petty merchant with a load of tin or cattle skins to sell the legions would be pressing hard to get his fingers into the unending flow of coin that would erupt from the Senate. Worse, he knew very well that some of the more enterprising tradesmen were perfectly capable of taking it upon themselves to help the Sanctiff reach the decision that would be of the most benefit to them.

What sort of fighting man could not be bought by man or elf?

Magnus reached over, took the bell from the table, and shook it. The bronze clang had barely stopped when a servant came rushing into the room and nearly collided with him, taken by surprise at his presence out of his recliner.

"Find Lucipor," he commanded. "I want him now. And bring that fool of a son of mine too. He may be useful for once, as hard as that is to imagine."

The slave bowed and ran off.

He did not, Magnus noted with mild irritation, seem to feel any need to inquire as to which of his sons the senator required.

Marcus awoke with a start. He sat up on his sweat-damped pallet. The sun was already risen, and a few rays of morning lightened the shadows cast by the thick walls of the domus. Looking around, he discovered that he was alone in the cubiculum, though he did not know if Marcipor had risen before him or, as seemed more likely, had not returned to the Valerian compound last night.

One of the house slaves brought him a bowl of water upon request. After he washed his face and hands, he determined to go to the baths as soon as he'd broken his fast. It might well be his last opportunity to do so in quite some time.

He found Sextus already in the triclinium, sprawled in front of a low table laden with fruit, bread, and meat left over from the night before. He was idly feeding his dog, a curly-tailed mongrel he'd acquired off the streets the year before. "You're up late," Sextus commented as he popped a piece of orange into his mouth.

"Yes." Marcus wasn't hungry, he realized. He'd eaten rather a lot after speaking with his uncle and his mother.

"How did Aunt Julia take the news of your departure?"

"Placidly." Marcus ignored the accusatory tone, somewhat surprised that Magnus had seen fit to inform Sextus of his upcoming travels. "Her eyes were dry."

"Another Aelia, she is," Sextus said wryly, then laughed. "You don't understand the benefit of a father gone campaigning and a mother uninterested in your affairs, Marcus. I wish Magnus would leave me alone like that. He's even forbidden me to ride out with you, although I suppose you'll have that sorry excuse of a slave to keep you company."

Marcus flicked a grape at his cousin. "You can't honestly tell me that you'd abandon Amorr for a long ride through the wilds of Merithaim, Sextus. You do realize that I'm part of an official Church embassy. There won't be any gambling or girl-chasing, and I don't recall ecclesiastical debate being one of your favorite pastimes."

"Chance is everywhere, my dear boy. And wherever there are guards, there you will find men who roll the bones. As for girls, I daresay that Elebrion is full of them!" Sextus's eyes gleamed wickedly. "Elven girls. I've only seen one or two, but they were lovely. Gorgeous! Tall, slender, skin like milk. If you look past the pointy ears and the haughty attitude, why, they might be Vargeyar maidens, and there's no harm in that!"

"No harm? You wouldn't survive your first day there. You'd make love to the first sorceress you saw and find yourself turned into a toad before nightfall."

Sextus paid him no heed. "Perhaps I shall marry two of them, no, three, actually, and found a new Pannonia. It's a pity there aren't more half-elves around these days. Why did we kill them all, do you happen to remember?"

"To spare their women your unseemly lusts," Marcus said dryly. He removed a piece of meat from the table, examined it, and tossed it to Sextus's dog. The ugly beast snapped the morsel down with noisy relish. "I have in mind to go to the baths today, since I don't think I'll find one along the Malkanway. Care to join me?"

"Gladly." Sextus raised a small pouch from under his couch. "We can do that after we take care of this. I have orders to drag you off to the Arena. Believe it or not, that's what got me out of aiding with the sportulae today. No fights, unfortunately, but since Magnus has correctly ascertained that you and Marce are able to defend yourselves about as well as a pair of declawed kittens, I've orders to take you to the stables and buy you a bodyguard capable of protecting your virtue from those hot-blooded elven slatterns."

"The Arena? A bodyguard . . . Do you mean a gladiator?"

"Uh, yes. I know you've never been, but you do know what they are, right? Big, bloody-minded brutes, usually knock about trying to kill each other?"

"Why would I need a bodyguard? If the Sanctiff sent six Redeemed to bring me home last night, I'm sure he will ensure that his ambassadors are well guarded in our travels."

"That's the problem. I think Magnus wants to make sure there's someone who couldn't care less about the perfumed princes of the Church and will remember to keep an eye on the embassy's most junior member."

Marcus shrugged. That made sense, he supposed, although he found it hard to believe that he could possibly be in any real danger. Except, of course, from the elven king. But if High King Mael decided to attack the embassy, one more bodyguard would hardly make a difference.

• • •

By the time they reached the gladiator stables in the shadow of the Colosseo, Marcus was pleased to step into the dark, low-ceilinged building just to get out of the sun.

His pleasure lasted only a moment; the smell of sweat, leather, and blood was so strong it almost made him reel as he looked around the interior of the wooden structure. Plaques and weapons adorned the walls, separated by the occasional rude shelf holding bronze and silver cups that Marcus supposed were trophies.

Seated at a makeshift desk was a big man laboriously attempting to write numbers on a scroll. They soon learned this was the training master working at his accounts. While the big man raised his eyebrows at Sextus's request to purchase a gladiator, he was clearly annoyed when Sextus asked to see only dwarves, and only those dwarves fighting under the aegis of the Red faction.

The time it took to summon them seemed like an eternity in that dark and odorous place, but finally the master begrudgingly presented nine of the stocky, broad-shouldered creatures. Marcus quickly realized the man's attitude derived from his correct notion that a quick sale was not in order. None of the nine would make for a good travel companion. These dwarves were bitter, angry individuals, degraded into a near-bestial state by the harsh oppression of their slavery.

"Perhaps one of the other factions might have dwarves as well?" Marcus suggested hopefully as the last of the sneering, scowling gladiators was escorted back to the factional cells.

"Not a one," said the training master. He was a tall, powerfully built man with a terrible scar across the left side of his face. "Whites don't take breeds. Greens do, but they usually go in for orcs and gobbos, and those don't mix real well with dwarves. Blues had twelve until last week, but they all got killed in the re-creation of the Iron Mountain siege."

"I saw that!" Sextus said. "It was incredible. Especially that catapult they built—for a moment there I thought they were going to turn it on the crowd! Say, why do you shave their beards?"

"Reminds 'em where they are. Reminds 'em *what* they are." The training master looked appraisingly at Marcus and Sextus, possibly wondering what these two wealthy young masters would want with dwarves in the first place. "They forget sometimes, else."

"Are these all you've got?" Marcus said. He was doing his best to keep the distaste off his face. Not for the dwarves, for whom he only felt pity, but for the training master. "Isn't there anyone else?"

The training master shrugged. "There's two more up in the infirmary. I don't know what you want with a dwarf, but neither one is up to putting up much of a fight. Unless that's what you want, of course."

Marcus stared at the man in disbelief. Fortunately, Sextus grabbed his arm and squeezed it before he could open his mouth. What did the man think they were, a pair of decadent thrill killers?

But then, this was Amorr, after all, and not even its public dedication to the Lord God Almighty enabled it to escape man's fallen nature. For every saint, there were ten sinners, and for every man genuinely devoted to faith, good works, and charity, there were three given over to the worst forms of depravity and sadistic decadence. No doubt this man, laboring as he did in this terrible place, saw the evil side of man far more often than its reverse.

"Take 'em back," the training master said to an overmuscled pair of assistants. Then he beckoned toward Marcus and Sextus. "Follow me. I'll take you to the ones in the infirmary. They're both good fighters, but one was lamed in the last spectacle, and the other one took a pretty good stick in the ribs."

They followed him up the stairs and into what could easily have passed for one of the lower circles of hell.

The one-room infirmary was dark. It stank of disease and decades of blood dripping from the wounded and dying to soak into the wood of the floor. Marcus was appalled, and he saw even Sextus swallow hard at the olfactory assault on their senses. There were forty beds. A third of them were full, attended by only one slack-jawed attendant who appeared half-witted, at best.

"We keep them alive if we can," the training master said, not blind to the reaction of his visitors. "Doesn't pay to let them die before their time, you know. And it's not every stable that puts poppy seed in the wine to take the edge off the pain."

Marcus resisted the urge to point out that the man was in the business of sending these poor creatures out to die. Still, it was true: there was none of the moaning and thrashing that Marcus would have expected from such a sad collection of maimed and maltreated individuals. Most were unconscious. The two or three who were not seemed to be lost in a dreamy state that left them blessedly unaware of their surroundings. Marcus did his best to avoid looking directly at any of the ghastly injuries, but even so he saw far more than he would have wished.

The training master stopped at the bedside of a grim-faced dwarf with deep-set eyes, orange-red hair, and a somber mien. He blinked in apparent surprise at being approached.

"This here's Lodi," the training master said. "He took a goblin spear in the side six days ago. But he's a tough old wardog. Took down four or five goblins and two orcs by hisself, just in that one fight alone. He's left-handed, likes a warhammer—no surprise—but he's not too shabby with a blade, neither. Not all that quick, but he's patient and makes for a mean counterfighter. What do you have, Lodi, eighteen wins?"

"Twenty-three," the dwarf answered in a deep, cracked voice. It sounded as if he had not spoken in days, which was quite possibly the case considering the level of neglect here. His eyes were glazed with either exhaustion or poppy seed, but he was coherent. "What do you want?"

"A bodyguard," Marcus answered, stepping forward and meeting the dwarf's eyes.

Those eyes were dark with suffering, yet contained none of the hatred or helpless fury that so indelibly marked the rest of his kin. There was a week's growth of reddish stubble covering his face, but it was clear that not even being clean-shaven had caused this dwarf to forget that he had once been free. Blood had seeped through the dirty bandage on his side, some time ago from the dark, crusted look of it, and there was no sign of green or yellow discharge.

"Can you ride with that?"

"Won't make for much of a bodyguard, I'd say," Sextus commented.

The dwarf's eyes narrowed. "A bodyguard?"

"Yes," Marcus said. "I'm going on a journey and will require one."

"Will that get me out of here?" the dwarf asked, glancing at the training master, who nodded. "You'll have to tie me to the beast, I think, but you'll hear no complaints from me, even if it chafes me raw."

"Or you bleed to death?"

The dwarf turned his head toward Sextus. "It takes more than a scratch from an orc to kill a dwarf. I'll live, and I'll keep your friend alive too."

Sextus glanced at Marcus and shrugged. If nothing else, the dwarf was certainly tough, and it was hard not to admire his determination.

"How much?" Marcus asked the training master.

"And we'll expect a discount, of course," Sextus said. "You have to admit, he's not quite in what you'd call prime condition."

Iᴬ Q. VII A. I ARG. II

Praeterea, homines in imagine Dei et ad
similitudinem Dei creati sunt. Aelvi in imagine
Dei et ad similitudinem Dei non creati sunt. Ergo
aelvi habent animae naturaliter sibi unita.

THE SUN HAD not yet risen, but Marcus was amazed by the number of clients that were already waiting in the courtyard of the Valerian house.

On a normal morning there were perhaps twenty-five or thirty men of quality gathered to perform their daily ritual of paying homage to the great man and collecting their daily benefice. But today there appeared to be twice that number, even discounting the numerous household and stable slaves who were busily arranging saddlebags, checking horseshoes, and otherwise preparing Barat and the other three horses that he, Marcipor, and Lodi would take on their long journey to Elebrion.

Magnus himself had not yet appeared, but the collection of clients, some important, some insignificant, stirred nevertheless at Marcus's approach.

One elderly man, a senator judging by the broad red stripe that marked his black tunica, was the first to greet him as the others fell back in honor of his rank, pressing a small leather bag into his hand. "We shall pray without ceasing for your mission, Marcus Valerius. Take this. It shall stand you in good stead, and may the hand of the Purified be upon you!"

"Thank you, Senator," Marcus bowed to the nobleman and stared quizzically at the bag.

"It is the knucklebone of Saint Ansfrid of Tolanon. It is said to be a powerful rebuke to the elvish sorceries. I hardly think it likely to be of much use here in Amorr, but perhaps you may find it otherwise."

Marcus, surprised, thanked the senator warmly, but before he could even inquire as to his name, the quiet murmuring of the waiting men abruptly rose to a hail of shouted greetings as Magnus at last deigned to grace his clients with his presence.

The great man was flanked by his three favorites as well as Lautus, his chief purser. All four slaves were carrying a quantity of velvet purses that Marcus assumed held the morning's *sportula.* His uncle held up a hand, though, and the crowd fell quickly silent, although one wag in a threadbare tunica drew some chuckles when he cried out. "You're too late, Magnus—we're here to pay our respects to the young dominus!"

Magnus smiled thinly, visibly unamused. He gestured at Dompor, who placed one of the red purses he was carrying into Magnus's hand. There was a clink of coins as Magnus flicked his wrist and the importunate client just managed to catch the small bag with both hands before it struck him in the face.

Amidst the laughter of his fellows, the man weighed the bag with an expression of surprise on his face, then he bowed deeply to Magnus as those around him realized that he'd been rewarded for his cheek instead of scorned. They cheered Magnus for his generosity.

"It's a pity you don't have the wisdom to accompany your wit, Gaius Trachalas," Magnus admonished him. "Now, do buy yourself a cloak and a new tunica. I should be extremely disappointed to hear that you managed to lose everything at the arena before nightfall."

"I hear and obey, *dominus!*"

The crowd of clients laughed. Clearly Gaius Trachalas was not unpopular despite his poverty.

Magnus did not allow them to greet him as was the usual custom. Instead he beckoned Marcus to join him, then as Marcus hastened to obey, he slipped a meaty arm around Marcus's shoulders and gestured toward the center of the city as he addressed the throng.

"Today, my friends, I ask that you do me the honor of accompanying my nephew and I to the Quadratus Albus, where the Sanctiff will be offering a public mass on behalf of an embassy to Elebrion, which departs this morning. You need not greet me now, but do join us, and one of my men shall be sure to attend to you as we walk."

As his clients noisily competed to be the most enthusiastic about the morning's departure from the ordinary routine, Magnus pressed Marcus forward. The men, senators and artisans alike, parted like the waves of a black sea before a twin-hulled vessel.

The gates were already open, and a pair of armored slaves waiting there smoothly wheeled and took their places at the front of the unruly formation, each bearing a long wooden stave for use in clearing out a path for Magnus lest the crowds around the Quadratus obstruct his way. Many of Amorr's nobles used litters borne by six, eight, or sometimes even twelve slaves, but despite his girth, Magnus, being long accustomed to all-day marches with the legions, preferred to walk.

"Gaius Trachalas's gibes notwithstanding, it is you they honor today, lad."

"Me?" Marcus was confused. He had little to his name, and certainly nothing worth giving an already wealthy client.

"Our house, if you prefer. I am House Valerius today, Marcus. Your father, perhaps, tomorrow. But in the weeks and years to come, it may well be the young pup who has already drawn the attention of Amorr's mighty that shall be the *dominus* to whom they apply for their supper. And then, of course, they are curious."

"Do you know, uncle, a senator gave me a saint's relic before you appeared. A bald man, of some years."

"Did he? Ah, that would be Publius Hosidius. A wise man, and quite right to be concerned for your health. That's why I wished to speak with you now, as there will be no opportunity after the mass. Now listen to me. You'll find a letter in your saddlebags that Lucipor wrote out. There's more detail in it, but what you must understand above all is that there is a very good opportunity that you will be in danger once you reach Elebrion."

"In danger? Me?"

"Yes, that's why I bought you the gladiator. The dwarf. I'd have preferred to send more along with you, but that would have attracted too much attention."

"From whom, the elves?"

Magnus snorted. "Have you learned nothing from your histories, boy? The elves? They're the only ones from whom you have nothing to fear. Unless, of course, King Mael takes it into his head to kill you all on sight. In which case no amount of bodyguards will serve."

"But from whom am I in danger, then, if not the elves?"

"Anyone. Everyone!" The procession halted abruptly behind them as Magnus stopped and spread out both his arms as if to encompass not only the street on which they walked but also all of Amorr. "This is a city built upon conquest, Marcus, full of men grown fat upon the conquered and enslaved. Oh, we manufacture and we trade, but first and foremost, we conquer!"

Magnus, suddenly realizing that the clients behind them were now listening to him, grunted in irritation and set off again, this time at a faster pace. He pointed toward the ground, to Marcus's riding boots, newly made only yesterday for his journey. "There are fortunes to be made in war, and not only by those who lead the legions. How much did you pay for those?"

"My boots? Sixty sestertii."

"And how many officers on horse in a legion?"

"Eight."

"So for each legion, there's five hundred sestertii to be had. More like a thousand, actually, since any tribune worth his salt will bring at least a second pair. Doesn't sound like much, does it? But *caligae* sell for fifteen sestertii, and there's five thousand men whose feet need to be shod. Add in the price of the armor, shields, and swords, to say nothing of the food required every day for that quantity of men, and a single campaign can give a man clever enough to obtain a procurement contract the means to purchase a knighthood or a villa in the country.

"And for the great, the temptations are even more sweet. There are commands to be sold, territories to be governed, slaves to be gathered—and above all, glory to be gained. Tanusius

Titianus may declaim as he likes, but Amorran blood is not so thin that men have forgotten that there is more honor to be won by the iron sword on the battlefield than by the silver tongue in the Forum."

Marcus adroitly stepped over a large canine deposit soiling the bricked street. "The history of Amorr is the history of war, uncle, I know. But even so, how does that place me in danger?"

"Think, lad! Half of Amorr is already salivating at the thought of sacking Elebrion if the Sanctiff is moved to declare holy war against the elves. Think how much wealth a city inhabited by near-immortals must have collected over the centuries! And now that the possibility has presented itself, the other half is dreaming up mad schemes to provoke a war if he doesn't. The minds of men are fertile ground, and you should be able to imagine what harvest would be reaped should the wicked elves slay a young Amorran nobleman they were guesting."

"That's why you insisted on a dwarf," Marcus said thoughtfully. "You were afraid that a man might be suborned by someone wanting to start a war between Amorr and Elebrion."

"Just so. I'd forbid you to take that slave of yours, except that he knows very well that your skin is worth more alive to him than dead."

"Marcipor would never betray me!"

"Every man has his price, lad." An uncharacteristically broad smile broke suddenly across Magnus's heavy-jowled face. "If I could only be certain the Senate would give me the legions, I daresay I might be tempted to arrange your death myself!"

When they turned the final corner and the high dwellings of the narrow street gave way to the expanse of the Quadratus,

Marcus nearly flinched, half-expecting to come face-to-face with a waiting gang of murderous would-be generals, governors, and war profiteers. The noise of the assembly was overwhelming. It struck him with an almost physical force, and the flames from the torches that lit the predawn gathering gave it an eerie and frightening air.

But the crowd filling the square was no threat. They had their backs to him, being interested solely in the gathering of luminaries upon the raised stone rostra.

The Sanctiff was there, of course, enrobed in white and seated on a massive silver throne, as were seven of the Azuli, along with Cassius Claudo, Father Aestus, and four or five other priests Marcus didn't recognize. But few eyes were on any of them or even the twenty gold-cloaked Michaeline warrior-priests that flanked the princes of the Church on either side.

Elves!

There were two of them, standing behind a large brazier on the Sanctiff's left at the west edge of the platform. They towered over the crowd, both being nearly a head taller than the soldier-priests despite the blue-dyed horsehair plumes that adorned the Michaelines' bronze-plated helms.

The elves were fair and attractive, although the flames that lit their faces cast weird shadowy tattoos that made them look more sinister and less human than normal. Perhaps it was those shadows or the strange glow from the fire, but they seemed less supernaturally beautiful than Marcus remembered from his childhood sightings ten years before. While the occasional elven merchant or adventuresome bard had passed through the Valerian summer estate to the northwest of the city, they had never been permitted to enter the gates of Amorr itself.

Even more astonishing than their mere presence was the fact that the taller of the two was wearing a silver circlet that indicated he was of noble blood. A noble and therefore a sorcerer, most likely, but one presumably wise enough to refrain from showing any other sign that he was a servant of evil. If he did, it would be a contest to see if the Michaelines would strike him down before the crowd tore him to pieces.

Marcus glanced at his uncle and saw that Magnus too had a look of surprised concern on his face. But the great man only shrugged and barked out an order to the two torch-bearing slaves standing on either side of them.

As before, they cleared the way, the mighty parting nearly as readily as their lessers had before. Any indignation they might have felt faded immediately once they recognized that it was Lucius Valerius's men who had moved them aside.

As they approached to within a few ranks of the rostra, Marcus suddenly realized that Magnus intended him to mount the stage and join the others in front of what appeared to be the entire population of the city gathered in one place.

He felt as if he had stepped outside his body, as if he were watching some other young man being lifted onto the well-worn marble of the elevated platform by the muscular arms of Magnus's bodyguards. It seemed unreal to him. The familiar expanse of the city stretching out before him might have been an alien place for all that he recognized it now. He could hear nothing, although he saw many of the mouths on a thousand faces before him moving and knew that the silence he was hearing was all but impossible.

And then it was as if something broke inside him, and the noise of ten thousand men speaking, shouting, whispering, gossiping, and conspiring rushed over him. The overwhelming sense of it nearly staggered him. There was cheering too, although it took him a moment to understand that what they were shouting was "Valerian, Valerian!" He raised a hand to acknowledge this honor to his house. As he scanned the crowd his eyes fell upon Magnus, who nodded approvingly as the cheers grew louder in response to his gesture.

Then a hand fell on his shoulder, and he found himself looking into the round and uncharacteristically somber face of Father Aestus.

"This is no time to announce your candidacy for the tribunal, Marcus Valerius."

Marcus, taken aback, had started to protest his innocence of any such ambitions, until the priest smiled at him and Marcus realized that his nose was being pulled.

He allowed himself to be guided over to the Michaelines standing on the left side and nodded respectfully as he met the hard, brown eyes of one warrior-priest with a scar that twisted his mouth into a seeming sneer. There was no time for introductions, though, and no sooner had Marcus turned around when the great gathering fell silent faster than Marcus would have believed possible.

The Sanctiff, Marcus saw now, had risen from his throne. He raised a hand to bless the Amorrans assembled before him, then announced his intention to make supplication to the Most High for the well-being of the embassy. Marcus felt astutely self-conscious as he clasped his hands and bowed his head.

"*Sancte Michael Archangele,*" the Sanctiff prayed, "*defende nos in proelio; contra nequitiam et insidias diaboli esto praesidium.*"

Yes, defend us, St. Michael, Marcus prayed with a will, for he suddenly felt a terrible sense of foreboding fill his soul. He seemed to sense a darkening cloud that appeared from nowhere to loom ominously over the buildings of the city. Indeed, there was still no light on the horizon. The distant dawn had not yet risen high enough to surmount the high walls that guarded Amorr.

Defend us, preserve your humble servants, O most pure and perfect Lord, even as we walk into the shadows of evil.

But he felt as if he was already there, trapped in the valley of the shadow of death. Though his head remained bowed, he could not help staring out over the masses assembled before him in the lifeless grey light of the false dawn.

How many of them were already enmeshed in conspiracies to amass wealth at the expense of human and elven blood? How many were plotting to use the Almighty's very viceroy to serve their own selfish and sinful purposes? How many of them wished to see Marcus himself murdered to justify their war?

The Sanctiff's voice interrupted his thoughts. His prayers rang out clear and strong even to the furthest reaches of the throng, amplified by the clever design of the marble and stone from which the rostra and much of the Quadratus was constructed.

Marcus glanced to his left and saw that the two elves were standing motionless on the other side of the platform, their eyes open and their heads unbowed. One of them noticed him staring at them and raised a slender eyebrow. Marcus flushed and quickly ducked his head as the Sanctiff brought his prayer to a close.

"*Imperat illi Deus; supplices deprecamur: tuque, Princeps militiae coelestis, Satanam aliosque spiritus malignos, qui ad perditionem animarum pervagantur in mundo, divina virtute in infernum detrude.*"

Yes, Marcus prayed, grant us wisdom, almighty God. Grant us knowledge to separate the wheat from the chaff, to cleave the sheep from the goats. Give us Your eyes, Lord God, that we may see the soulless spirits of evil that seek nothing but ruin and distinguish them from the souls that may be saved for Your glory.

"Amen," said the Sanctiff, and the amen was echoed by a thousand voices just as the sun rose above the walls to spill the golden rays of dawn over the white dome of the palace behind the square.

Marcus cried out in wonder as the brilliant light reflected down into the crowd, banishing his fears with the darkness. And he was not the only one to marvel at the beauty of the morning and exalt in the sudden warmth that banished the cold along with the darkness.

His exhilarating feeling of spiritual release lasted but a moment. When he looked over again at the elves, he saw them staring at the Sanctiff with expressions that mingled contempt with amusement.

Their pride and arrogance showed in their alien eyes—but was it truly the pride of demons? He found himself wondering if despite the most holy blessings of God's own viceroy, it was possible that he was about to embark upon an embassy that had more to do with man's fallen evil than truth and divine justice.

Iᴬ Q. VII A. I ARG. III

Praeterea, ille Psalmographus Deum rogat, "quid est homo quoniam recordaris eius vel filius hominis quoniam visitas eum?" Responso huic quaestioni inquit, "minues eum paulo minus a Deo gloria et decore coronabis eum dabis ei potestatem super opera manuum tuarum cuncta posuisti sub pedibus eius;" Quo discernamus homines apud summam rerum corporearum subsistentium praestare. Ergo aelvi habent animae naturaliter sibi unita.

IT TOOK NEARLY an hour for Hezekius, the Michaeline commander, to extricate the party from the horde of well-wishing senators, cavalars, priests, and archbishops. In the end he'd managed it with the help of Cassius Claudo's famously sharp-edged tongue.

Marcus was relieved to see both Marcipor and Lodi waiting for him with the baggage train. It was bad enough to worry about holy wars and murderous merchants without having to contemplate months on the road without a friend or even a single change of clothing. Somehow he wasn't surprised to see that Marcipor had talked the stablemaster into providing him with a rather better mount than human slaves were generally permitted.

Lodi wasn't actually tied to the mule upon which he sat like a bag of potatoes, but Marcus thought it wiser to leave dwarven pride unchallenged rather than bring up his wounded state again. The heavy chainmail worn by the dwarf would probably suffice to alert the entire party should he fall, at which point the matter could be addressed.

As he had promised, Lodi bore his suffering in stoic silence, only emitting the occasional grunt of pain when the mule to which he was securely fastened made a false step on the cart-rutted road. As poorly stitched as the wound was, it had not broken open, and, thanks to the healing ministrations of one of the Michaelines, a healer of some skill, the dwarf looked to make a full recovery. Fortunately, this first day's ride was expected to be an easy one.

Marcus was fascinated by Lodi. The dwarf was a short but powerful creature, so similar to a man. For all his reading, Marcus knew very little of Lodi's race, which had not endowed Selenoth with a written history or even a literature worthy of note.

There was, of course, the song of the great siege of Iron Mountain, an epic saga that had taken all Amorr by storm five or six years ago and had inspired the battle re-creation in which Lodi had been injured. But even that had been penned by a Savonder, and though it was supposed to be derived from the dwarven oral tradition, the scholarly consensus was that it was of questionable verisimilitude.

The embassy traveling party was rather larger than Marcus had imagined it would be. The acerbic bishop was attended by no fewer than two priests, six slaves, and six guards wearing the green-and-black livery of his diocese. Appropriately more humble, the Jamite priest Father Aestus was accompanied by only two slaves—one rotund and jolly like him, the other tall, gaunt, and taciturn.

The nineteen Michaelines, led by Sir Hezekius, were unattended by slaves or squires. It seemed the warrior-priests were accustomed to serving themselves, which was, Marcus thought, admirable and in keeping with the custom of the less militant orders. Indeed, no sooner had they reached the baggage train at the northern gate of the city than they doffed their gorgeous panoply in favor of stained and weathered riding gear. Only the rich blue leather of their scabbards and the bright bronze hilts of their swords gave the casual observer any indication of their unique vocation.

Marcus had little fear that those swords would need to be drawn anytime before reaching Elebrion. The soldier-priests weren't Redeemers, but the Michaelines' uniformly close-cropped hair and military bearing would give sufficient pause to any bandit gangs tempted by the party's excellent horses and well-loaded wagons.

Two outriding Michaeline priests scouted the road ahead, so far in advance that they could barely be seen, while two more brought up the distant rear lest they be overtaken unaware.

Both Marcus and Marcipor wore their swords, as well. Marcus's was a fine blade, though never tested in battle. And Marcipor's was a gaudily decorated thing more suitable for the theater than the battlefield.

Lodi wore two thick butcher's axes from his belt. No battle-axe, as the training master had indicated. And there was a very large crossbow strapped to the back of his mule as well. It looked like a siege bow, a weapon designed to be mounted on a wall. Marcus wondered if this had been pulled from secret armory of his uncle's or if he'd had ordered it for Lodi especially for this embassy. No human could use the cumbersome thing afoot, but after glancing at Lodi's scarred, tree-like arms, Marcus decided that the dwarf might very well be able to.

Marcus rode near the end of the column. Only the three supply wagons and the rearmost pair of Michaelines were behind them. A fourth wagon, in which the archbishop, Father Aestus, and the two other Churchmen rode, was positioned ahead of them, in the middle of the line. Marcus had been worried about Lodi's mule being too slow, but fortunately, all four wagons were drawn by teams of four mules that kept their pace to a relative crawl.

They rode for two hours through flat coastal plain on a road flanked by hills that gradually rose toward the horizon on either side. The land had been burned dry by the merciless summer sun. The hilltops were brown and treeless, and what vegetation managed to survive was mostly scrub brush. Every now and then in the distance they would see a gnarled tree standing alone, stubbornly digging its exposed roots into the soil, like an old, leather-skinned farmer refusing to abandon a family farm long gone fallow.

That pitiless sun was now rising toward its peak, and it was apparent to Marcus that he was not the only one getting bored with their slow progress over the roads. Even the dwellings they passed seemed lifeless—tall, narrow, stuccoed-stone structures painted in various shades of yellow that had long ago faded into a cheerless goldenrod.

He was eager to speak again with Father Aestus. Perhaps the friendly priest could help him know how he was supposed to behave as the Sanctiff's personal proxy. But Aestus was riding with the bishop, Cassius Claudo, near the front of the column. And Marcus wouldn't dream of approaching the bishop without an invitation.

It occurred to him then that the Sanctiff hadn't offered him any servants for the trip, or even a letter of introduction that identified Marcus as his representative. When he'd been summoned to the palace, he'd thought his position had risen high indeed. But now, riding behind a long line of horse's rumps, he felt again like no more than a young priest yet to prove his value.

How to do so? That was the challenge he faced, and with some dismay he began to realize how large the gap between potential and accomplishment appeared to be once one seriously contemplated that gap with an eye toward leaping it.

Even as a boy Marcus had dreamed of writing a text that would astonish the world with its brilliance. Heroes of the Coliseum were lauded one year and disregarded the next. Few could remember who been seated at on the consular thrones more than two or three years ago. Even generals accorded the signal honor of a Triumph were usually forgotten within a decade. Only the scholars—great scholars such as Augustinus, Oxonus, Depotapolis, and the Castrate—were granted the immortal gift of burning their memory into the minds of men.

A text, it must be. But where to begin? One day Cassius Claudo had stared at a blank parchment and then written that first word from which had sprung the magnificent *Summa Spiritus*. Presumably Aestus had also done the same with his *Ordo Selenus Sapiens*. It was like planting a seed, only he did not know from whence the seed would come. Did one simply wait for inspiration to strike? That seemed insensible. After all, a man might wait all his life for inspiration to arrive of its own accord.

And why should he wait? There were few men who knew the elves well, and not since his grandfather's grandfather's day had man been permitted to enter the High City. Claudo's masterpiece was based entirely on human sources. If on this journey Marcus might somehow be granted access to the works of great elven philosophers whose very existence was yet unknown to the scholars of the Empire, he might well hope to write something of interest, if not of note.

The elves must be his subject, then, and the elves alone. He would focus solely on them, a subject deemed well worthy of contemplation by the mere fact of the Sanctiff's particular interest, in the place of the wider scope of the *Summa Spiritus*. It would be a second *Summa,* an *Elvic Summa.* A *Summa Elvetica!*

The Castrate's method would not suffice. Marcus had no authority. His words bore no intellectual weight. He could not just proclaim a thing and expect men to hold it to be true. Perhaps his *Summa* could be in the form of a dialogue. No, too pretentious by far. Only an arrogant and supercilious soul like Depotapolis with his bent for mendacious manipulation would think that his carefully orchestrated playing of the two sides toward an inevitable, if not necessarily logical, end was a conclusive form of argument.

Marcus could rely upon neither reputation nor authority. Therefore he required a more systemic and methodical approach to the matter. Yes, that was the way. A systematic consideration of the issue would force him to begin at the most natural place to begin, namely, the beginning.

Does an elf have a soul? No, that was taking it too far at the start. In the beginning was God, who made man in His image. God also made the animals, albeit not in His image. God also made the elves, but were they then more properly akin to man or to the animals? He already inclined toward the former, but upon reflection, there were significant points to be made on either side. What really was needed was a—

"You have an interesting servant there."

Marcus jumped in his saddle, coming only reluctantly out of his contemplations. He turned to see who had spoken to him. It was one of the younger Michaeline priests. He rode up alongside Marcus and indicated the dwarf.

"Hmm? Oh, yes."

Marcus searched his memory for the Michaeline's name. He'd been introduced to them all but it was hard to remember which of the twenty names belonged to this particular priest. Nehemin? No. Zephanus, that was it. He blinked, realizing that the priest was still talking.

"You don't think the elves will object?"

"About what?"

"Why, about your dwarf, of course." Zephanus flushed as the sorcerer-elf, seemingly far enough ahead of them in the train to be out of earshot, suddenly turned around and glanced at him. Then the sorcerer shrugged and turned back to his conversation with his elven companion.

"Apparently not," Marcus said, stifling a smile. Marcipor was riding ahead, engaged in an animated conversation with three of the Michaelines and gesturing in a lordly manner.

"Well, what do you know?" Zephanus said. "Those long ears really do serve a purpose after all!"

"All things serve a purpose, brother," Marcus said. "Our inability to discern that purpose does not indicate its absence, only our shortcomings."

Zephanus eyed him speculatively. "Ah, a philosopher. So, I assume you're the Valerian. The Valerian who does not prefer war. Do forgive me. I thought it was the other lad up there."

"You're not the first to make that mistake. My man Marcipor hasn't quite mastered the art of servility."

"I suspect your dwarf hasn't either," the priest commented dryly, glancing at the taciturn Lodi, who had yet to utter more than a grunt to Marcus or anyone else throughout the morning. "I should have known you'd be less grandiose. Your father isn't one to throw his weight around, either. It's probably just as well. I imagine one Magnus in the family is enough."

"You know my father?"

"Yes," Zephanus said. "I served under General Valerius last fall in the Garmaghal River campaign. He brought two of his legions across the river—Seventh and Ninth, I believe—and the Abbott-General sent him three squads of Michaelines as reinforcements. I remember he wasn't very pleased to see us when we arrived. He'd asked for four. But happily, as it turned out, we didn't have to do much more than suppress their shamans and so forth. Their infantry didn't show much stomach for a fight once we crossed and smashed their center. I doubt we lost more than fifty or sixty men, all told."

Marcus nodded, remembering his father's letter that had, he'd said, been dictated as the first legion crossed the river, supposedly while under fire from goblin archers and artillery.

For all that he was an undemonstrative man, his father did seem to have somewhat of a flair for the dramatic when it came to writing letters. Nearly half of the letters Marcus had received from Lucius Valerius were allegedly written during the course of battle. Marcus wasn't sure if it was because the proximity of danger caused his father to think of his family or if he merely sought an easily impressed audience to appreciate his casual heroics.

"They had an illusionist, did they not?"

Zephanus laughed. "They did indeed! The wretched little beast conjured up a vision of a terrible flash flood just as the first Century reached the far bank and scared half the Seventh to death. We probably lost as many fools to drowning as fell to any of their quarrels that day. It could have been real trouble. Had they counterattacked at that moment it would have hit us hard, but fortunately, by the grace of God, they held their ground."

Marcus frowned. He didn't like to hear that his father had apparently come so near to failure, especially in such a minor action. The victory at Garmaghal had barely registered in Amorr. Had his father's legions not been involved, he probably wouldn't have known about it himself. His displeasure must have been evident, because Zephanus stopped laughing and raised a finger.

"No, lad, it was hardly the general's fault. He'd warned us to watch for mischief with the waters. But we were looking for elementals and the like. We weren't expecting goblins to have an illusionist. There's not so many vauders among the gobbos, you see, it being mostly mortal men who go in for the more abstract sorceries." He glanced forward at their alien companions, shaking his head. "Or elves. Especially elves."

"I don't know that I understand the distinction," Marcus said. "My tutor, Father Aurelius, isn't enthusiastic about us learning about magic of any kind, not even the battle magics.

I've picked a few things up from my father's tales or from a few historical accounts of the classic engagements, but I'm not even sure what the difference between an illusionist and a shaman is."

"No, I can't imagine your tutor would be," Zephanus said with a smile. "Not if he's ordained. He's right about that, with regards to most students. Your average priestling has no need of such information. It would serve no purpose to dangle the evils of a fallen world in front of young minds being honed for the higher purpose. But you, on the other hand, on this journey are going to be surrounded by enchanters, illusionists, sorcerers, and even archmages in a matter of weeks. So before you offend the wrong elf, it might behoove you to have some idea of which ones are capable of turning you into a turnip and which ones aren't."

"Don't concern yourself on my account." Marcus grinned and pointed at Marcipor. "Now he, on the other hand, could likely use your instruction. Without it, we can safely assume he will be in turnip form before nightfall on the day of our arrival."

"Is it possible he might be more useful as a turnip?"

"I'd say probable," Marcus responded.

They both laughed, and for the first time since he had mounted his horse that morning, Marcus began to feel that perhaps the embassy might not end in death and debacle. He found himself rather liking the young Michaeline, whose mien was not at all as holy or as grim as he'd expected of a warrior-priest sworn to celibacy and slaughter.

"What did you think of my father?"

"The general?" Zephanus said. "Well, I can't say that I saw very much of him. This may surprise you, but generals seldom make a habit of consulting with their *fideleists*. They tell the Michaeline captain where the enemy magic is and what we're to do, then the captain tells us. Still, it wasn't hard to see that your father had a lot of experience and that he was a good commander of men. He's intelligent, he's straightforward, he knows how to use what he's got, and he knows how to fight. The legions seek that in a general above all else. Now, perhaps he's more respected by his men than he is loved, but I imagine he prefers it that way."

"Yes, I imagine he does," murmured Marcus.

The comment drew a raised eyebrow from Zephanus, but the young priest continued as if he hadn't been interrupted. "General Valerius doesn't give a lot of speeches or try to inspire the troops with words, like some generals do. My first campaign, we were serving under Nonius Messius. Now there was a man who was well-enamored with the sound of his own voice. He didn't talk: he orated! He even had a scribe following him around, writing down all of his interminable speeches for posterity."

"Were they any good?"

"Certainly, if you wanted your soldiers well rested. I can't say they weren't effective, either. Listening to Messius was how I learned to sleep on my feet. If you can find a scroll of his speeches when we return to the city, I do recommend you buy one. You'll find them more effective than warm milk and honey on a sleepless night. After Messius, your father's notion of an inspiring pre-battle talk came as a real surprise."

"And what was that? His style of speech, that is."

"Succinct. And pertinent. At Garmaghal, he rode in front of the Centuries in the vanguard, drew his sword, and pointed at the far bank of the river. 'You can see that they're over there,' he said. 'Go kill them.' There were no cheers. The drummers didn't even start in. No one realized he was done! But as it turned out, that was all he needed to say. We certainly killed enough of them that day."

Marcus smiled, thinking about his father's characteristic laconism. Marcus had argued with him before his father had left to take command of the legions two years ago. General Valerius had intended to bring him along as a staff aide in order to season him and expose him to battle for the first time, but Marcus had been fixated upon the idea of a career as a Church scholar. Fortunately for him, his mother, Father Aurelius, and Magnus himself were all of the opinion that Valerians had shed enough blood for Amorr and that Marcus was destined for something other than battlefields and bloodshed.

At the time, Marcus had felt almost disdainful of his father's brutal profession. But now, having come to understand both the need for such men and the high regard in which they were held by others he respected, he was beginning to wonder if perhaps he had missed a unique opportunity.

"How does one . . . " he hesitated, unsure of how to phrase his request. "How do you balance the demands of your ordinate with the requirements of your profession?"

Zephanus smiled at him and shook his head as he answered the thought that lurked behind the question rather than the question itself. There was a flicker of what might have been pity in his eyes. "No, Marcus Valerius, our brotherhood is not for you. Should St. Michael ever call you to his banner, you will know that call for what it is and you will have no such questions."

"I don't understand!"

"Of course you don't. Have you ever seen purple whorls of sorcery spinning in the air as an archmage gathers his evil magic together? Have you seen the sky darken under a cloud of imps, sprites, and demons as an army of ahomum shake their spears and chant their guttural thick-tongued summonings? Can you see the aura of green, black, and gold that surrounds yonder elf?" Zephanus pointed to the shorter elf, the one wearing the sorcerer's robes.

"No, I've never seen anything like that. Can you really see such things?"

"I see them, whether I will or no. I can no more not see them than I can avoid seeing you." Zephanus grinned as Marcus glanced back and forth between him and the elf, obviously trying to see what was not apparent to his eyes. "I don't jest, young Valerius. The Fifth Eye is how the saint calls us to his service."

"The Fifth Eye? That sounds . . . esoteric."

"It's nothing of the sort. It's merely a turn of phrase in honor of Saint Oculatus, whose birth name was Quintus Tullius. He was the first to be given the gift of the holy vision. His men were being slaughtered by elven archers hidden behind an invisibility spell, and when he cried out to God his prayer was answered and he was given the eyes to see behind the accursed veil. Haven't you heard stories of some lad or other accused of witchcraft because he saw what his elders could not? Fortunately, the brotherhood keeps watch for such promising young men, and they usually manage to intervene before any harm is done."

"Usually?"

"To be honest, I've never heard of anyone blessed with the Fifth Eye being burned. Saint Michael does protect his own. But then, one can't be sure of what one doesn't know."

"No, that's true. Is it only boys, then, who are called by the saint?"

"To date it's only been men and boys. I don't know what we would do should a lass be given the gift. Or what purpose that would serve—a woman can't ride to war, after all."

"Elvesses fight," a gruff voice, redolent with gravel, spoke behind them.

Both Marcus and Zephanus craned their necks to stare at the dwarf, who stared back at them, expressionless, from the swaying back of his fat mule.

"Yes, they do, don't they, sir dwarf? I beg your pardon. I fear I have forgotten your name."

Lodi shrugged. "'Dwarf' will serve. We're not likely to encounter many of my kin on the way to the Elflands."

"His name is Lodi," Marcus said. "He's supposed to be the less useless half of my bodyguard, but he's still recovering from a wound he received at the Colosseo."

"Ah, a gladiator, then?"

Lodi shook his head.

"Not by choice," Marcus added. "Nor of my doing. I bought him from the Reds."

"Did you now? I am curious. How does a dwarf of sufficient martial talents to survive the arena find himself battling criminals and animals for the pleasure of the good people of Amorr in the first place?"

"Never you mind that, priestling," Lodi muttered. "Sounds as if you've fought them too, though."

"The elves?" Zephanus said. "No, I am too young to have had the honor. And may God and St. Michael grant that does not change throughout the course of this trip. Seeing as we have no eagles to spare, I'd prefer the High King didn't take my head as a trophy."

"What would the elf want with eagles?" Lodi asked. "They're a mite small for his skyriders."

Marcus laughed. "Not the birds, the legionary standards, Lodi. The elf king still has the two his father took at the battle of Aldus Wald. They're the only ones Amorr has ever lost that we didn't manage to take back. My uncle wanted the Sanctiff to trade them in return for the Church recognizing that they are ensoulled."

Zephanus gave him a skeptical look. "And your uncle is?"

"Lucius Valerius, called Magnus."

"Hmmm, I should have known. Well, that's not a bad idea, actually."

Marcus suppressed his first, indignant protest and contented himself

> To see the battle of Aldus Wald as it happened, read "Birth of an Order" in Appendix Aelvi at the end of this book.

with a mild observation. "It would appear Michaelines don't go in for a lot of theology. Or philosophy."

"I wouldn't say that," Zephanus protested with a grin. "Why, sometimes our debates over who to kill first can last for hours!"

Marcus smiled. "Still, I wonder if anyone here actually know how to fight them. Elves, I mean. Not that we want to, but it seems to me that perhaps it might be useful to know something more than the year in which Saddranus fell to the orcs."

Marcus glanced at Lodi, but the dwarf was staring off into the horizon with an expression that seemed to indicate he was done speaking for the nonce.

Zephanus, on the other hand, was rather more loquacious. "Happily we have with us someone who is said to have battled them on at least one occasion. Do excuse me for but a moment, noble sir and dwarf, and I shall return."

The young warrior-priest urged his horse into a brief trot, until he reached the side of two of his fellow Michaelines, who were riding in companionable silence farther up the narrow column. Their party stretched out along the road as the sun rose toward its apex.

Zephanus returned, bearing in his wake an older Michaeline with a close-trimmed beard that was shot with grey. His receding hairline was lined with a white scar that nearly spanned his forehead, as if he'd been wearing a helmet so long that it had left a permanent mark upon him. Or, as was much more likely the case, some long-ago enemy had nearly removed the top of his head with a sword or axe on a battlefield that was now otherwise forgotten. His horse was a magnificent chestnut very nearly the equal of Barat, Marcus's own mount.

"Marcus Valerius," Zephanus said, "I present the Blessed Sir Claudius Serranus."

Serranus nodded and Marcus returned the greeting, a bit more deeply. It wasn't hard to remember to be properly respectful to a veteran soldier who looked as if he had breakfasted on raw orc legs earlier that morning.

"An honor, Blessed Sir."

The scarred Michaeline flashed his teeth momentarily. "Call me Serranus. That, or 'Brother Serranus' will do. Heard you were a courteous young pup. Perhaps you won't forget to curtsey to King Caerwyn or such and get us all killed, eh?"

"I shouldn't like to displease the Sanctiff, Brother Serranus."

"Yes, I'm sure it's fear of his displeasure that will make your bowels clench and the acid burn in the back of your throat when we reach the heights. Or when you stand in the place where the mountain meets the sky, darkness falls, and you hear the cries of the High King's warhawks soaring unseen somewhere high above you."

"Are you so certain that I shall need to wait until then? I don't think it's the lack of breakfast that seems to have soured my stomach."

Serranus smiled, a more genuine smile this time. "It takes a brave lad to admit that he's afraid. I think you'll do well, Valerius, should it come to swords and elvish sorcery. It won't make a difference, mind you, but at least you won't shame your name. Probably."

"I'm confident I shall sleep better for the knowledge."

"Brother, Marcus here was eager to know more about how the elves make war," Zephanus said. "And since I'm told you have some experience with that, I thought perhaps you might further his education."

Claudius Serranus waved his arm, his gesture taking in the road disappearing into the horizon before them. "I don't seem to have anything better to do," he said. "This is a dry and dusty business. Give me a skin to wet my whistle and we shall see if the stories of an old war dog can while away a mile or three."

Marcus dutifully produced a wineskin, which the old warrior-priest took.

He opened it and expertly sprayed a stream of Valerian Primus into his mouth without wasting a single drop or further soiling the sweat-stained tunic that he wore open down to his chest. His greying brows rose with surprise. "That's a good vintage you've got there, lad. Yours, I'm thinking."

"It's of the House, yes." Marcus nodded in respectful acknowledgment. "Please keep it, Blessed Sir, as a small measure of the regard House Valerius bears for the noble Order of St. Michael."

"'The Order,' the man said," Zephanus pointed out as he leaned over his horse's neck with a hand extended. "That means me too. Let me try it!"

"I couldn't allow that, little brother, not in good conscience. It's far too early in the day to risk sun and grape addling such a young pate as yours." He saluted Marcus with the skin, gave it one more healthy squeeze, then twisted the carved spout closed and slung it off the horn of his saddle. "Now, as to your question, can either of you tell me the defining characteristic of an elven army?"

"Archery," Zephanus answered. He didn't seem inclined to complain about being denied a taste of House Valerius's best. "Their archers have far greater range with their longbows than we can match with our slings and spears, which makes it hard to come to grips with them."

"That's true, to be sure, but it's something more basic than that."

Marcus racked his brain, trying to think of every military history he'd ever read that mentioned the elves. *The Taktika of Leus* contained several accounts of famous battles with them, including Ardus Wald, Bremulon, and Tarphoris, but elven involvement aside, there wasn't a single similarity between the three battles that he could think of. An ambush, a battlefield, and a city defense.

As Zephanus had said, it was the superiority of their deadly longbows that sprang first to Marcus's mind. The historical accounts were no doubt exaggerated, but there had to be an element of metaphorical truth, at least, in the descriptions of how their arrows could darken the sky.

If it wasn't the archers, what could it be? Their dark magic was superlative, but even the men of Savonderum used mage-craft in battle, the peril to their souls notwitstanding. Would an experienced veteran like Serranus find it worthy of such particular note?

Then another thought occurred to him as he happened to glance in the dwarf's direction. It struck him that the two old warriors might be evenly matched for who bore more scars.

"Is it that they have no infantry?" he suggested.

"Of course they have infantry," Zephanus said dismissively. "Most of their archers are on foot, and even their light cavalry usually dismount when they fight at range."

"No, I mean they don't have any heavy infantry. We do, the Savonders do, the dwarves do, the orcs do, even the goblins do, if you think of how the orcs use them as auxiliaries on the wings when they're not mounted. The Troll King doesn't have anything *but* heavy infantry. But the only elves that wear proper armor are their lancers, and they're mounted."

"Aye, General Valerius!" Serranus barked in response. The grizzled warrior thumped his chest in what was obviously a sardonic salute, but his eyes were sparkling with good humor. "The young scholar has it in one, little brother, for all that he's never bloodied a sword. And that, my dear young novices, tells you very nearly all you might possibly need to know about the elves—their cowardly tactics, their pernicious culture, their spiritual enervation, and their ultimate fate. More importantly, it also tells you how to kill them."

"It does?" Marcus looked at Zephanus, but the younger Michaeline clearly had no idea what Serranus was telling them either. If the two elves riding far ahead of them could hear their conversation, they weren't letting on.

"Aye, it most certainly does. Didn't your tutors ever force you to think, young Valerius, or did they merely set you to memorizing Psalms, catechisms, and philosopher's speeches? Here, let me give you a hint: who has the most heavy infantry?"

"The orcs," Zephanus answered immediately.

"The orc tribes," Marcus echoed just a moment later.

"Quick on the draw, brother," Serranus said approvingly to Zephanus. "There are scores of famous orc heavy foot regiments: the Black Orcs, the Red Hand Slayers, the Ghinghis Mountain Bhoys. Now, why do they spend that infantry with such profligacy? Their tactics, such as they are, are essentially minor variants on the straightforward charge."

"Because they're orcs," Zephanus said. "They're stupid."

"No," Marcus objected. "Well, I mean it's true that they're not very intelligent, in comparison with man, dwarf, or elf. But mainly they're wasteful of their infantry because they can afford to be. Orclings breed and grow to maturity so quickly that no chieftain of the tribes cares much if he loses half his warriors—so long as enough survive to bring him victory that day. In fact, he probably hopes they'll kill themselves off by fighting external enemies before they get caught up in internecine strife. That's why the tribes are always at war, either raiding human lands or fighting amongst themselves. Just too many orcs running around."

"And that's why they're always invading dwarven territory," Zephanus said slyly, but Lodi failed to rise to the bait and continued to ignore the conversation.

"Now," Serranus said, "with that in mind, what can you conclude about the elven lack of infantry, Marcus Valerius?"

"The opposite. They value their lives too dearly to dare risking them in melee combat."

"Precisely! That's why they fear to meet the legions at close quarters: they can't match our numbers and our discipline. That's why they will always run before the heavy horse of Savonderum, and why even the spears of the peasant levy present them with a problem.

"The orcs' heavy infantry haven't discipline and their armor is shoddy, but their speed, strength, and numbers make up for that and make them dangerous in close combat. As for the dwarves, well, there isn't an infantry in the world that is their equal, one for one, except the mountain trolls. So, it is fear of losing their precious long lives that dictates the elves' approach to warfare. This not only reveals a tactical weakness that can be exploited, but is also a cultural sign that speaks volumes about the state of their race."

"I bet they aren't afraid of goblin infantry," Zephanus commented.

"No one is afraid of goblin infantry," Serranus said with a snort. "Nor should anyone be, unless they happen to outnumber you fifty to one. Fortunately, that doesn't happen very often since the little rats take every chance they get to desert whatever orc chieftain has rounded them up to serve as front line fodder. So, Marcus Valerius, what does this tell you about Elebrion?"

"I'm not sure. They fear death, they will only fight from afar, they have only three kingdoms where there were once seven . . . " The realization struck him suddenly. "Oh! I should think their society is probably highly decadent then, that they've likely become amoral pleasure seekers like the men and women of whom Flavius Mundus wrote in the tales of the plague days. Do you think they are in decline?"

"No, it's more than that," Serranus said. "I believe they are waiting to die. Fear has a specific object—not unlike hope, usually. But the object of hope is a future good. A difficult one, perhaps, but always something that is possible to obtain. The object of fear, on the other hand, is a future evil, an evil that irresistible only because it is desired."

Even in the heat of the near-midday sun, Serranus's ominous words struck Marcus with chilling effect. Waiting to die? Fear of death that was born of an irresistible desire for extinction? Although he knew that war between Amorr and Elebrion was a real possibility, it had never occurred to Marcus that it might be the elves, not men, who were wishing for it.

"Truly?"

"Should the Sanctiff in his wisdom decide that they are creatures unfit to serve Our Immaculate Lord," Serranus said, "I suggest it will be a mercy to put their cities to the torch and the remnants of their race to the sword. The High King will not lift his hand against us—not because he fears us, but because he desires what we can give him and his people in the same way that a mortally wounded soldier welcomes the last kiss of steel."

Marcus rode in stunned silence, the hoof-falls of the troop and the creaking of the wooden wagons the only sounds. The road had begun a slight incline and the horses were breathing harder than they had before. Fortunately, there were dark lines running parallel to the road in the distance that promised the possibility of shade once they crested the rise.

Zephanus chuckled. "And here I'd always thought you won that pretty face fighting them in the borderlands, Claudius Serranus. I had no idea that they did nothing but bare their throats to your blade. If the elves are so ready to die, how did you get that scar on your face, then? Were you foolish enough to let Caulus Phillipus shave you?" Zephanus laughed at Marcus's expression and held up a right hand with two fingers folded down. "Phillipus lost half his hand to an orc's axe at Goxlims. Don't let him shave you."

But Marcus wasn't thinking about how Serranus had been scarred. He was more curious about *where* he'd been when he had been scarred.

"Amorr doesn't border on Merithaim, much less Elebrion," he pointed out. "And the elves haven't raided Imperial territory for one hundred years. So, either you are much older than would seem possible, Claudius Serranus, or you are telling us tall tales. Or . . . you were fighting on behalf of someone other than the Senate and People of Amorr."

Serranus laughed. But before he could reply, the horses at the front of the column abruptly pulled up. Marcus rose in the saddle to see over the bishop's wagon. The lead horses had halted at a stone bridge passing over a shallow stream. In a booming voice that carried all the way back to their reguard, Sir Hezekius announced that they would halt long enough to refresh themselves and water their horses.

Normally it would be a slave's job to help Marcus from Barat's back. But although Marcipor was already cantering back toward him, Marcus didn't wait for his help to dismount. With a groan he lifted his right leg over the saddle and dropped awkwardly to the ground. Lodi grunted and followed his example. The two of them locked eyes for a moment, then the dwarf grimaced and rubbed at his thick thighs. Marcus shook his head. It was going to be a long, long ride to Elebrion.

I^A Q. VII A. I ARG. IV

Praeterea, homo in Die Sexto creatus sunt. In ordine naturae qui in narratione Creationis descriptus, perfectius praestat. Ergo homo est perfectior quam aelvi. Tum, perfectissima res animae est separatio ab corpore, quod in illa re similior Dei angelorumque, et purior, quod separatur ab ulla aliena substantia. Quandoquidem non aeque perfecti atque homines, aelvi ulterius quam homines ab perfectissima re animae. Ergo aelvi habent animae naturaliter sibi unita.

THEIR REPRIEVE FROM the road was far too short, but at least his stomach was full of bread, meat, and cheese now, Marcus thought. More importantly, his parched throat was well wetted by the cool waters of the stream. The brook flowed down from hills that were just beginning to become visible on the horizon.

They wouldn't reach them by nightfall, but everyone was looking forward to reaching them all the same, even though the incline would slow their progress. Somewhere on this side of those hills was a monastery where they hoped to spend one night not sleeping on the ground. And on the other side of the hills . . . the mountains of the elven kingdom.

"Douse your head in the water before we ride on," a dripping Zephanus suggested before mounting his horse and joining his brethren.

When the stentorian roar of the Michaeline captain ordered the party to their mounts, both Marcus and Marcipor were quick to follow Zephanus's advice.

"Do you think this will help with the insects?" asked Marcipor, pushing his water-darkened hair out of his eyes as he urged his horse to a walk. Throughout their repast, he had complained of the small cloud of gnats that had pestered him since mid-morning.

"Yes, certainly. Until you dry off and start to sweat again."

"I'll try not to, then." Marce nodded toward Zephanus, who was riding a distance ahead of them now. "You like that priest?"

"I suppose so. With whom were you riding?"

"Ecclesiastus and Habbakus. They're both of Tedes descent, like me."

"Is that so? Which one has the red hair, Habbakus?"

"No, he's the other one. And actually, Ecclesiastus is only Tedes on his mother's side. His father is an Amorran citizen."

"He doesn't look very Amorran to me."

"I said he was a citizen, not that he was of the city. Ecclesiastus said he was from Elkos, I think." Marcipor glanced back at the dwarf. "How is our old billy goat bearing up?"

"As well as I am, I think. His idle chatter is lifting all our spirits. I say, are your legs beginning to chafe? My thighs are rubbed nearly raw. It's been too long since I've ridden so much as an ora."

Marcipor grinned mischievously. "That's just as well. Father Aurelius tends to frown on his pupils spending time in ora-houses."

Even Lodi groaned at the weak pun. Thankfully, before Marce could attempt to surpass himself, they saw Zephanus and Serranus riding back toward them. At their approach, much to Marcus's surprise, Marcipor fell respectfully silent.

"I see you followed my advice," Zephanus noted approvingly. His own dark hair was still damp from the stream.

Serranus leaned over, extending an unexpectedly full wineskin to Marcus. "The Order of Saint Michael wishes to express its gratitude to House Valerius for its meritorious service on behalf of this humble priest." He handed the wineskin to Marcus. "Don't marvel, boy, there's no miracle—it's just water in there."

"Oh," Marcus said, feeling embarrassed. "I trust you found it satisfactory?"

"Very much so," Serranus answered, slapping Zephanus on the back. "Excellent stuff. Didn't you think so?"

"I might have if you'd spared me more than a mouthful, old miser."

"Wisdom and wine are wasted on the young, little brother. Now, Marcus Valerius, I believe you were interested in hearing more of the elves and their way of warfare, were you not?"

"Indeed, Claudius Serranus. If you would be so kind."

Marcipor stifled a yawn.

"Bored already, laddy?" Serranus said to him. "You needn't listen if you don't want."

"Please ignore my bodyguard. He's much more fierce than he looks. It's just that he's slain so many scores of *sottum* that he finds such tales most tedious."

"Indeed?" Claudius Serranus dismissed Marcipor with an audible snort and turned his attention to Marcus. "Well then, as you correctly surmised, in my youth I did not march with the legions. I marched under the banner of the King of Savonderum. In the summer of my fifteenth year, my father died and my elder brother inherited our little farm. He wished to marry, and I wished both to see the world and avoid living under my brother's patriarchy, so it seemed a propitious time to depart.

"I quickly learned that I had no skills that commanded more than a pittance, since the only work available was the sort of work I'd thought to leave behind at the farm. But I was a big lad, and on the third day after I'd left the ancestral village I met a man in a pub who was recruiting for a company of wardogs.

"He said the Red Prince was planning a campaign to teach the cursed elves a lesson. It was something to do with the Collegium Occludum, if I recall correctly, but I wasn't listening closely since my only interest was in the notion of a monthly wage. Plus, I'd wanted to see the world, and marching through it with a sword in my hand accompanied by a band of armed men seemed to be a reasonable way to do it.

"So, I made my *X* on what the recruiter told me was a contract that ran only through the harvest, and thought myself rather clever for it when he generously agreed to pay for the next two rounds." He grinned at Marcus. "Not the wisest move I've ever made."

Marcus feigned surprise. "An illiterate young farmer signing a contract he can't read? Or rather, marking it. In all the tales I've read, such things usually turn out splendidly!"

"Precisely. As it happens, the contract was actually an indenture in which I had sold my body to become the deeded property of one Captain Hilderus, who owned the Bloody Crows. It was a small consortio, only forty-five men, more than half of whom barely knew which end of the sword to hold. Or rather, spear. Although what I was given was little more than a long, pointed stick.

"The Savonders make war in the strangest fashion. Their king doesn't want the expense of a standing army, but he doesn't want to become too dependent upon the great lords, either. So while he provides the engineers, the mages, and perhaps a third of the heavy cavalry, the nobles provide the other two thirds.

"The infantry is a haphazard collection of royal levies taken from wherever the king chooses, land levies taken from the estates of the great and lesser lords, and the 'auxiliaries,' which are simply whatever mercenary companies happen to hear that the king wants men. So, there's a fair number of captains who make a living turning foolish young farm boys into corpses every summer.

"Only two weeks later I found myself marching with the rest of the Crows under the banner of a baron from the other side of Savondum. The baron—his name was Gourgaud, if I recall correctly—was charged with capturing a group of elven raiders that had been burning farms near Voyence.

"We were one hundred horse and six hundred foot, and there were only supposed to be sixty or seventy raiders. Therefore the baron and Captain Hilderous were far more worried about being able to find the enemy and run them down once we did find them than they were about what those sixty elves might be able to do to us. But, you recall what I told you about them before we stopped today?"

"They prefer to keep their distance?" Marcus said.

"Just so. After five days of sighting them and chasing them all over the hills, our outriders ran into their scouts on the edge of an old forest near the western border. In retrospect, I realize they had been leading us around by our noses just to keep us occupied while their commander prepared the ambush. When we finally encountered it, it proved to be as well prepared as any ambush I've seen since.

"The baron thought we'd have the advantage in the hills since they wouldn't find it as easy to use their archers at long range. I'm not sure what he was thinking when we finally brought them to bear with their backs to the forest. My best guess is that he thought they were afraid to run since they were all afoot and outnumbered by our horse. They formed their line with their backs to the trees. It was a double line, but it didn't look very impressive since they were so badly outnumbered and they didn't have much in the way of armor."

Serannus chuckled without amusement and patted the armor packed behind his saddle. "Not that I did, either. I was standing in the third rank with my stick in my hand and nothing but a smelly old red tunic with a shapeless black thing sewn onto the front. It had two big tears in it. Suddenly, and as I watched that small group of elves raise their bows toward us, it occurred to me that I was probably wearing a dead man's shirt. The tears were probably arrow holes. Maybe it was even a shirt that had been worn by two men dead before me."

Serranus stared across the sea of sun-scorched grass and the shapeless, straggly bushes that dotted it like small islands scattered at random. "When the elves loosed their arrows the first time, most of them struck home. It's a terrible sound, an arrow striking a man. Have you ever heard it?"

Marcus shook his head.

"A hiss, a thump, and then usually a scream. But sometimes there's not even that. One man was one rank in front of me and two men to my left. I could have reached out and touched him with my pike. An arrow hit him in the throat. And the way he fell, I figure he was dead before he hit the ground.

"A funny thing, battle, especially when you're just standing in the ranks and people are falling dead to your left and your right for what looks like no good reason. There's a lot of screaming and shouting, but you don't really hear it, and part of you doesn't really believe that you're there at all. It's as if all of the blood and the madness and the shrieking just happens to be taking place around you.

"They loosed their second volley just as our horn sounded the charge. The captain shouted at us to charge with the rest, and like the fools that we were, we ran forward, screaming like a mindless horde of damned souls. I didn't watch how I was holding my pike and nearly stabbed the man in front of me, although I can't see how it would have done him much harm—it wasn't sharp enough to scratch bare skin. But no sooner did we start moving forward when both of the elf lines began to melt back into the trees.

"It was a trap, of course, as I said before. A few stadi in, there was a great defile that was disguised by the brush and trees. It was hard to see where most of the elves were. But when at least a score of them were seen fleeing down into a large defile, we followed them down in the hopes of cornering them at the end of it.

"No one noticed that all the rest of them had slipped to the sides and were hidden above it, on the ridges. I wouldn't be surprised if their confounded mages had disguised them somehow, although elves can move quietly when they want, and they're hard to see in the woods anyway.

"Whoever had prepared the ambush had strung a pair of ropes hanging down from large trees on either side of the ridge. One moment we were chasing them and thought we had them, and the next we found ourselves stacked like cordwood at the far end of the defile just as the very last elves were climbing up the ropes right in front of our eyes. At that point, they began to loose their arrows again. And this time they didn't run away after a pair of volleys. We lost three hundred men that day, most of them in that forest. Only fifteen of the forty-five Crows survived."

"How did you make it through?" Marcus said, imagining the slaughter.

"Mostly cowardice. When I saw that the captain had no more idea what to do than I did, I dropped that useless spear and hid under a fallen tree. I cried, wet myself, and vowed I'd go home to the farm and live my whole life as a better man if only God would spare me from the arrows of the elves."

"Did you?" Marcus could understand the experience of surviving such a terrible ordeal would naturally tend to drive a man to seek the Most High.

"No. If anything, I went the other way. You see, lad, there's no promise less likely to be kept than one made by a frightened man. You'll do well to remember that, should you ever find a frightened man making you one."

"But I thought that was how you came to become a priest. How did you become a Michaeline?"

Claudius Serranus smiled. "That's between me and St. Michael, Marcus Valerius. And until today, it had nothing to do with elves. Now, do you want to hear how we beat that very same group of long-eared devils? Better yet, let me ask you. How do you think the baron went about it?"

Marcus stared at the scarred, sun-leathered face of the old warrior. But the Michaeline's half-mocking smile told him nothing that he did not know already. He viewed Marcus as a noble, still wet behind the ears and innocent of battle for all that he might well be expected to send men to die in it—if he did not take refuge in the Church.

"I don't know," he admitted. "I expect you found a way to trap them between the horse and your surviving infantry, but I don't know how you could manage it in such broken ground. Especially since you implied that they had at least one battlemage, who would've been better than any the king would have given a minor noble charged with pursuing a small group of raiders. And while the cavalry would have been faster on the plains, I would think a well-trained elven force would move more quickly through hills and forests."

"All elven forces are well trained," Serranus said. "Between their long lives and the experience of their commanders, which no man can hope to match, no troop of men has ever been an equal, man for elf, to any elven force. But, perhaps due in part to that very excellence, they are more prone to a weakness of character that makes them vulnerable. Hubris."

"Pride? But all the strategists write that soldiers must be proud in their service, particularly in their units, if they are to fight well."

"I said hubris, not pride. God hates the arrogant and He hates the proud. But not all pride is out of place. There is a pride that would rule and a pride that would serve. The pride that makes a man hold his ground and refuse to be the first to run when his cohort is being pressed hard by the foe, that is a good thing, a needful thing. It is a strength. The pride that causes a commander to despise his enemy counterpart, that is a fatal flaw."

"How did the elven commander despise the baron?" Zephanus asked. "I can only assume that's what you're implying, but I still don't see how that helped him beat them."

Serranus glanced at his brother in the order and the irritation in his eyes silenced the younger priest. "I'm not concerned whether you see it. I'm seeking to determine if the scholar here can ascertain the answer, given the suggestions I've provided."

"The elf despised the baron," Marcus answered. "He'd beaten him, beaten him badly, and so he must have assumed that the baron would fall back into a defensive position. The elf had already been raiding the area for some time. So, having accomplished whatever he'd come there to do, he'd think he could withdraw with impunity, without any serious risk of being attacked again."

"So what would you have done if you were the baron?"

"I would have done just what the elf expected. I wouldn't have wanted to risk losing any more men. I'd have tried to defend the villages most likely to be attacked. I'd garrison those villages with my remaining infantry and half my cavalry, then station the rest of my horse in a central location from where they could react to the first sign of a fresh incursion."

"Conventional, but sound. And yet you seem noncommittal."

"I already know that the baron didn't do that because you suggested he *attacked* the raiding force somehow."

"Very well, what would you do if you were ordered to prevent the elves from withdrawing?"

"I know where they're withdrawing to?"

"Of course. They were from Merethaim. If they were from Kir Donas, they'd have been around the coasts, not near the western border. The High King never risked his elves on raids and such."

Marcus tried to remember his geography. He could almost picture the scroll upon which a detailed map of Savonderum had been painstakingly inked. He remembered it had a red border that ran the length of the scroll and the ornate compass on the bottom left had two animal heads facing east and west. A wolf and a unicorn?

He forced his mind's memory to travel north from the compass, up past the very road from Amorr they were currently riding, but east of the mountains that within days would appear in the distance to block their path. The eastern half of Savonderum consisted of flat, rich-soiled plans that produced the kingdom's wealth. But the west was covered by the hills and forests that led to the Elflands and the savage wilds.

There were no large cities in the west, for the land would not support it. Only small towns and villages scattered haphazardly over the hillsides. In the south, the border was relatively open and was marked by a large lake that devolved into the marshes inhabited by the swamp goblins and a few degenerate orc tribes.

In the north, however, the hills swelled into proper mountains, through which only a small number of high country passes might offer transit for a force the size Serranus had described. It was through one of these that the withdrawing elven raiders could have been relied upon to use as they returned to Merithaim and safety.

Marcus smiled. He had it!

"Your baron withdrew his infantry to defensive positions near the key villages to discourage further attacks, then sent his horse to block the passes before the elves could reach them. He had them dismount and fight as infantry, where their heavy armor would help protect them from archery and give them the advantage when the elves were forced to close with them."

Marcipor beamed at him and he felt a measure of triumph when Serranus nodded.

But then the Michaeline held up a finger. "Well done, but there are four passes through the mountains between northern Savonderum and Merithaim. The baron had only one hundred horse. How did he know which pass they were going to use?"

"He guessed and got lucky?" Marcipor said.

"What would have prevented the elf commander from simply withdrawing and attempting a different pass once he found his first choice blocked?"

"Oh," Marcipor made a face, disappointed.

"The boy's forgetting something," Lodi growled unexpectedly. "You were there, priest-man. And you weren't on horseback neither."

Marcus's jaw dropped. He was too surprised by the truth of the comment to rebuke Lodi for the lack of deference the dwarf had showed for 'the boy' who was, after all, his present master. He'd forgotten that Claudius Serranus must have been there for the fight, based on his earlier comments, and as a lowly auxiliary pikeman he certainly hadn't been with the cavalry! And hadn't Serranus said something about the cries of warhawks in the mountains?

"I know," Marcus said excitedly, waving his arm and nearly causing Barat to shy. "He didn't send his horse. He force-marched the infantry and divided them between the four passes. And he didn't take any defensive positions. He used the horse to trail the raiders until they gave up and decided to go home. Only, when they did, they found their road blocked by fifty or more spears!"

"Gourgaud divided us into three groups, not four. Groups of one hundred each. He knew they wouldn't use the southernmost pass because that would take them quite far out of the way on the elven side of the border.

"My group marched for six days, stopping only to sleep and eat. Eighty-two of us made it to the top of the Summus Nufeninus, the highest and most narrow pass of the three. Think yourselves fortunate that we won't be riding through any ground as difficult as that confounded goat trail. We reached it just as night was falling. So exhausted we were from the march up the winding path that we didn't even post guards.

"When the first man woke up the next morning, he saw the sun reflecting off the shields of our cavalry approaching the base of the pass. Which meant the elves were closer still. Indeed, the elves were already more than halfway to the summit, so we had no time for anything but to clear the camp and position three lines of twenty men just below the crest of the pass, with the other twenty behind a huge boulder that marked the summit on the southern side.

"The Savonder who led us would have liked to hit them from both sides as they came over the top, but there was no shelter on the north side. There was nothing there but a drop of three or four stadium from the ledge."

"I should think sweeping them off that ledge would have been an effective measure," Zephanus said.

Serranus nodded. "It was, to an extent. Pursued as they were by the cavalry, the elves hadn't happened to notice the marks of our recent passage. We hit them just as they crested the rise. The men hiding to the south killed ten or twelve of their vanguard as they broke from cover, but the difficulty of the climb had caused the elven line to extend itself to the point that the ambush wasn't as devastating as it might have been otherwise.

"I was in the first line blocking the pass. But only a few of the elves, four or maybe five, came our way. We killed them, of course. I stuck one through the leg with my wretched stick before two other Crows got him in the chest and throat. But they were tremendous fighters. Fast and deadly, wielding two longswords more easily than a legionary uses his gladius. It was six to one, and they still managed to kill four of us and wound eight more before we brought the last one down.

"The rest of them retreated back down the trail and behind a curve. A few of our men followed, but they went down with arrows in their eyes. At that range, no elf was going to miss. So we fell back and waited, thinking that once the cavalry worked its way up the pass on foot, the elves would be forced to try to break through our line at the summit."

"Where did the warhawks come in?" asked Marcus.

Serranus smiled at him, but there was no warmth in it. It was a grim expression of recollection, a remembrance of deaths past. "Armored as they were, the cavalry wasn't able to climb as quickly as we had. I daresay they were a little reluctant to climb too, knowing that they'd be climbing into range of the elven archers. Regardless, they'd barely passed the second switchback when we saw a huge bird flying over the mountains to the west.

"The elves must have had scouts out every day flying over the passes to see when their raiding parties would be returning. From below us, their mage sent some sort of flare high into the air. There was a burst of red light, and the bird swooped down upon us. I'd never seen a warhawk before, but I can tell you, they're much more frightening than you think a bird could be.

"It had wings more than four perticae wide and a beak that could crush a man's head like a seed. But the real danger was its rider. I later learned that only sorcerers are permitted to be sky riders, so I didn't know to take cover when the bird dove down at us. I can still remember he was wearing some sort of leathers covered with fur—I suppose it must get cold so high in the sky—and he threw a ball of fire at us just as he swept past.

"It was fire from hell, it must have been, because it wasn't like a normal fire that burns away a man's clothes before his flesh. This magefire no sooner touched a man than it burned right through him. I was lucky: it barely singed my left arm. But four others died screaming within seconds." He pushed back his sleeve and, with a mild flourish, extended his arm toward the others.

Marcus could see a strip of puckered, twisted skin, the mark of a burn made long ago. He shivered with horror, thinking of the heat that could produce such a scar so quickly and what it would be like to be engulfed in it.

His eyes shot to the two elves riding ahead of them. What madness it seemed to court the ire of these inhuman devils. And yet, was it not equally unthinkable to suffer them to live proudly in their high mountains, scorning both God and the kingdoms of man with their dark, demonic magics?

Or was it possible, as the heretic Brutus Giordunus wrote, that what the Church claimed was elvish sorcery was merely a tool, a physical construct no more evil in itself than an onager or a gladius? A gladius was shaped in a forge, Giordunus noted, where elements of earth were cunningly woven together with elements of air and fire in a mysterious sorcery known only to the smith, and yet its evil resided solely in the thoughts of its wielder.

Perhaps elven sorceries were only clever tricks developed over the ages by a long-lived, close-mouthed race and viewed with awe by man in much the same way that barbarians marveled at the great walls of Amorr when they saw them for the first time.

But Giordunus had never seen with his own eyes the elven magic he defended with his contorted logic. Claudius Serranus certainly believed in its sorcerous reality, and who would know the truth of the matter better than the warriors of St. Michael?

"Yes, the baron could see the sky rider," Serranus was answering Marcipor. "He saw it land, which told him where the elves were trapped. He already knew he had to reach that spot before nightfall, when their vision would give them the advantage over us at the summit. But when the bird left almost immediately and flew due west, that told him the elven commander thought he could get reinforced by air before then. So, we had very little time."

"He didn't have his men ride their horses up the trail, did he?"

"No, Marcus Valerius, that wasn't possible. In fact, what he did was order them to dismount and remove all of their armor so they could move at speed. They marched double-time up that path with nothing more than their shields and their helms to protect them from the archers. The elves, seeing their advantage, began targeting them as soon as they passed the next switchback.

"They had to endure five more switchbacks and had lost ten or fifteen men to the arrows before we realized that if we couldn't take the pressure off them somehow, they weren't going to make it. So we gathered as many rocks as we could find, climbed to the edge, and started hurling them down at the elves below. It didn't harm them much, but it kept them from being able to aim so well at the men-at-arms climbing the pass.

"Finally, when they reached the turn that would take them right beneath the place where the elves were trapped and expose them to murderous archery, the horn below sounded the charge. We took that as our sign to rush down the path, but we left ten men above to keep up the barrage of rocks. We lost a few men coming down, and the baron lost even more on that final stretch, but we hit them fore and aft despite the best efforts of their archers.

"It didn't last long, but it was a supremely vicious fight. I've never seen the like since. Nearly as many from both sides died from being thrown from the heights as did being pierced by swords or those wretched sticks we carried. But in the end, we killed every long-lived devil on that mountain."

Serranus patted the scabbard at his side, then drew his weapon forth from it. It was a longsword, but it was not the Amorran cavalryman's blade Marcus was expecting. It was a thin, delicately engraved sword with the famous blued edge that indicated its elven heritage.

Marcus heard himself gasp in chorus with Marcipor. Even Lodi grunted with surprise. Few had ever laid eyes on an elvensword except in battle. The few captured blades that weren't claimed by kings and great lords on the battlefield were usually purchased by their agents within weeks of their whereabouts being discovered. Moreover, the length of these blades precluded them being used by any Amorran soldier who fought with the legions on foot.

"I took this off a prettily-togged devil that was wearing a golden lorica and helm. He'd killed Captain Hilderus and three others, but his left-hand sword stuck in the last man's ribs and gave me the chance to jam my stick right into his mouth. He choked on that, he did! One of the baron's men finished him off. The confounded sergeant claimed the armor and one blade for the baron afterwards, but he let me keep this one. I've worn it ever since. There's no magic in it, not according to the Master Dower of the Order, but it's a fine blade and keeps an edge like nothing I've ever seen."

The old warrior-priest ran his thumb lovingly down the line of the sword, over the elvish runes that spelled out some unintelligible message, most likely the deeds and lineage of the elf who had borne it.

Caught up in admiring Serranus's trophy, neither Marcus and his bodyguards nor the two Michaelines heard the rider on the white horse approaching from the front of the column until he was almost upon them.

It was the elf wearing the circlet, the aristocratic sorcerer, and from the bloodless appearance of his face and his rage-filled silver eyes, it didn't require a master of elven lore to see that he was furious. Claudius Serranus half-raised the blade in an instinctive gesture of defense, so threatening was the violence of the elf's demeanor, and Marcus reined Barat in and urged him off to the side lest he find himself caught between the priest and the elf.

"How dare you bear that weapon!" the elf hissed. "Were this not an embassy sealed before the High King by vows of salt and silver, I would flay the flesh from your bones this very day, cursed human!"

Serranus's eyes widened with shock and confusion. But the elf's threat didn't cow him. Instead it seemed to bring him back to his hardened nonchalance. His scarred face twisted scornfully as he glanced from the sword to the elf, shrugged, and slid the blade back into its scabbard.

"How dare I bear it? I daresay I may claim that right seeing as I killed him who bore it before me, Sir Elf. But that was long ago, in a place far from here. What's this blade to you, and how have I caused you any offense?"

The elf stared at Claudius Serranus for what seemed to Marcus like a very long time. Neither man nor elf blinked, until the elf's long left ear twitched and he broke contact, staring briefly up into the sky as if coming to a decision. Then he spoke in icy tones that testified to an anger far too great for mere words.

"My name is Fáelán u Flann. I am cousin to King Mael. That sword was forged as a name-day gift for my sister's son, the High Lord Cathan u Treasach. Rest assured, Blessed Sir, I shall contest your claim to it, and soon. Thank your dead god that I do not do so this day."

Lord Fáelán turned his horse and kicked it forward, leaving an appalled silence in his wake. Claudius Serranus stared at the elf's departing back as Zephanus groaned and buried his face in his hands.

All through the aches and pains of the long, hot day on horseback, Marcus had wondered if he had the physical where-withal to survive the month-long ride to Elebrion. But now he found himself contemplating the possibility, remote though it must be, that the embassy might not even survive its first week.

High in the sky above him, the sun began its slow descent toward evening. And the shadows cast by the trees lining the brick road lengthened, bit by bit.

Iᴬ Q. VII A. I S. C.

Sed contra est quod Oxonus dicit quod in rationalus animalibus appetitus sensitivus obedit rationi. Ergo inquantum ducitur quadam aestimativa naturali, quae subiicitur rationi superiori, scilicet divinae, est in eis quaedam similitudo moralis boni, quantum ad anima.

MARCUS DID NOT stir when the bells for Matins rang throughout the monestary. Nor did he wake when Marcipor shook him, first by the foot and then, more firmly, by the shoulder. He did, however, come to his senses with a distinct sense of alarm combined with an even greater feeling of confusion when Lodi finally picked him up by the front of his tunica and held him on his feet until he was conscious enough to stand on his own.

It was dark. Marcus could see little but shadowy black figures moving quietly amidst the barely lighter grey background, from which he concluded that it was sometime between prima and altera.

Light flared unexpectedly, and he shielded his eyes as Marce swept a torch around the small chamber they'd been given.

"Careful with that, boy," Lodi snapped. "Some things in my baggage don't take kindly to flame."

"What are you talking about?" Marcipor said.

Lodi snatched the torch and placed it in the iron holder near the door.

Marcus groaned at the discovery of how stiff his legs were, for all that they'd slept cool, dry, and comfortable on straw mattresses laid over clean stone. It was downright cold now, though, as the night's chill had penetrated the brick walls of their chamber.

He wondered if they were expected to appear for the morning prayers and if he'd be able to stay awake through them if they were. He thought about having Marcipor ask one of the monks moving through the adjacent corridor, until he recalled that the question would serve no purpose. Although the Quiricusian monks had proven to be excellent hosts, they were not very talkative ones, being sworn to silence this month in mournful memory of their martyred child-saint.

"Good morning," he said to Marcipor and Lodi. "I don't suppose either of you remember how to get back to the dining hall?"

Both of them thought they did, although Marcus had more confidence in Lodi than Marce. He supposed a dwarf had to be born with a good sense of direction or else develop one quickly living a life that consisted of wandering through unlit caverns miles underground. He sat down on the still-warm mattress, pulled his boots on, then reluctantly stood back up and glanced around to ensure that Lodi hadn't missed anything when repacking their personal effects into the large leather bag that held them. He hadn't.

"Onward to Elfland it is. Lead on, good sir dwarf, if you would be so kind."

Lodi nodded. If the dwarf wasn't the most respectful of servitors, he was at least obedient and hadn't murdered Marcus and Marcipor in their sleep when given the opportunity. Although he'd never been given much occasion to think about it before, he found that an absence of murderous intent was a quality to cherish in a slave. It had probably been foolish, given his brief acquaintance with the dwarf, to permit him to stay in the chamber overnight. But Marcus had simply been too tired last night to care.

The dining hall was dark, lit only by two torches and the grey predawn light that entered through the windows that overlooked the stables. Twelve Michaelines already dressed for the road sat at two of the rough-hewn wooden tables in the hall, breaking their fast with what looked like a hot oatmeal. Serranus was there, but not Zephanus.

In the middle of the room was a stack of wooden bowls accompanied by wooden spoons. Steam rose from a much larger bowl that Marcus guessed held the oatmeal. When he followed Marcipor over to the table, he saw there were also two smaller bowls, one holding salt and the other honey.

Roast goat in the evening and honey in the morning. These monks fed their guests well, he thought. It was a pity they wouldn't find hosts like this again until they crossed the mountains. Of course, it wasn't often that the abbot was given the chance to host a bishop who was known to hold the favor of the Sanctiff himself.

They sat at the table next to the Michaelines, but found themselves eating in silence. The first time Marcipor opened his mouth, one of the Michaelines cleared his throat and pointedly shook his head. Marcus was rather relieved. Marce's commentaries on the quotidian peculiarities of Creation were best endured on a full stomach well after daybreak. The echoed chanting and singing of the monks at their morning prayers was a much-preferred accompaniment to the meal.

A Quiricusian brother emerged just as the first Michaeline finished his meal and rose from the table. The warrior-priest bowed in polite thanks as he handed the robed monk his empty bowl, and the gesture was returned. It seemed there was rather more respect than rivalry between these two very different orders, although there was little similarity to be found between the creaking, armor-clad Michaeline and the slender Quiricusian. And yet, Marucs thought, there is as little similarity between the eye and the stomach, though a man is wise to value both. In the service of God, who is to say which is the more needful?

It was an interesting thought. But could the analogy be stretched so far as to encompass the likes of the elves, much less orcs and goblins, let alone trolls? Difficult.

In the courtyard outside, they discovered that the Quiricusians had thoughtfully prepared their horses for them already. They also discovered that Serranus and the other Michaelines they'd seen in the dining hall were the tardy ones. The rest of the warrior-priests were already mounted or standing near their horses. Marcus ordered Marcipor to check the cinch on Barat even as he checked Bucephalus. All was in order, from which he concluded that the monks had some proper horsemen in their stables.

The sun was just beginning to send its first long, flat glints of crimson out like scouts roaming across the horizon when the bishop emerged from the left side of the main building, accompanied by his entourage. Father Aestus was there too, looking sleepy. Beside him walked the abbot and a pair of elderly monks. They had been given separate accommodation befitting their standing, as had the two elves.

Bishop Claudo glanced around the courtyard sourly and his eyes narrowed. "Where are those elves?" he said, with a hint of irritation in his voice. The abbot silently dispatched one of his companions to fetch the laggards.

"I see you survived yesterday's ride." Marcus turned around and saw Zephanus, already astride his big white gelding.

"Good morning to you, brother. You look eager to get back on the road."

"I am refreshed, Marcus Valerius. My soul is restored. Let everything that hath breath praise the Lord indeed, for do not our brothers the birds greet the new day with a song sweeter than any sung by man?"

Marcus forced a smile, but he feared it was a thin one. Dear Lord in Heaven, have mercy—the friendly young warrior-priest was a morning creature! Such beings were far more alien to him than elves.

"I know a few of the brothers were hoping we'd be permitted to wake after Matins ends, but then, we'd have missed the best part of the day!" He gestured east, toward the red glow of the imminent sunrise. "And look, it seems our silent brethren have located our long-eared friends at last."

"I fear they don't share your preference for an early rise, brother."

"Nor, I think, do you, Marcus Valerius. Either you're particularly fascinated with that chestnut tree over there or your stare is a bit fixed."

Marcus blinked as Zephanus grinned.

"If you think he's a night bird, you should see Sextus, his cousin," said Marcipor, who was still yawning and rubbing at his own eyes. "Now that the elves are here, we should probably mount, don't you think?"

Marcus agreed, but it seemed the abbot had other ideas. He, at least, was obviously not subject to his order's vow of silence. First he made the bishop a pretty speech about the honor his holy presence had bestowed upon the humble order of Saint Quiricus. Then he turned toward Captain Hezekius and said a few words about the noble example of the Michaelines and what an inspiration they were to the lesser orders. Both men were presented with small silver reliquaries, which he assured them were pieces of marble from the very steps that had shattered the blessed skull of their child-saint.

Then, to Marcus's and everyone else's surprise, the abbot turned to the two elves and pronounced a blessing on them, before wishing the entire party a safe and peaceful journey.

Marcus noticed that the elves didn't seem particularly inclined to speak with anyone. And while Lord Fáelán appeared to be pointedly ignoring the Michaelines, at least he greeted the bishop with appropriate civility. After a nod from the bishop, Captain Hezekius ordered the party to mount, and those who had not already done so were quick to obey.

Marcus couldn't help groaning as he stepped into the stirrup and threw his leg over the saddle, but he reminded himself that it was only a matter of time before his body began to adjust. Until it did, he would simply have to bear the pain that nearly everyone but the Michaelines were feeling.

The grey-robed guards at the monastery gates bowed deeply, but silently, as the bishop rode past. How strange it would be to keep one's thoughts to oneself for an entire month! Marcus doubted he could do it. Perhaps a week would be possible, but any more and he'd be desperate to say something, anything, to anyone who would listen. He grinned, thinking of Sextus, who couldn't last an hour without opening his mouth if he wasn't sleeping. Which, he thought enviously, was assuredly what his cousin was doing right now rather than riding out at dawn on a fool's journey to Elebrion.

"I do say, it's a bit brisk out," Marcipor said. "But I imagine we'll be sorry when this morning chill burns off."

"Yes," Marcus said, "I certainly hope there will be some clouds today. I felt rather like a pot baking in the kiln yesterday afternoon."

"That tall elf lord doesn't seem to still be upset today," Marcipor said, albeit in a manner that made it sound as if he was trying to convince himself, not Marcus. "After all, it's hardly Claudius Serranus's fault that he happened to encounter the elf's kin on the battlefield."

"I suspect the elves might have a different way of looking at it than we might, Marce. From what I understand, they have a very different way of looking at many things. Stratius writes that whereas we view events as taking place within the framework of a vast and essential order, as a part of the fabric of the world, the elves see them as being of no consequence in themselves. Events only take on meaning insofar as they are given meaning by mind."

"What does that have to do with Serranus killing the elf?"

"Very little, I should think. He killed much like an animal does, fighting to survive in the face of death, and he apparently ascribed no more meaning to his taking of the elf's life than he did to any other death in battle. He was a soldier, and that's what soldiers do in war. However, his decision to claim the elf's sword as a trophy, to say nothing of his subsequent use of it as a marker of distinction—which you'll note is most unusual in a priest, even a priest of a martial order like the Michaelines—indicates that the event must have been of some degree of significance to him."

"I see," Marcipor said in a way that made Marcus doubt very much that he did. "So what is the meaning, then?"

"The meaning of the event of his taking the elf sword and subsequent bearing of it?"

"Yes."

"I haven't any idea at all. I may not even be correct. Perhaps Lord Fáelán simply wishes to see his nephew revenged. Although I doubt that. Familial relationships aren't quite as close among the elves, I understand. One can see how living several hundreds of years might encourage a certain amount of distance between the various members of a family. It's bad enough having to listen to Sexto tell the same five jokes over and over again. After one hundred years of them, I think I'd have to take vows with the Quiricusians before I murdered him."

"Don't you think he would have made for a better travel companion than the one we've got?" Marcipor asked softly.

Marcus glanced back at Lodi. The dwarf still sat his mule heavily, but when they'd changed his bandage upon arrival at the monastery, there hadn't been any ill-hued stains indicating infection. And if the dwarf didn't take much away from the tedium of the road, he also didn't add to it. Sextus, like a sword, could easily cut either way. While Marcus knew he'd eventually miss his cousin, at this early hour the dour silence of the dwarf was much to be preferred over what would have been a long and energetic listing of grievances.

Neither Zephanus nor Claudius Serranus rode near them this morning. In fact, as the morning wore on, it became apparent that the Michaelines had been commanded to stay away from the two elves—and anyone else who didn't belong to their order. Marcus couldn't blame Captain Hezekius for the change, in light of yesterday's disastrous near-altercation. But he regretted it all the same. Riding a horse could be a great pleasure when one was galloping through open fields, but this slow, monotonous walk over mile after mile of unchanging road was about as tedious as anything Marcus had ever encountered in his life.

The scenery was little changed from the day before. The mountains in the distance seemed no closer, and the scrub brush harbored little in the way of interesting fauna. Fortunately, the promised clouds made their appearance and shielded their necks and faces from the worst of the mid-morning sun. Marcus hoped they would not burn away before the oppressive heat of the afternoon.

He found it hard to imagine what it must be like for the legionaries, marching along these roads for days at a stretch, scorched by the sun while carrying all of their supplies, armor, and possessions on their backs. No wonder they were so fearless in battle! Facing an army of howling orcs and shrieking goblins would almost seem like paradise after weeks on the unforgiving road, especially if one could wait in the comfort of the shade for their attack.

He wondered why the legions didn't march at night and sleep during the day. Why didn't they ride at night themselves, come to think of it? Surely that would make more sense than to subject themselves to this brutal regimen. His saddle creaked as he shifted in it trying to find a spot on his thighs that had not been rubbed nearly raw the day before. But why bother? It wasn't midday yet and they had at least six more hours to ride today, so by the time they were permitted to dismount for the evening, whatever spot he'd managed to miss yesterday would be thoroughly chafed.

Marcipor rode along beside him, his head cast down and his eyes half-closed. He'd made a game attempt to keep up the conversation at first, but now he too rode in a shell of silent contemplation of his own misery. Ahead of them, a few of the Michaelines began to sing, but their voices faltered when an older warrior glared at them, and soon the column was silent again except for the interminable clop-clop-clop of the horses' hooves on the flattened stone-and-mortar *crusta*.

A gravelly voice interrupted his morose moss-gatherings.

"Forget what the priest told you."

"About what?" He was too surprised to hear the dwarf address him to say anything else.

"The elves. Yesterday."

"You don't think Claudius Serranus killed the elf lord? If not, then where did he get that sword? That Lord Fáelán doesn't seem inclined to doubt him."

"I meant his idea that the elves are dying because they want to die. Nonsense."

"Quite possibly. But Serranus does seem to have some experience of them. And you must consider that they've lost half their kingdoms too, more than half, actually, and five of their seven royal lines have failed. There aren't anywhere near so many elves as there used to be. Perhaps they exhausted themselves in their war against the Witchkings. They never really recovered from that."

"Five of the seven?" Marcipor asked. "I thought there were still three kingdoms?"

"There are, but the House of Silverspume isn't royal. King Ithamar's father succeeded the last Deeptide king after he was killed in a battle with the Tritonian Mer."

"The Witchkings wasn't just their war," Lodi growled. "The dwarves fought too. So did the orcs and men. But elves aren't dying out because of the Witchkings, or the fish-lovers, or because they read too much poetry. It's that cursed elven pride that'll do for them in the end."

"It is written 'pride goeth before a fall,'" Marcus admitted. "But I find it difficult to imagine that you spent much time immersed in Holy Writ during your employment by the stables of the Reds. Or anywhere you happened to find yourself before your inadvertent visit to our great city."

"I wasn't visiting, I was a slave!"

"As you say," Marcus nodded, too interested to hear what the dwarf was saying to bother correcting him. "Do continue."

"They're arrogant beyond all reason, probably arrogant beyond your capacity to believe or understand. They won't change, they can't change, because doing so would mean admitting that they're not a race of demigods superior to dwarf and man alike."

"What about orcs and goblins?"

"That goes without saying."

"Of course. Why do they have to change, though? What is the problem?"

"I don't think your old priest noticed. He was probably too busy just trying to stay alive. That, or he can't tell one pretty, beardless face from another. But do you know how men say that dwarves are all alike, that there's no difference between dwarf and dwarva?"

"Dwarva?"

"A female dwarf, a dwarf-mother."

"Ah, I've heard it said that they have beards too, and they fight like the men. Or rather, dwarves."

Lodi smiled thinly beneath the orange stubble of his growing beard. He made a sound that was somewhere between a snort and a cough. "That's not true. Few men have ever seen a dwarva, for they seldom leave the safety of the mines and mountains. But it is true of the elves."

"I can only assume you are referring to the fighting, and not the beards?"

"I am that."

"The elf maidens fight? Really? I've never read a single scholar who made note of that. And Magnus never mentioned it in any of his old stories either. How do you know?"

Lodi gestured to his bandaged side. "The training master told you I got this during the Iron Mountain spectacle."

"Yes, I recall."

"I was there."

Marcus stared at the dwarf, amazed. He glanced over at Marcipor and saw that he too was surprised by Lodi's casual statement.

"You were there, during the great siege?" Marcipor asked. "But that was so long ago!"

"We may not live as long as elves, slave boy, but we aren't as short-lived as men either. I was there from the start to the end, seven years all told. I saw the Troll King die, I saw the great duel between Grokthorn and Gorbag, and I couldn't tell you how many orcs and goblins and spiders and wolves fell before my axe. Could tell you how many trolls, though, that I could tell you."

"How many?" Marcus asked.

"Not a one. Never managed to kill a single rockhead in all that time, if you can believe it. Leastways not by my axe."

"What does this have to do with the elves?" Marcipor wanted to know.

"Not much. But do you want to know about elves, or do you want to know about Iron Mountain?"

"Both," Marcus answered. "I want to know about both."

So, as they rode beneath the grey shield of the clouds, Lodi told them.

I^A Q. VII A. I CO. I

Respondeo: De hac quaestione, variae opiniones erat. Imprimis, si anima sua natura absoluta res esset, quae creata fuisset sola, probaretur quod anima neque homo neque aelvus esset. Sed, cum anima natura particeps in forma corporis necesse sit suae creata sit, non separatim, sed in corpore. Siquidem anima res absoluta esset, simillima angelorum. Attamen quod anima particeps in forma corporis, considerandum est, secundum iusta principia, particeps in genere animalium. Ergo non potest illa base statui, sed necesse est considerare praecipuam naturam generis aelvi.

MARCUS RODE ALONG the dusty road at the back end of what he hoped would turn out to be an important historical expedition. But at the moment the momentous journey was secondary to the every clop and shift of Barat beneath him. He was endlessly grateful that Lodi was suddenly willing to speak more than two sentences at a time. And as the dwarf spoke, the miles passed by and it was as if his words fell away and Marcus could see the events happening in his mind's eye.

It was the Savondese knight-errant, Sir Alwys d'Escard, who was responsible for the fame of the seven-year siege spreading throughout the wider world, Lodi said. He was not, as it was sometimes reported, the only man to have fought for the dwarves during the vast and terrible war that was waged between the armies of the Troll King and the dwarves of Iron Mountain. He was, as a matter of fact, merely a royal ambassador from the king of Savondir to what passed for King Guldur Goblinsbane's court.

There wasn't another king in Selenoth so rude or so cruel as to entertain himself by juggling the skulls of courtiers with whom he had grown discontent. Even if there had been, no king would have been capable of doing so with skulls he had personally removed with his bare hands only moments before.

D'Escard's version of the great siege, written in a dactylic hexameter worthy of the heroism shown there, was long on vivid details that captured men's imaginations, such as the terrible climb of The Twenty, who braved orc slings and goblin catapults and troll-thrown boulders to trigger a massive avalanche that buried the proud gates of Iron Mountain beneath masses of stone just as Guldur's rams were about to shatter them.

His rendition of the Breaking of the Elves, which recounted the dashing Prince Everbright's doomed attempt to drive off the besiegers, was known to have brought even the most hard-bitten men-at-arms to tears. And few would forget D'Escard's telling of the epic brawl between Bergulmor and Oskrug Orceater that followed the Goblinsbane's sudden death, a titanic battle that not only broke the siege but divided the newly born kingdom of the trolls in twain as well.

Too bad most of it was hogswallop.

What it lacked, Lodi said, was the greater part of the story, namely the story as seen through the eyes of the dwarves. It was not merely that D'Escard's *The Siege of Iron Mountain* lacked a true dwarven feel, composed as it was in High Savondese. But as a foreign member at the Troll King's court, D'Escard had simply never been witness to the ugly, bloody struggles that took place within the dark roots of the mountain, the violent battles deep beneath the surface that comprised the greater and more decisive aspects of the lengthy siege.

And so Lodi made to right that wrong for Marcus and Marcipor.

Lodi was a young dwarf of fifty-two on the day that the first scouts reported that the rumors of an immense troll-led army massing near the foothills of the Volpiscenes were actually true. This was unthinkable for three reasons. First, the orc tribes weren't in the habit of following the orders of their own grand chieftans, let alone a goblin or troll. Second, trolls didn't lead armies.

And third, only a fool or a madman would attempt to invade the mountainous Dwarflands, where much of the terrain was impassible and there was virtually nothing of value that was accessible to an invading army. There was great wealth throughout the four dwarven kingdoms of the Underdeep, of course, but that was a vast, uncharted, and lightless series of mazes. It was no place for anyone without a reliable source of light and an unerring sense of direction underground—of the sort possessed by nearly every dwarf and hardly any other sentient creature inhabiting Selenoth.

Lodi had been a miner, he said, a successful one who, despite his youth, owned two silver veins, one of which was possessed of enough promise that he had thought of proposing marriage to a certain dwarva named Geral. Geral's father owned a shield-factory that supplied King Hammerstone's Iron Guard.

Lodi was there paying court to Geral, intending to gift her with a small bit of ore from his most recent shaft, when one of the guardsmen, in full armor, entered the factory and told Geral's father that all of his spare shields were required immediately, even those still lacking the king's regalia worked in gold that customarily served as the boss.

Furthermore, the guardsman said, the factory was to begin working around the clock so that as many shields as dwarvenly possible would be produced, and Geral's father was to make a list of the materials he required and they would be delivered at the earliest opportunity. A second list would also be required of him, one consisting of the names of his workers, so they could be spared the forthcoming levy so that they might supply not only the Guard, but the militia, the levy, and any other dwarf who might raise a shield in defense of their mountain.

"You look like a dwarf who knows how to swing a hammer," the guard told Lodi. "A warhammer is much the same, except it's easier to crack a skull than a rock."

"I can swing a hammer," answered Lodi.

"Then I advise you to come with me. Either you can fight with the King's Own, or you can fight with young dwarves like yourself who don't know an orc from a goblin on either side of you."

Lodi decided that his chances of surviving an encounter with the enemy were probably higher if he encountered them in the company of experienced warriors rather than fellow neophytes. And he also wanted to impress Geral. So he did as the guard suggested. First, though, he begged a shield from Geral's father, who gruffly waved away any offer to pay for it, and for his efforts won a kiss on the cheek from a duly-impressed, wet-eyed Geral.

He found it hard to regret that kiss even now, he said, although he cursed it many a time when the Iron Guard was once more summoned in the dead of the night. Again and again they were called to stand in the gap and cover the retreat of some lesser regiment or sometimes the militia when they'd been beaten back by a mighty troll, an elite force of orcs, or sometimes just the sheer numbers that the Troll King was able to throw at them. More than once he'd marched shoulder to shoulder with his grim-faced companions through a dark tunnel toward the enemy as fleeing dwarves streamed back to safety on either side of them, and he thought that he very well might be among those dwarves—were it not for that kiss.

Usually, it wasn't long before the Guard found themselves engaged and pressing forward over the bodies of dead dwarves who hadn't been fortunate enough to fall back in time. Lodi realized that it was just as likely that he would have been numbered among those unfortunates.

His training had consisted of a rudimentary fitting that saw his iron armor welded to fit him, more or less, and the receipt of a helm that neither fit him nor quite matched those of his fellow guards. He also received a hammer that had a heavier, broader head and a lighter shaft than the one to which he was accustomed.

Then he was given a short lecture from a grey-bearded sergeant who informed him that if he ran, he'd better run toward the enemy because they'd treat him a good deal better than the sergeant would. Lodi saw no reason to doubt the dwarf, whose misshapen skull proved that he was very tough indeed. There were few who had survived even a glancing blow from a great orc's spiked mace, but Sergeant Malvern of the Iron Guard was one of them.

After a meal and a brief swearing-in ceremony, which involved holding an iron chain and kissing an engraved image of King Hammerstone, Lodi found himself enlisted. In the company of twenty other armored dwarves he stood in the midday sunshine on a ridge that jutted out above the huge gates that were the primary means of entry to Iron Mountain.

The gates were not the only means of entry, but they were the only ones that were easily spotted, and certainly the only ones that were large enough to permit entry to even a small portion of the great mass of movement that was pouring through the two passes that lay to the east between Mount Bray, Mount Saelenheil, and Toadfall Mountain like a pair of black rivers swollen by the wintermelt.

The wolf-riders came first: goblin lancers astride the backs of lean, grey killing machines. Lodi stopped counting after he reached five hundred. Then came the boar-riders, foul-tempered orcs on the backs of even fouler-tempered swine. They were about twice the size of the goblins, but they carried swords and maces rather than lances. The stench of them, even from a distance and high above, was incredible, and Lodi found it hard to imagine how unbearable it had to be in their actual vicinity.

The infantries followed, with regiment after regiment of unarmored goblins followed by countless club-dragging orcs. Thousands, tens of thousands of them trudged into what appeared to be predetermined positions. The large gaps they left caused some discussion among the guards for who, or what, would fill them.

They soon learned. First came the elite orc regiments, heavily armored great orcs marching with a discipline and elan that had not been seen in any of the preceding regiments. Then came what Sergeant Malvern had said he feared most: a long series of wagons being drawn by powerful horned auchs containing what had to be the Troll King's artillery, as well as an amount of supplies that would normally have been considerable had they accompanied an army one-tenth the size.

Finally, there came what had never been seen before on Selenoth—three regiments of giant, granite-hewn monsters, each standing more than fifteen feet tall, most marching out of rhythm but indubitably marching together. Trolls. Three regiments of trolls.

At that point, Guldur Goblinsbane was little more than a name mentioned in passing to Lodi. But already, even to his unsoldiefly eyes, it was clear that the Troll King was a creature of truly unusual power and vision. Lodi could not conceive of anything that would have enabled anyone, least of all a rockheaded troll, to assemble an army of this magnitude and keep it together long enough to reach the gates of Iron Mountain.

What riches had he promised them? What spoils did he dangle before them to motivate them to do his will? Why did the orcs and goblins follow him, or rather, march before him, when surely they would just as soon have fought him, as they had always fought his kind?

The Troll King's cognomen hinted at the answer, of course. But at that time Lodi was simply not capable of comprehending the slaughter that Guldur had wreaked, first upon his own kind in enforcing a crude form of species unity upon his fellow trolls, and then among the orc tribes he'd encountered next.

Goblinsbane was the overlord of less than one-third of the teeming masses of orcdom. None of the most powerful tribes such as the Hagahorn or the orcs of Zoth Ommog had been subdued by him, but the third he commanded still outnumbered the sum total of all the dwarves in all four dwarf kingdoms. And finally, he won the submission of the goblins by an eight-year display of brutality that was unmatched in the memory of all the sentient races of Selenoth.

As for the countless hill, plain, and swamp goblins that made up the greater part of the Goblinsbane's army, it soon became clear that they were intended to serve as more than mere fodder for the hidden dwarven cannons that were embedded deeply into the mountainside. They had been brought along to feed the army.

Any thought that the mighty army was too large for it to remain long in front of the gates vanished as the guardsmen watched two great orcs, Red Claw Slayers by the look of the black banner that waved over their encampment, grab a young swamp goblin foolish enough to walk too near to their campfire. The goblin shrieked wildly, but his screams didn't stop the Slayers from rending him limb from limb and popping the pieces into their boiling cauldron.

The guttural laughter that rose from the nearby orc encampments sent chills of fear down Lodi's spine. How could they possibly hope to drive away an army that was just as willing to slaughter its own warriors as it was to slay its foes? And although Iron Mountain was supplied with limitless water and well stocked with foodstuffs, the indiscriminate palate of their besiegers meant that they couldn't count on the siege ending until literally every last goblin had been both killed and eaten! How long could sixty thousand dwarves, of whom perhaps a third were males of fighting age, hope to withstand an enemy army that appeared to be beyond count?

Gulder Goblinsbane had the dwarven gates razed to cinder. After the gates were buried, he commanded the removal of the many tons of stone and other debris that covered them. But the work went slowly, as dwarven miners tunneled from inside the mountain to snatch and slay workers by night and lay explosive traps that slew scores of them at a time during the day.

And when the great gates were finally uncovered and the three mighty rams meant to smash them were brought up at last, a terrible crashing noise was heard and the gates seemed to bulge from the inside out. After much repeated bashing proved to be worthless, the chief goblin engineer finally managed to convince a skeptical Troll King that the dwarves had set off a second landslide, this one inside the mountain, sealing the entrance more solidly than before.

Then began the long and terrible War in the Deep, to which D'Escard devotes but a few suggestive stanzas. But for Lodi, that *was* the siege—the desperate battles fought in narrow passageways and black, unlit tunnels, where often there wasn't even enough room to lift your arm, let alone raise your weapon.

The first time he found himself crawling through a rathole and sensed, rather than saw, the presence of an enemy immediately before him, he vowed that he'd have a spike welded on top of his warhammer. Fortunately, the goblin miner had been too occupied with digging to realize that he'd broken into a dwarven crawlspace. Lodi managed to get one hand around the goblin's skinny neck before it could shriek out a warning to its fellows. He killed five diggers that night, and never once did his hammer leave his belt.

Night after night, the Iron Guard dug tunnels, killed, and then refilled the tunnels to hide their tracks. They planted mines that exploded at random intervals during the day as unlucky orcs and goblins encountered them. They slipped out of hidden exits high up on the mountain and climbed down to launch hellish mortar fire on the camps far below. They slew thousands, tens of thousands, but always there were more goblins, more orcs, more implacable enemies to replace those that fell. The enemy encampment grew to surround the mountain as if it were a pyramid erupting from a field of hateful monsters.

After the initial terror of realizing that they were surrounded by foes, the dwarves of Iron Mountain gradually became accustomed to their peril. Vigilance was required, but as days turned into weeks and weeks turned into months, abject fear changed to morbid nonchalance.

At first, the size of the enemy army dwindled visibly as the ruthless dwarven tactics wreaked lethal havoc on the foe. But the enemies that survived grew more careful and cunning, and soon Lodi noticed that two or three of the Troll King's elite regiments would disappear, sometimes for a month or more, and return with entire tribes of raging orcs or sad-faced goblins marching before them. Thus did Goblinsbane replenish his forces faster than the dwarves could kill them. And every night, two or three irreplaceable dwarves died.

The first year passed quickly, an unending nightmare of slaughter in the darkness. The second and third years passed more slowly, as the attackers appeared to become almost bored, and the besiegers fought nearly as much amongst themselves as they did with the besieged. In the fourth year, Guldur detached a large body of wolf-riders accompanied by ten regiments of heavy orc infantry and launched a secondary attack on the human kingdom of Savondir. Only a third of those troops returned to Iron Mountain.

In the fifth year, Goblinsbane increased the pressure on them again, actively digging a series of shafts down from the mountain itself in an attempt to locate the great underground halls in which the dwarves lived.

But in the sixth year, the Troll King finally stumbled upon a tactic that promised eventual success. Though it was unusual for a troll to be an initiate of the Deep Magic, there was one in Goblinsbane's army. He was pressed into service when, even more unusually for a troll, he had a bright idea. Mastery of the basic elementals was expected of initiates, and this one realized he could use the ability to summon and speak with earth elementals to map out the tunnels used by the dwarves.

Since neither trolls nor elementals tended to be particularly intelligent, and Guldur had only one initiate at his disposal, this development was not as devastating as it might have been in the hands of another besieger. But from that day on, dwarven warriors fell at a faster rate than they had since the siege began.

More families began taking advantage of the Long Passage, the deep emergency tunnel that extended for leagues under the Volpiscenes out to the west, fleeing for the safety of one of the other dwarven kingdoms. After six years of unstinting war, their numbers had dwindled to around eighteen thousand, with only seven thousand effective fighters. Meanwhile the attacking army actually appeared to have swelled in size as more orc tribes were captured, enslaved, and hurled against the unyielding mountain fortress.

Knowing that the collapse of his defenses was rapidly approaching, the dwarven King Hammerstone sent out two delegations of noble dwarves to plead for aid. One went to the Collegium Occludum, and the other traveled to the royal court of Merithaim. Calling for the restoration of the old alliance that had defeated the Witchkings, he offered half the gold and silver of his kingdom if only they would come to the assistance of his people.

The wizards of the college ignored the desperate request. It was not their habit to interfere in wars that did not disturb their studies. But Caefall Everbright, the king of the elvish kingdom of Merithaim, was moved by the dwarven pleas and swore to ride to their assistance. The Goblinsbane would fall before a hail of elven arrows, he vowed, and promised that his army would be on the move before the new moon.

Everbright was true to his word, and Lodi was one of the scouts hidden way high near the treeline when the shining helms of the elven lancers first gleamed from the heights of the Saelenheil pass. They were too far away for him to even distinguish individual riders, but he watched as the gleaming column halted at its first sight of the enemy. They beheld a massive, sprawling encampment, more populous than all but the greatest cities of man, spread out below them at the foot of Iron Mountain.

Lodi, long inured to the unspeakable horrors of the huge and stinking hell-city, didn't understand at first what was happening when the column turned about and retreated back through the pass. He lay in his rocky shelter, uncomprehending, as the silvery figures disappeared, never to return.

It was, of course, absurd to expect the elven king to hurl his meager forces—only five thousand cavalry accompanied by twenty-five thousand archers—against a dug-in army more than ten times its size. King Everbright had been told that the Troll King's army was enormous, but his imagination was unable to comprehend the reality of what fighting such an army would entail until the moment he laid his eyes upon it. And in that moment, his heart quailed. He issued no order. He commanded no trumpets. He simply turned his horse and began the long ride back to the safe woods of Merithaim. After a moment of stunned surprise, his knights made haste to follow suit.

This was what D'Escard had called Everbright's valiant attempt to drive off the besiegers, the tale that could bring warriors to tears.

News of the cowardly elven betrayal hit the dwarves of Iron Mountain hard. In truth, there had been little expectation that even the combined forces of elf and dwarf could have defeated the Troll King, but now even that ember of hope was extinguished.

King Hammerstone ordered plans for an evacuation. Only he and the Iron Guard would remain behind to defend the caverns so that his subjects could flee to safety deep under the mountains. After ten days, which was the length of time required for a traversal of the Long Passage, the king himself would light the explosives that would hide the escape route forever from those who might otherwise attempt to follow.

But even as he told the Iron Guard of his intentions, a sulfur-maker turned guardsman named Arkli Powdergrit suggested one last, reckless throw of the dice. An appeal to the goddess Fortune in the hopes that she might favor them with her blessing when all the gods of the dwarves had turned a deaf ear to their unceasing prayers. The king smiled at the young dwarf's idea, shrugged, and granted his approval. There was little chance the plan would succeed, and even if it did, there was no telling what the consequences would turn out to be. It seemed difficult, however, to imagine that anything could make matters worse at this point.

So it was that in the seventh year of the war, Lodi found himself crawling through a small tunnel, wearing a leather harness and dragging a long, wooden pole longer than he was tall. Somewhere in the darkness ahead of him a pair of dwarves laboriously carved through the hard rocky foundation of Iron Mountain. There were twelve others behind Lodi, most trailing different but equally heavy burdens. Only two of them were armed, and they were the Guards' most proficient killers, silent assassins who had sent thousands of orcs, goblins, and even trolls to the icy hells over the last seven years.

It took them three days of digging and crawling to reach their destination, where they spent an anxious day waiting for the sun to set and hoping that no emaciated goblins would be searching for sustenance and dig down in just the wrong place. When darkness fell, the two killers were the first to emerge from the earth. They moved slowly, nearly indistinguishable from boulders as they crept about the vicinity, making sure that no enemies, whether restive, sleeping, or festive, were there to give the alarm. They were already well within the bounds of the enemy encampment, but they had surfaced in the great boneyard that had begun with a few spindly, well-gnawed goblin bones seven years before.

They were surrounded by the sight and smell of death on every side. But strangely, Lodi felt safe inside the jumbled pile of broken skulls, femurs, ribs, and tibias. It was quite literally the only place where they could make their preparations within range of their target. So he worked with the others to clear out a rectangular space free of bones that was large enough for twelve dwarves to lie down side by side. That accomplished, they began assembling the various items they'd been dragging behind them through the tunnel. In less than an hour, they had reassembled a huge scorpion catapult, with its single iron-tipped stinger mounted in the slide.

As the red rays of dawn began to spill down the mountainside, the lead engineer began winching the skeins taut. The wooden pole that Lodi had dragged now served as the shaft of the giant bolt. It was marked with inscriptions and enchantments that supposedly ensured its aim would be true. The catapult was aimed at the large pale-green leather tent that sat nearly a third of a millarium away in the center of the encampment. There, the Goblinsbane slept in a large shelter made of flayed goblinskin.

The camp was stirring and there was movement on every side, but the stacks of skeletal remains shielded the motionless dwarves from view. Lodi hardly dared to breathe. It seemed as if many agonizing hours passed as they waited, fearing that discovery and death would arrive at any moment. But in truth it was well before noon when the Troll King emerged from his hideous lodging and stood before it, looking out over his abominable domain.

He was immense, as tall as five dwarves, and he looked almost like a mountain in his own right. His heavy-featured face was crude and craggy, the color of dark granite shot with yellow veins. He wore very little. Only a blue scrap of leather covered his loins, while on his head sat a massive crown of solid gold boasting a circumference to rival a beer barrel's.

For all his palpable power, it was said that the most frightening thing about Guldur was his eyes. D'Escard wrote of their strange intelligence and intensity that seemed so eerily out of place in such an extraordinarily physical brute. Lodi could not possibly have seen them from so far away, but the alert way in which the Troll King glanced around his surroundings suddenly filled him with terror that they had been spotted, and in moments that huge right arm would rise to point at them and send a thousand orcs to kill them and with them the last hope of Iron Mountain.

It seemed to Lodi that Guldur must be able to hear the creaking of the skeins as they were winched tighter and the rattling of the claw as the engineer secured yet another notch of progress. There were hurried whispers as one of his companions threw his body against the giant weapon at the engineer's direction to shift it a little to the left, adjusting for the windage.

Then there was a clacking sound followed by a mighty thrum, as if an immense bird had flapped its wings once right over their heads. The scorpion leaped violently backward, not unlike like its living namesake, which sent a rattling cascade of miscellaneous bones down upon their heads. But the cascade wasn't loud enough to drown out the sound of a sickening thud in the distance, followed by the most glorious sound Lodi had ever heard in his life.

The howls of the Troll King echoed off the stony slopes, howls that sounded more of rage and disbelief than pain as he staggered backward, pierced through the right side of his chest by the huge wooden bolt, then collapsed, crushing the blood-spattered goblinskins of his tent underneath his mighty weight.

"Hammerstone!" a dwarf shouted in ecstatic triumph.

"Hammerstone!" Lodi and the others roared back, barely daring to believe that they had slain Guldur Goblinstone himself. "Hammerstone!"

Their victorious roars were soon drowned out by a rising tide of bestial fury that seemed to surround them on every side. Hearing that, Lodi left everything behind, rushed for the entrance to the tunnel, and dove into it with reckless abandon, heedless of the jagged edges of the broken rock that tore at his skin. He crawled faster than he'd ever crawled before, knowing that it wouldn't be long before the smaller, faster goblins would find the entrance and follow after them.

But before they'd gone very far, he heard a deep voice chuckling from somewhere in the darkness behind him.

"Relax, dwarrows. You needn't crawl like white salamanders fleeing a light. They won't follow. I've left them somewhat of a surprise." It was King Hammerstone himself, there to greet them.

There was another chuckle, and then a deafening crunch. The ground shook and trembled, and for a moment Lodi feared that the tunnel might collapse. It didn't, though, and after a long three hours of retracing their previous route, they emerged victorious. King Hammerstone shook their hands, embraced every single one of them, and gifted each dwarf who had been part of the assassination team a royal gold vein in perpetuity.

The end of the siege came quickly, much more quickly than Hammerstone and his generals had dared to dream. Before noon of that very day, the Troll King's two most powerful warleaders—Orzuth Stoneshaker and Mulguth the Mighty—had come to blows over who would succeed Guldur.

The fight was inconclusive, but it was not without consequences. Orzuth and his followers folded their tents, shouldered their packs, and departed for the homeland they had not
seen in ten years. Rightly fearing Orzuth's intentions to declare
himself king of the trolls, Mulguth himself quickly followed
suit, accompanied by seven regiments of heavy orc infantry and
three regiments of war boar-riders.

Realizing that the trolls who had enslaved them were no
longer paying them even the least bit of attention, hundreds
of thousands of goblins slipped away under the cover of darkness that night, with tribe after tribe fleeing desperately for the
homes from which they'd been driven. Most of the orc chieftans did so as well, albeit in better order.

When dawn rose over Iron Mountain the next day, Guldur
Goblinsbane's great horde was gone, as if scattered by the
western wind. Only a few thousand orcs remained amidst the
wreckage of the foul encampment, busily engaged in picking
over the abandoned campsites for whatever bits of treasure they
might find. They paid little heed to the dwarves who emerged
from their stone citadel, and the dwarves were content to like-
wise leave the scavengers to their scavenging. Most of them
were gone the following day, and on the third day, the Iron
Guard put the last malingerers to flight without once drawing
blood.

Guldur Goblinsbane's head—sans the crown that Mulguth
the Mighty had taken for himself—was carefully cast in
gold, and to this day remains on display, impaled upon the
great scorpion bolt that killed him, behind the throne of Iron
Mountain.

The sun was low in the sky when Lodi finally fell into a
contemplative silence. Marcus and Marcipor looked at each

other, amazed by the way in which the true story was more dramatic than the epic version they knew, and surprised at how easily the long day had passed.

"What happened to the dwarf-maiden, the one whose father made the shields?" Marcipor asked.

"Dead," answered Lodi. "She died in the fifth year when a few hundred goblins found an air passage and got past the levy dwarves guarding it. By then, the queen had organized a whole reserve of shield maidens. Geral was a captain, and her squad responded first. A goblin warlock who didn't know any better threw fire and ignited the whole cavern. Killed her, her squad, and every single goblin too."

"I'm sorry," Marcipor said.

"A long time ago." Lodi shrugged. "But now you understand, see?"

"Understand what?" Marcus said.

"About the elves." The dwarf snorted contemptuously. "They talk fine. They screech about valor and honor, and their bards concoct ballads every time an elf-lord manages to cross a stream without wetting his boots. But it's only words. It's nothing but words, there's no steel underneath it. That Savonder, Alwee D'Escard or whatever he's called, he sung about the breaking of the elves like they rode in to try and rescue us, and how they was so brave that they attacked the Troll King when they was outnumbered ten to one."

"But they didn't," interjected Marcipor.

"No, they didn't do nothing of the kind," Lodi said. "They turned their backs and rode away. The dwarves, we had to save ourselves."

"I don't understand," Marcus said. "How can you reasonably blame the elf-king for not throwing away his army once he saw that there was no way they could break the siege?"

"Believe what you want, Master." Lodi shrugged. "Just remember that when an elf says something, it don't mean no more than wind blowing through trees."

Iᴬ Q. VII A. I CO. II

Secundum, conditio hominum in statu innocentiae non erat dignior quam conditio Angelorum. Sed inter angelos quidam aliis dominantur, unde et unus ordo dominationum vocatur. Ergo non est contra dignitatem status innocentiae, quod homo homini dominaretur. Quandoquidem hic homo subiectus illo homini possit, et factum non statum animae subiecti afficiat, ita aelvi possint subiecti dominationi homini et factum non statum animarum aelvorum afficiat.

T WAS THE twenty-second day of their journey when they finally entered the elflands. They were days ahead of schedule, but it was still none too soon as far as Marcus was concerned. Each of those days had been long and arduous, for Captain Hezekius had demanded an ambitious pace throughout, particularly for a party containing several men on the far side of sixty.

The third and fourth days had been the worst, leading Marcus and Marcipor to seriously discuss the possibility of riding sidesaddle, as did Bishop Claudo and three of the other prelates. But the sight of their dwarven companion grimly swaying with the gentle motion of his mule inspired them both to clench their teeth and bear the burning torment. It was halfway through the fifth day when Marcus realized that he was not subconsciously bracing himself for each step of his mount. His body had adjusted at last to the demands of the journey.

Their progress slowed once they reached Merithaim and the Shadowald. The great forest before them was the largest on Selenoth, stretching across the borders of several nations, and it served as a natural barrier of sorts protecting the inland elven cities from the human bandits that lived in the mountains the embassy had just finished crossing.

Despite regular patrols by Savondese and elven rangers alike, this was a wild and ominous place in which the more aggressive orc tribes regularly gathered to stage their vicious raids against more civilized lands to the north, west, and south. The practical Amorran Senate, of course, had simply built a wall south of the mountains, kept it manned by three cohorts, and remained mostly untroubled.

Nevertheless, the way forward was clear, and the towering trees were quite beautiful. The embassy rode forward, feeling as if they were finally making progress.

Three days deep into the forest, riding along what looked more like a deer trail than a proper road, an inhuman scream caused the captain to call a halt. Moments later, it was followed by several howls that sounded like wolves.

"What's that?" Marcus asked Lodi.

The dwarf hadn't become what one would call *conversational* after breaking his silence three weeks before, but these days he was much less reticent than before. In fact, at times Marcus preferred riding in relative silence next to Lodi instead of Marce or one of the more loquacious priests. He feared that if Zephanus told him one more time the story about how he'd killed the orcish shaman by severing the link between the orc and the demon it had just summoned, he might not be able to resist the temptation to stab the cheerful Michaeline in the leg.

Perhaps, he thought to himself, my vocation is not as strong as I think it is. One thing the journey had taught him was a deep and profound respect for the Quiricusian order and its custom of regular vows of silence.

"Elf," the dwarf muttered, staring narrow-eyed into the trees. It was getting dark, and Hezekius would be calling a halt soon. "The first scream, anyhow. Don't know about the second."

"Wolf-riders?"

"Maybe. But it sounded too purposeful to me. They're usually not real disciplined."

Five Michaelines broke from the column at the command of the captain, their swords gleaming brightly in the deepening shadows. Marcus cursed as he saw a sixth rider follow them. It was Marcipor, and he was waving his gaudy sword as if he were leading a cavalry charge. The idiot had spent so much time around the warrior-priests that he practically considered himself one of them now.

"Stay here," Marcus barked at Lodi.

He wished he had time to retrieve his shield from his pack horse, but if he stopped to grab it now he'd never be able to catch up with his lunatic slave. He spurred his horse after Marce's, wishing for a third eye as he tried to blindly unthong his blade while keeping one eye on the trees and the other on the riders ahead. Happily, he soon learned that it wasn't particularly necessary to see them, since the way they were crashing through the underbrush, they sounded like an army in front of him. They certainly weren't going to surprise anyone.

He ducked under one low-hanging branch, narrowly avoided a pine tree, then, at the top of a small rise, found himself looking down over a small valley. He reined in his horse, watching with alarm as the five Michaelines, with Marce not too far behind them, charged down the hill toward a bowman who was taking shelter behind the half-exposed roots of a large oak.

No, they weren't charging toward the man, Marcus saw now, but past him. They galloped on toward two large, shadowy shapes above the bowman on the far side of the depression. Marcus couldn't tell if the creatures were orcs or goblins, but they were throwing rocks, one of which narrowly missed braining his idiot slave. The sight of the riders alarmed them, though, and they melted away into the gloom before the horses were halfway up the hill.

Marcus quickly dismounted, tossed his reins over a tree branch, and ran down to assist the bowman. He jerked back, startled, as the man whirled around—not only because there was now an arrow aimed at his chest, but because the bowman was not a man at all, but an elf.

"Who are you?" the male elf asked in strange but understandable Savondese.

He was tall, but that was about all Marcus could distinguish at the moment. The arrowhead, on the other hand, was a bodkin-pointed iron cap with a three-blade cross-section, affixed to a wooden shaft that was painted red. The fletching was white, and there were two rings on the white-knuckled hand that held the bow just under the motionless point of the arrowhead pointed at his chest. Marcus wondered if at this distance, the arrow would pass clean through him or if it would remain buried in his chest like the dwarf bolt that slew the late unlamented Guldur Goblinsbane. He dropped his sword and spread his hands slowly, very slowly indeed.

"We heard the screams," he said. "We came to help. I'm from Amorr. We're an embassy from the Sanctiff to the High King in Elebrion."

"Amorran, yes, I can see that. I thank you." The arrowhead lowered a bit. "They will not stand before your knights. They fear those who ride horses. Please, take up your sword. I must see to Ferlathel."

Still holding his arrow nocked, the elf stepped out from behind the tree. Marcus, breathing a sigh of heartfelt relief, leaned down to retrieve his blade, then followed the elf a little ways down the hill.

He saw it—him, he corrected himself—kneel before a body sprawled amidst the leaves. It was another elf, and from the amount of blood pooled around its head, it seemed the back of its head was caved in. Marcus swallowed hard and steeled himself against his stomach's urge to purge itself.

The living elf merely shook his head in sorrow. "We were stalking them, but they must have noticed us. They took Nylia in an ambush. They were too strong. We fled, but they can track better than us with their keen sense of smell."

What are they? Marcus was about to ask, but Barat's alarmed snorting alerted him a second before the elf's shout did.

He began to turn around, but something very heavy hit him hard and sent him tumbling to down the hill.

Vafala! He pushed himself up with his free hand, but then a large dark shape leaped at him. He brought up his blade in reflexive self-defense and somehow intercepted the thing.

But he was smashed back to the earth again and his sword was torn from his grasp as the full weight of the impact knocked the wind from his lungs. His ears were filled with alarming snarls and growls, and he had the terrible impression of something very heavy, very furry, very smelly, and very intent on ripping his throat out.

It was a wolf, he realized, when its giant jaws yawned wide and white in front of his unprotected face. A very large wolf!

He managed to reach his dagger. He jerked it from its sheath and drove it deep into the beast's furry side. He was more shocked than relieved when the beast froze in mid-snap, jerked back, and thrashed side to side a few times before slumping lifeless on top of him.

Marcus lay there for a moment, trying, mostly unsuccessfully, to breathe, while wondering how he'd managed to kill the monster. Had his sword pierced its heart on that first lunge? He didn't think so. His dagger? Did wolves have some sort of vital organ on their left side?

Without warning, the crushing weight was removed from his chest. The fresh air that replaced the awful lupine stink was better than incense. He inhaled it with greedy relief.

Lodi loomed over him, holding a bloody axe in his hand. "Are you hurt?" he asked, looking concerned.

"I don't know," Marcus said as the dwarf pulled him to his feet. Everything hurt, to tell the truth, especially his ribs and his left shoulder, and there was blood everywhere. "I don't think so. I don't even think any of this is mine, actually."

"Your shoulder," Lodi said, as his thick finger probed at the left one. Marcus winced in sudden pain, but Lodi shook his head. "It's not too bad, but you'll want that cleaned out all the same. More of a gash than a proper bite."

Marcus stared at the wolf and shivered with horror. Not a wolf: a wolf-thing. It had a wolf's head, but was bipedal, with clawlike hands instead of paws. Fur covered its body and it wore no clothes, but a carved black stone adorned its neck. It was no true beast. It looked more like a child of the dead Witchkings, the demonspawn from the far north that had driven the brave Darlarn from their homes across the White Sea.

A massive blow from Lodi's axe had nearly severed it in two at the base of its spine. That, and not the insignificant stab-wound from the dagger that still jutted from its side, had killed it. Marcus's sword was lodged in its right leg, and an elven arrow pierced its arm. Not far away, a similar abomination lay dead, pierced by arrows in its throat, chest, and eye.

The elvish archer, looking none the worse for wear, nodded at him. "The dwarf got the one on top of you. I killed the other." He retrieved his arrows. "How is it that you travel with a dwarf, human?"

"It's a long story. You'd have to ask my uncle."

"I see. Then where are you bound?"

"Elebrion," he answered.

The elf smiled. "Then we are well met indeed. As you have done me a great service, I am pleased that I can return the favor. If you were following the trail that lies nearest here, it may interest you to know that it heads not toward Elebrion but the Ogran wilds."

Marcus started to laugh, but it came out as a coughing fit. Still, he had survived his first battle, and by the sound of the triumphant whoops of the returning riders, so had Marcipor and the Michaelines. But as the blood leaked slowly from the wound in his shoulder, he found himself wondering if there were any basis in truth for the grim legends of the werewolf's bite.

Falmithal, as the elf archer was called, was not only indebted to the Michaeline warriors, he was impressed by them. Mainly because they had actually managed to capture one of the wolf-beasts after killing its three companions.

The beasts were called Ulfin, Falmithal said, and with Lodi's help the Michaelines constructed a crude cage of sorts that carried the bound creature between two very unhappy horses. Of course, to hear Marce tell it, you'd think he had not only caught the beast himself, but tamed it to boot.

"If you would win the favor of the High King," Falmithal told Marcus and the others that night over the campfire, "make the Ulfin a gift to him. There's word he's offered a reward for one captured alive, though no one knows why."

The two elves from Elebrion remained as aloof and distant as ever, but after a quiet conversation with their woodlands cousin, they bent enough to offer a formal thanks to the Michaelines, and to Marcus, Marcipor, and Lodi as well.

Marcus passed Falmithal's recommendation along to Bishop Claudo, but the ascetic old priest only nodded impassively and betrayed no indication of whether he intended to follow the elf's advice or not.

With Falmithal's help, Captain Hezekius corrected their course, and it was not long before the ominous massed pines gradually began to fade into delightful copses of ash and oak trees.

They were passing through the elven kingdom of Merithaim. Their destination was beyond this land, in the neighboring elven kingdom of Elebrion, where the High King dwelt. Still, it afforded Marcus the opportunity to study elves closely.

The royal court of Merithaim was not, like the High King of Elebrion's court, resident in a fixed location. Its lords and ladies lived a traveling existence, moving about the Shadowald Forest for most of the spring, summer, and autumn, before retiring south to the king's mountain palace in the winter.

King Caerwyn Everbright was its liege, a relatively young elf and the son of the elf king who had so outraged Lodi and the dwarves of Iron Mountain. Thanks to Falmithal, they were greeted at court with exquisite courtesy, and the king gifted Marcus, Marcipor, and Lodi with silver-hilted daggers.

He also attempted to similarly reward the six Michaelines, but they politely refused to accept the elven blades. Marcus had the impression that after the debacle with Lord Fáelán, the Order would be adding to what was likely a long list of monastic rules—including, perhaps, the prohibition against owning or carrying elvish blades.

The two days they spent with the Merithaimi court was a magical time for Marcus. It was a much-needed break from the rigors of the road—both for him and for Barat. During the day, Marcus was free to roam as he pleased, accompanied only by Falmithal, whose impeccable manners steered Marcus clear of most social blunders and smoothly extricated him from those that could not be avoided.

The elven maids were beautiful beyond anything he'd ever seen: tall, slender, and preternaturally fair. They were also too shy to speak with the young humans, for the most part, but they were tremendously curious about Marcipor's golden beard. Marcipor claimed that he'd stolen a kiss from one of them, but Marcus was skeptical. He wouldn't have dared himself, even if he weren't bound by his intended vocation. They probably weren't all sorceresses, but a man had no way of knowing which was and which wasn't.

He was frustrated, and not only because of the way the elven beauty filled him with serious doubts about the purity of his soul, to say nothing of his vocation. Whereas he'd previously imagined exposure to the elves would help him reach a sound conclusion about their nature, the more information he acquired, the more any sense of certainty receded from his grasp. When he looked into that alien gaze with its strange, inhuman pupils, could he see a soul lurking behind it? One could see life there, certainly. One could see intelligence, animation. But was there *anima*?

Elven beauty ascended toward physical perfection, but that counted for little in matters of the spirit. The Dalarn too were beautiful. Were not those tall, fair barbarians so thick of feature and large of frame, one might even confuse one for an elf if one were far enough away. Importantly, there was not a single unimpeachable reference to elves throughout the Holy Writ. One might make a better case for defending the spiritual immortality of sparrows and leviathans on the scriptural basis.

As for their intelligence, upon which he'd thought to lay the foundation of his *Summa,* a passage from Augustinus troubled him deeply. For demons were also intelligent, and yet the philosopher called them "animals of the atmosphere" due to the way in which their nature is akin to that of aerial bodies. Marcus sighed as he watched a pretty elven girl pass by the fire. This was not going to be a matter quickly solved.

The evenings were given over to debate between the theologians. Marcus was entranced by the bloodless but pointed duel fought nightly between the two evenly matched combatants.

The jovial Father Aestus was inclined toward impassioned classical rhetoric, of which he was a master. His silver tongue wove a spell of words that were always compelling and entertaining. But Marcus sometimes found it hard to remember exactly what the father had said or to retrace his train of logic.

Bishop Claudo, on the other hand, was a living, breathing encyclopedia of literary quotes and obscure references. He could cite Aristotle and Augustinus with equal ease, knew well the prophets and philosophers, and once reeled off an entire cantos of Eurymenes without resorting to his notes. Marcus did not like his imperious demeanor or his droning, high-pitched voice, but his logic was like a remorseless battering ram, smashing again and again with devastating effect against the Jamite priest's beautiful, but delicate, web of words.

"What is man that thou art mindful of him?" Claudo said, quoting the Psalmist.

"A little lower than the heavenly beings," Aestus replied with a chuckle. "Above man: the angels. Below him: the beasts. Can it be said that there is room between man and angel, or between man and beast? Can it be said—"

"Your *Ordo* has already conceded the latter," Claudo broke in before Aestus could get started. "And if you recall, I have written the same in the *Summa*. Furthermore, I have already demonstrated this line of thought is inconclusive. It proves nothing."

"A little lower than the angels," Marcus repeated, and sighed as he thought of an elven maid he'd seen that afternoon. Her long hair was crimson shot with gold and fell to reach a waist so slender he thought he could probably encircle it with his hands. "Truly, they are as beautiful as angels."

"And why should they not be?" asked Father Aestus with an impish grin. "They are created by angels, fallen angels, not by God. What appears perfect can make its own likeness, and immaterial creatures are more perfect than material creatures, which nevertheless can make their own likeness. For fire generates fire, and man begets man. Thus you see that an immaterial substance can make a substance like to itself."

"Like to itself," agreed Claudo. "But angels are an immaterial substance, while elves, as we can readily observe, are material. *Entirely* material, one would say, assuming that they do in fact lack a distinct and animating spirit. Augustinus agrees, for has he not written that that neither good nor bad angels can create anything?"

"He has," Marcus broke in. Three weeks of listening to their discussions had emboldened him sufficiently to allow him to take part sometimes, although he was careful not to take sides if he could avoid it. "However, from that, Augustinus concluded that since angels are incapable of creation, neither can any other lesser creatures create anything." He drew the silver elvenblade. The edge was traced with fine etchings, which he'd been assured were nonmagical in nature. It was manifestly a beautiful creation and a wordless refutation of the great philosopher.

Father Aestus nodded approvingly. "Immaterial substance can be made only by God, since it has no matter from which to be made. Its creation can be the action of God alone. But as Petrus Lombardus writes, God can communicate to a creature the power of creating, so that the latter can create ministerially, not by its own power. From this it follows that the first separate substance created by God created another after itself, in a process that continues to this day. Thus was the substance of the world created, and thus is it that the substance of the world creates the matter of inferior bodies, such as the elves."

"How can you say they are inferior when their beauty exceeds that of man?" Marcus asked.

"Beauty? Pah!" Bishop Claudo glared at him over the dancing flames of the fire as he recited the words of Jeremaeus the prophet. "'And your heart became proud on account of your beauty, and you corrupted your wisdom because of your splendor. I am against you, O Sidon, saith the Lord.'"

"Nevertheless," Marcus replied, and he turned his back on the endless debate.

His blankets were warm, and that night his dreams were filled with the laughing vision of elven girls with white skin and green, green eyes.

On the evening of their second and last day with the royal court of Merithaim, Marcus was sitting by a fire, gnawing on a roasted rabbit haunch, when Marcipor sat down to join him. On the morrow, they would leave and travel the final stretch of their long journey, where they would finally see Elebrion and meet the High King of the elves.

From what Marcus had slowly gathered throughout their travels, Bishop Claudo would present the high king with a peace offer from the Amorran Senate, formally ending a war that had, in truth, ended three generations ago. It seemed a strange thing to do, considering how quickly afterward it might well be rendered meaningless by the Sanctiff's forthcoming decision. But then, Marcus had grown to manhood in a proconsul's house. He well knew how little diplomacy sometimes had to do with the actual situation.

Marcus nudged Marcipor and pointed the rabbit at Lodi, who sat at a nearby fire staring into the flames. "This is as close to the dwarflands as we're likely to get, Marce. Do you think I should free him?"

"Free him?" Marcipor looked aghast. "Why?"

"Well, he did save my life. I understand it's customary."

"Only in the theatre! How many times has your father's man, Black Arcus, saved him? Ten times? Twenty? Did your father ever free him?"

"Maybe he should have. No one ever said Corvus was perfect."

"You idiot." The flames danced across Marce's face. With his golden hair and his ragged beard, he looked like a pagan idol. No wonder the elven maids were curious about him. "Corvus gives Arcus whatever he wishes whenever he asks. The only reason he hasn't manumitted him is because Arcus doesn't want it."

"He doesn't?" Marcus was shocked. "Don't you? I always thought—"

"Don't even say it! What, do you hate me? Do you have any idea what I would do to survive if you freed me?"

Marcus shrugged. "I don't know. I suppose I assumed that Corvus would adopt you. You could do whatever you liked."

"Valerians only adopt within the House, Marcus. And I do whatever I like now, for the most part. But suppose you did free me and Corvus adopted me. What then?"

Marcus took a bite of the rabbit and considered the question. He offered it to Marcipor, who waved it off. "Well, you're not so interested in the Church, obviously, but whether Corvus adopted you or not, you'd still be his client. And mine. We'd certainly get you a commission in the legions."

Marcipor laughed and shook his head. "That's why I can't ever be a free Valerian, Marcus. That noblesse oblige is so bred into you, down to your patrician bones, that you can't even imagine doing anything but your cursed duty. A slave of the Church or a slave of the State—either way, Marcus, you're far more of a slave than I could ever be! I don't want to spend the next twenty years of my life tramping around the borderlands killing a wide variety of people who've never done any harm to me. I want to live life, to love beautiful women, and go to the theatre whenever there's an actor worth watching!"

"There's not a lot of theatre here."

"Are you blind? There's nothing but theatre on every side of us! If not the pageantry of the elves, what about the dialogue that transpires when you and those two old priests start yammering away about whatever old Paleoscrivus wrote on his goatskins back when Amorr was nothing but a pair of stone huts on either side of the Tiberius? That's theatre! And Marcus, think about what we're doing here. This is the first time, and probably the only time, I'll ever be anywhere this close to the center of events before they happen. I'm on the front row of one of the biggest theatrical events of our time."

Marcus chuckled. "I hope things don't get any more dramatic than they've already been." He rubbed his shoulder wound. "Well, then, what are you going to do when I take my vows, Marce? I always planned to free you then, but if you hate the idea so much . . . "

Marcipor shook his head. "You're never going to take them."

"Everyone else thinks I am."

"I don't. Sextus doesn't. And no one else knows you as well as we do. The truth is that Corvus doesn't want you to, so you won't. You may want to please God, but you want to please your father even more." He grinned. "Anyhow, if you do, you'll give me to Sextus. We've already settled it."

Marcus laughed. The thought of losing Marcipor to his cousin's service did cause him a slight pang of jealousy, but that was drowned out by the amusing thought of what exceeding mischief the two of them, unfettered by the solitary voice of reason in the domus, could get into together. If the Senate had even the slightest notion of what Amorr might be in for, it would pass a law exiling both of them to separate provinces. And they'd have to punish Marcus as well for the treason inherent in creating such a threat to the Republic.

"And, Marcus, I have to ask you something."

"What's that?"

"Before you free Lodi, if you decide to free him, you have to tell him to flog me."

Shocked, Marcus stared at his oldest friend. "Why would I do that?"

"Because this stupid slave forgot his responsibility back there in the forest. Marcus, you treat me like a brother, and sometimes I forget I'm really not. I wasn't thinking about you when I took off with Justin and the other Michaelines when we caught that wolf-thing. I was just curious. But you, you never forget, and you came after me, like a good master should."

Marcus was suddenly furious. "Are you implying that I was chasing after you because I wanted to protect my property?"

"No, no. I'm just saying that you remembered your duty to me, and I forgot mine to you. A slave is supposed to look after his master, not nearly get him killed by putting him in needless danger. If Lodi hadn't disobeyed and followed you, you'd be dead. So, you have to have him flog me."

"I have to do no such thing! I'm not having you flogged."

"But you should!"

"Well, I'm not. I won't hear of it."

"Just do it, will you?" Marcipor sounded as if he wanted to cry.

"No, you idiot! Who's the cursed master, Marce? I am, right? Now, shut up or I'll . . . I'll . . . "

"Flog me?" Marcipor suggested sarcastically.

Caught up in a raging temper, they stared angrily at each other for a moment, until Marcus burst out laughing.

"Look, Marce, you're just feeling guilty. But a whipping isn't going to make you feel any better. Really, it isn't. I understand why you're asking for one, but you must remember, we are freed from the chains of guilt by the blood of the Immaculate." Marcus shook his head and sketched the sign of the cross in the air. "*Ego te absolvo.* There, it's done. Forget it."

"I don't think that counts until after you take vows."

"I'll take them just to get away from you if you won't shut up." He glanced back at Lodi, who was still sitting there in silence, seemingly unaware that anyone else was nearby. "But what makes you think he feels the way you do? He's a dwarf, not a man."

"Ask him, I suppose. You know, it's a good thing we saw him shaved in Amorr, back before that bird's nest of a beard grew back. Otherwise, for all he talks lately, you'd never know he had a mouth."

Marcus did ask Lodi if he wanted to be freed. That very night.

As it turned out, Lodi had no burning desire for freedom. Like Marcipor, he was more concerned about the problems that freedom would present him at the moment than its future promises. The elven wood of Shadowald was not a place where a lone dwarf could expect to survive long. Lodi might bear the king of Merithaim's gift-knife, but he was surely the very last individual in the party to be inclined to place any trust in the value of the elven king's goodwill.

He also pointed out that as Marcus's bodyguard, he was expected to save Marcus's life from time to time. He had no desire to have one of Amorr's most powerful magnates placing a bounty on his head for shirking what was, after all, nothing more than his duty.

"Your uncle told me to bring you back from Elebrion or he'd have my head. So, I'll bring you back, one way or another. Alive, I hope. Once I get you back to your uncle, then we can talk about freedom." Lodi stared into the flames. "It's not the words that matter anyway. Call me free or call me slave, but either way, I'll need enough gold to buy passage to Malkania. From there I can get back to the Volpiscenes."

"Ask for it and it will be yours," promised Marcus. Even if Magnus didn't want to free the dwarf for his own incomprehensible reasons, he'd have to if he didn't wish to cause his nephew to be foresworn. A Valerian's word wasn't merely binding on the Valerian, it bound all of House Valerius.

Four days later, they began the long approach to the High City of the elvish kingdom of Elberion. If the city was not truly one of the great wonders of the world, it deserved to be. The twisted forest pathways of the Shadowald slowly gave way to the foothills of the Montulae and finally to the climb that would lead them to the forbidding walls of the royal elven city.

There was now a chill in the air, even at the height of summer, as they traversed the seven gorges that had swallowed entire armies during the War of the Three Peoples. After crossing Ol-Oropon, the sixth bridge, Bishop Claudo halted the train and, in his pinched voice, led the Michaelines in a ceremonial mass for the two thousand noble souls that had been lost here.

Marcus knew their splintered bones moldered unburied somewhere in the cruel, unhallowed depths below. "I wonder if anyone has ever crawled down there?" he mused, as he and Marcipor peeked cautiously over the edge of the rocky chasm. The drop was tremendous, on the order of three thousand cubits.

The wily elves had allowed half the Amorran Legion to cross the bridge, then their sorcerers had destroyed its moorings while the latter half was still crossing. A surprise cavalry charge, its approach masked by illusion, had then swept those already across the bridge down into the gap, while Octavius Severus the Elfslayer helplessly gnashed his teeth on the other side. The Battle of the Sixth Bridge was one of the great disasters of Amorran history.

It was the elves' lethal use of battle magic in this engagement, taken in company with the rout of the three legions at Aldus Wald, that had been one of the chief spurs in encouraging a dubious Sanctiff to allow the Michaelines to pursue their potent anti-magic skills as a much-needed countermeasure.

"You'd probably find some useful things down there if you did," replied Marcipor thoughtfully. He shrugged off Marcus's dismayed expression. "It's not doing them any good now, is it?"

Each waystation they came to was a sort of small community in its own right. The elvic guards, four at each bridge and twenty at each waystation, were civil, but markedly less friendly than their forest brethren had been. Judging by the flicker of curiosity in their pale eyes as the Amorrans rode slowly past, Marcus judged that very few men ever dared pay court to High King Mael. The path was paved at this point, and despite the incline, it was a broad and easy way.

"How come it's never been taken?" asked Marcipor on the tenth day of their climb. "Even if you couldn't get past the bridges, I haven't seen any farms or livestock since we crossed the first one. Couldn't you simply lay siege and starve them out in a season or two?"

Marcus shook his head. "No, there's an underground river that links Elebrion to the sea, somewhere near Kir Donas. I've read that they even have a fish market."

"Brrrr." Marcipor shivered. "Swimming to safety in an underground mountain river? That would be a horribly long row—in the dark, no less. It must be two hundred leagues to Kir Donas!"

"It's not dark," Lodi said unexpectedly. "It's lit by lights enspelled five hundred years ago and still shining. No magic older than elvish lore."

Marcus and Marcipor looked at each other. "Have you been there?" Marcipor asked. "Have you seen the river?"

"No, but I been plenty of other places underground. I've seen elf-lights. They never stop glowing, so there's no night down below. Some say they been put there by their *diableristes,* burning souls caught by their filthy soul-drinker swords. Lights of the damned, some say."

Lodi scratched at his thickening stubble, which was now almost long enough to qualify as a beard by human standards, if well short of the dwarven. "Dwarves don't hold with such. Pyromantic lanterns don't work so well or last so long, but at least they're not witchen filth."

One of the Michaelines glanced back at them.

Marcus shushed the dwarf. "Lodi, don't talk about such things, at least not like you know something of them."

"Me? I don't know more than any other dwarf. We're not afraid of magics, but we don't hold with it."

"That's good." A dwarven slave might be permitted some license that a human slave was not, but no one except those expressly granted permission by the Sanctiff could practice magic in Amorr—under pain of death by fire and water. Even the unknowing possession of an ensorcelled object might suffice to land one in speedy exile, or worse. A slave—especially a breed slave—caught practicing any form of magic would be immediately put to death.

"Except, of course, for the smiths," Lodi said. "They're powerful great magicians. If that priest of yours thinks much of his elvenblade, he should see a dwarf-worked sword!"

"Lodi!"

Fortunately, the Michaeline had lost interest in their conversation. Marcus breathed a sigh of relief and shook his head. He wasn't entirely sure, but he didn't find it hard to imagine that being put on trial for suspicion of sorcery would be detrimental to any future career in the Church.

I^A Q. VII A. I CO. III

Cum in omnibus creaturis sit aliqualis Dei similitudo, in sola creatura rationali invenitur similitudo Dei per modum imaginis, in aliis autem creaturis per modum vestigii. Id autem in quo creatura rationalis excedit alias creaturas, est intellectus sive mens. Unde relinquitur quod nec in ipsa rationali creatura invenitur Dei imago, nisi secundum mentem. Gregorius, in homilia Epiphaniae, nominat aelvum rationale animal, ergo aelvi similius hominum angelorumque quam animalium irrationalium.

THE MASSIVE WALLS of the great elvish city were in sight when they reached the seventh and final waystation. Drenched in the crimson light of the setting sun, the walls looked invincible. Far above the Amorrans' heads, two giant eagles circled aimlessly, and the sun glinted off the polished armor of their riders, who were surely armed with longbows, Marcus thought. The sight of the high patrol soaring over their heads made him very glad that there were two elves wearing unmistakable silver helms riding at the front of their train.

They entered the city in the afternoon. The great gates parted as they approached, and they rode in to the haunting fanfare of the strange elvic pipes called *caslai*. The pipes were long and white, carved from bone, with three separate tubes joined in irregular fashion. They produced sweet, high-pitched tones that echoed eerily off the surrounding mountains like an eagle's cry in the thin air.

An honor guard awaited them inside the gates. The elves of Elebrion were taller and even paler than those of Merithaim. Their hair bore closer resemblance to the white of their snow-capped mountains than to the yellow flower-colored hair of their brethren in the lowlands. They also dressed more formally than their woodland cousins. All were wearing cloaks dyed in rich hues of royal blue, sumptuous purple, and blood red.

There was an ethereal quality to them—they showed little emotion in welcoming their guests, and their silver armor was so elaborate that it bore more resemblance to lace than to steel—and to their city as well. Together, Elebrion and its inhabitants left Marcus with the impression of a tomb guarded by beautiful, barely animate statues. It was a city of dead angels.

From what he'd seen in approaching it from below, Elebrion was perhaps only two-thirds the size of the city-state of Amorr. But now he saw that the elvish city was not nearly so crowded, which gave it the impression of being rather larger. It was spacious and regular, laid out in quadrants and wholly devoid of the serpentine vici streets that wound through Amorr like woodworms boring through a rotten log. There was a feeling of emptiness about the great marble-floored squares through which they rode. The citizenry seemed outnumbered by ornate fountains and intricately carved statues of past elven heroes and strange geometric shapes.

They passed a large building that seemed more alive than most. It seemed almost to have a golden aura emanating from its arches. It was marked above the entrance with what Marcus recognized immediately as the elven symbol for truth. The building drew him, as if it were a mighty lodestone and he nothing but the merest flake of iron.

He stopped, staring slack-jawed at what simply had to be the great library of Elebrion. It was one of the greatest storehouses of earthly knowledge in all the world, second only to the notorious Collegium Occludum itself.

How Marcus yearned to enter, to read those precious histories spanning times now lost to man, to learn the truth of all those centuries preceding the Black Age of the Witchkings. To Marcus, the worst of the Witchkings' horrific sins—which were beyond number—had always been their wanton destruction of every script, scroll, and chiseled tablet that preceded their dark rule.

The doors of the library were remarkably plain. It might have been the entrance to a supply store. What spell-warded treasures there must be hidden away behind those deceptively nondescript doors! What ancient tales and histories lay there, patiently waiting, unseen by human eyes for four hundred years or more!

A horse bumped into Barat from behind, breaking the spell that held him transfixed.

"Get on, Marcus," barked Jorim, the Michaeline who'd been following him. "There's time enough for gawking later."

Marcus apologized, but when he looked toward the front of the train, he could see that he was not the only one for whom the great trove of elven lore held a powerful, if perhaps illicit, allure. Bishop Claudo too was staring back toward the library with a wistful expression that was most strange when seen on that pinched face. Marcus grinned. Knowing that the bishop had a weakness not unlike his own made the old scarecrow seem almost likeable for a moment.

The elvic guard finally stopped in front of an enormous building that thrust high into the sky, with five delicate tines arching upward rather like a hand stretched forth into the heavens.

It was symbolic, of that Marcus was sure, but of what he did not know. It couldn't be the five aspects of truth as taught by the Pannonian philosphers, unless perhaps the half-elves had inherited that concept as part of their subhuman paternity. Was it possible that the elves worshipped a secret god, a quintine one? Or perhaps they revered five distinct divinities—false gods, of course—although Marcus had no idea if that was the case since he'd never read anything that described the tenets of any elvic religion.

Scholastic inquiry into false faiths was not banned, precisely, but neither was it encouraged. And there was very little source material available to a young scholar regarding human heresies, let alone subhuman ones.

Of course, it was entirely possible that the geometric arrangement was simply ornamentation in the mode of the abstract sculptures he'd seen in the squares. It was impossible to say, but he made a mental note to ask an elf about it if the opportunity presented itself.

A jangling of metal drew his attention down from the skies, and he realized that he was the only one still seated on his horse. Marcipor was tugging at his left stirrup. Feeling vaguely embarrassed, Marcus quickly dismounted and joined the others.

The elven guards were relieving the Michaelines of their ornate blue scabbards, stacking them neatly near the white marble steps, oblivious to the begrudging acquiescence of the warrior-priests. Marcus quickly unbelted his own sword and smiled as he offered it to a silver-armored elf. But except for taking the weapon, the guard paid him no notice. Pale inhuman eyes flickered over his face and past him as if he was of no more interest than his horse.

He saw that the Michaelines were taking their brilliant blue-and-gold cloaks out of their packs and using them to cover their stained riding leathers. Glancing down at his own filthy clothes, he wanted to kick himself for not realizing that they might be given an immediate audience with the High King. He had a cloak somewhere in his pack, but he couldn't remember if it was in any better shape than the tunica and trousers he was wearing now. He wished he was wearing the somber black of the bishop and his men—at least that way the dirt wouldn't be so obvious.

Noticing that Marcipor was more than a little reluctant about giving up his ludicrously encrusted parade sword, Marcus couldn't resist taking out some of his annoyance at himself by adding salt to Marce's wounds. "I shouldn't be surprised if the bishop set that aside for a host gift. Don't you think it's pretty enough for the High King?"

"Do you think they'll give them back to us?"

"I wouldn't worry about it. As I understand it, it's quite common for rulers who wish their rule to continue to take a dim view of unknown visitors being armed in their presence."

"You'd better be right! Or I'll—"

He was suddenly silenced when Marcus's leather glove closed over his mouth. Marcus smiled and removed his hand as the elvic guard holding their blades gestured toward where the human party was forming two lines behind Bishop Claudo and Father Aestus. Marcus rather doubted that the High King of the elves was likely to be much concerned about improbable threats of retribution from an unarmed human slave, but regardless, it was surely unwise to utter them in front of the king's own palace guards.

They entered the palace through an arched entrance populated with the figures of elves and other beings. Unlike Amorr, where the stone statuary was always left untouched, these carved figures were painted in great detail. Fair-haired warriors slew raging beasts with crimson tongues, bards plucked at golden lyres, and lovers embraced, pressing their pink lips together in sensual abandon. The diverse figures seemed to leap out of the white marble from which they had been released. So realistic were they in their various pursuits that more than once Marcus was forced to avert his eyes in the interests of chastity.

They were marched through a series of similarly decorated rooms and led into the throne room to be presented to the High King and his queen en masse.

High King Mael's throne room was an imposing chamber of white marble that brought to mind a mausoleum. Unlike in the Sanctiff's palace—the only other such structure Marcus had ever been inside—the lights here were cold and burned with a blue flame that gave off light without heat. Were they the witchlights of which Lodi had spoken before?

On two thrones sat an elegantly clad pair of elves. Marcus knew King Mael was more than five hundred years old, but he looked no more than forty. His hair was darker than most of his subjects, though still much lighter than that of most of the

Amorrans. His eyes were a blue so dark they almost appeared to be black.

His queen sat at his side. Where he was dark, she was so fair as to be almost alabaster, with a long, narrow face, straight white hair, and deeply slanted grey eyes that were outlined in scarlet. In her white dress she looked rather like one of the marble figures on the entry arch, albeit one that the artisan had only just begun painting.

Marcus followed the rest of his group as they were escorted before the thrones and arrayed in three rows. Elvish palace guards wheeled in the draped cage that contained the Ulfin. This they placed behind the Amorran party.

The court herald, dressed in the livery of the High King, stepped forward from beside the thrones. "The emissary of the Sanctiff of the Holy Republic of Amorr and his retainers, accompanied by the Sky Lord Fáelán u Flann."

Cassius Claudo gestured at the others to stay where they were and stepped forward to make a deep and appropriately respectful bow. Marcus was struck by the strange likeness between the elf king and the bishop, a likeness that had nothing to do with their dissimilar features and everything to do with the way in which their intense personalities seemed to have burned away everything that was weak and soft and prone to mercy inside them.

"High King," Claudo said, "it is my humble honor to bring you—"

"I know what you bring to my realm," the elf king interrupted. "You bring judgment. You bring conceit. You bring arrogance, and you bring the promise of war between your people and mine."

Claudo blinked, but showed no other sign of being discomfited. He reached his right hand into his left sleeve and withdrew a scroll with gilded caps. "My instructions were to present a treaty to formalize the peace between our peoples, your Majesty, one that is long overdue in recognizing the real peace that has prevailed for more than forty years."

The king sniffed. "The Sanctiff sends a declaration of peace? Are not matters of war and peace concerns for the Consul of the Legions and the Amorran Senate, rather than its High Priest?"

"In most circumstances that is indeed the case, your Majesty. In this particular instance, however, there are certain aspects that fall within the Church's bailiwick. Therefore, under Amorran law, the sanction of the Sanctiff is required. Sanction, your majesty, which has now been duly, if belatedly, granted."

"And how was this 'sanction' justified?" King Mael asked. "I am curious, my lord bishop. Perhaps you can inform me why the viceroy of your god was moved to grant us this favor. Did the god speak to him? Or was it merely inspired wisdom of the sort that has granted your race with an ever-increasing body of divine literature?"

Marcus was frightened by the cruel amusement that flickered sporadically across the face of the High King. Mael was toying with Cassius Claudo. He obviously knew the true purpose of the embassy and was throwing it in their faces, daring them to admit it. Was he looking for an excuse to take offense and send them away—or worse? Perhaps, but how would that serve him in any way? Marcus's thoughts raced as he tried to understand the icily polite battle with verbal stilettos that was taking place before him.

"I couldn't possibly say, your Majesty. The Sanctiff answers to none but the Immaculate and acts as he sees fit. It is for me to obey, not to question."

"Then well done, faithful and obedient servant. Lord Hwysfeith, please take the treaty from the Amorran ambassador and see that it is placed before my council for review. As the last clash between our two peoples took place one hundred and ninety-eight years ago, I expect there will be few surprises in the document."

As an elderly elf approached Claudo and took the treaty scroll, Marcus mentally translated the king's words: "Your Senate can forget about getting back that pair of eagles we took off their legions two hundred years ago." He shrugged. No doubt military men like his father would be outraged by this, and one or two legions might even riot, but having met the Sanctiff twice now, he found it impossible to believe that the man possessed even the slightest concern for two centuries-old pieces of legionary insignia.

"Your Majesty," Claudo said, "as an example of the esteem with which you are held by the Amorran Senate and people, and furthermore as what, God willing, may be an omen of the friendly relations and cooperation between our two kingdoms in the future, I beg your leave to present you a most particular gift that this embassy happened to acquire in the course of our journey to your realm."

The High King nodded, his face impassive. Marcus assumed Mael had to know what was in the large cage that had been dragged in by the guards and placed at the rear of the hall already, even though it was completely covered with a thick cloth of bright blue silk.

But his dark eyes narrowed with curiosity as ten Michaelines, under direction from Hezekius, knelt down, lifted the cage, and carried it forward before the throne. After placing it carefully on the marble floor, they arranged themselves in two lines standing at attention, five facing the cage and five facing the throne. Muffled snarls and whines could be heard from under the cloth, but the cage barely moved.

"Your Majesty!" an elven guard called from the rear of the hall, his hand gripping the hilt of his sword.

King Mael raised his hand, unconcerned, and the guard fell silent. "I hardly dare to hope that you have brought me what I have sought for twenty years," he told Cassius Claudo. "If you have, then rest assured, you shall know the royal favor of Elebrion."

"May it be so, your Majesty." Somehow, Cassius Claudo managed to prevent any hint of smile from touching his lips. He pointed to the cage, and two Michaelines stepped forward and whisked the cunningly constructed cloth off it with an effortless flick of their wrists.

Inside the cage was the horrid beast very like the one that had nearly killed Marcus, chained to iron clasps with its arms and legs fully extended. The Ulfin was thin and bare patches of skin were exposed where the fur had been worn away by its chains, but its rage-filled spirit remained unbroken. It bared its large canines in defiance of the royal figures seated before it.

"A princely gift, lord bishop!" The High King's eyes lit up with excitement as he took in the beast. "Wherever did you take it?"

"I am informed there were six, your Majesty. We encountered them unexpectedly in the Shadowald where they were engaged in battle with some of your kindred from Merithaim.

I should have preferred to have brought you more, but I am afraid that my men were careless and killed the other five."

"A pity. You have my thanks even so, however, as one is all that I require. Perhaps you will accept these small tokens of my appreciation." Mael gestured with a finger.

Marcus couldn't stifle a gasp as two weathered brass eagles suddenly appeared in the air in front of Cassius Claudo. Then two small red pillows appeared on the floor beneath them and they fell down upon the pillows with a soft thump.

A small token? They were the sacred standards of the Tenth and Twelfth legions lost with Lucius Varus almost two hundred years ago at Ardus Wald! For their return, the Senate would have gladly traded ten thousand Ulfin, even if they'd had to march across the White Sea to collect them. The elf king's use of magic to deliver them was somewhat of a sardonic poke in the eye, of course, but not even the most fervent witchhunter in the Church would have objected to it at that moment.

"Your generosity is without limits, your Majesty," Cassius Claudo said in a voice gone strangely hoarse. He made a surreptitious sign, and the entire Amorran delegation bowed with him. Marcus could feel tears welling up inside his eyes as the bishop then knelt, made the sign of the Immaculate One on his chest, and rose to his feet with the long-lost standards in his arms.

The elf king smiled in satisfaction, though without warmth. It seemed to give him gratification to see the effect his gift had had on the Amorrans. "My lord bishop, it is our pleasure to invite you and your entourage to dinner in honor of the Amorran Senate and people tonight," he said. "Will you be so good as join us?"

"With gratitude, your Majesty." Cassius Claudo cleared his throat and bowed one last time. "With the utmost gratitude, High King."

There was barely time to stow their packs and change from their well-stained travelling clothes into attire that was worthy of the High King's table.

Nevertheless, Lodi somehow managed to acquire a bowl of hot water. With this and his dagger the dwarf adroitly shaved Marcus, insisting that there wasn't sufficient time to enjoy the usual spectacle of watching Marcus butcher himself. Despite fingers that were thick and stubby, the dwarf had a surprisingly delicate touch. The shave Lodi gave him compared quite favorably to the best shave Marcus had ever received from an Amorran barber. Rubbing his smooth and unlacerated face afterward made him think for the first time just why dwarf-worked weaponry was valued so highly.

The feast was held in a different building within the palace grounds. This was a wide, rectangular edifice that appeared to be used for some sort of theatrical events, perhaps musical performances. A broad set of stairs led to large auditorium with stages on either side, although the tiled floor made Marcus think that music was probably unlikely. One stage held a large, ornately carved wooden table. The other was hidden behind a green curtain.

The floor tiles were ornate, laid out in intricate patterns that appeared to be runic. They were painted in a light, attractive color scheme that reminded Marcus of peaches and apricots. Colorful banners embroidered with scenes of elves at the hunt and at war—usually, but not always, with orcs—hung from the ceilings to obscure the unadorned stone walls. The entire chamber was well-lit with the bluish flameless torches that Marcus had come to think of as elf-lights.

Marcus was seated at the third table, the one to the left of the royal table at which the bishop, Father Aestus, Captain Hezekius, and one of the older Michaelines were dining. Claudius Serranus was one of the five Michaelines at the second table, while Lodi, Marce, and Cassius Claudo's two priests were seated with Marcus, in addition to two elf lords and three noble elvith.

The latter were exceedingly beautiful, excrutiatingly so, comparing favorably with their woodland cousins in much the same way that the great ladies of Amorr outshined the female villagers dwelling in the country. Their hair was impossibly long, first sweeping up in a variety of strange, sculptured figures, then falling down nearly to their waists. Marcus estimated that without whatever magic it was that held their hair into place, they would be unable to walk without stepping on it and falling.

The elvish ladies' clothes were equally impractical, making use of an incredible amount of fabric to do such a poor job of concealing the alabaster skin beneath it. Fortunately, they were not voluptuous—an Amorran woman wearing such daring clothes would look more like a sausage exploding in the fire. Although their high cheekbones and elegantly sculpted features were inarguably beautiful, all in all, Marcus found the elvith too alien to be attractive, let alone irresistable.

Lodi sat grudgingly at the table, silently refusing to so much as respond either to the elf lord across from him or to the elvit at his side. Whatever disinterest Lodi and Marcus were showing to the elvish beauties around him, Marcipor was more than making up for. Marce's eyes were devouring the slender beauty sitting next to him. Meanwhile, the younger of the two bishops revealed an unexpectedly dashing aspect to his personality as he engaged in what could only be described as a flirtation with the very elvit Lodi was studiously ignoring.

Marcus found his eye drawn to a pretty elvit at the table below him and to his left. She was dressed more simply than the other elvith, and her white hair was tied into two simple braids joined together at the ends by a clip in the form of a golden hawk. She wore a dress that would not have drawn notice anywhere in Amorr, being little more than a black sleeveless tunica. Sitting amongst the colorfully, strangely attired elves and rich blues and golds of the warrior-priests at her table, she stood out as starkly as a Quiricusian grey-robe surrounded by Michaelines.

Her eyes met Marcus's. They were green and filled with a lively intelligence. He nodded politely, feeling more than a little embarrassed. In return, she favored him with a flicker of a smile, and then, to his shock, she winked.

Astonished, he looked to both sides and behind him, assuming she must have been looking at someone else. But no one was looking in her direction. He turned back to face her and saw that she had turned her attention elsewhere. There was, however, what looked suspiciously like a self-satisfied smile on her face.

The food set before him was less foreign to him than the fashions. After all, meat was meat, vegetables were vegetables and grain was grain. The elves did make use of some unusual spices he couldn't identify, but they only added an exotic flavor to what was a very good meal. Of course, after nearly a month on the road, almost anything would be a treat.

However, there was one dish that looked as if it was supposed to be some sort of Amorran noodle served with slices of barely cooked fish. But the noodles had been left to boil too long and were far too soft to the bite for his liking. The wine, on the other hand, was quite good, although sweeter and served cooler than most Amorran wines.

As dessert—green shards of sweet flavored ice—was served, the High King rose to his feet and offered a toast. "To the Amorran Senate and people. Long may they prosper . . . in peace."

Elf and man alike raised their glasses and drank to the peaceful prosperity of the Republic. Not a man there missed the significance of the royal stress placed on the final word, though.

Cassius Claudo then stood and raised his glass in return. "To the High King and queen of the fair realms of Elebrion, Merithaim, Kir Donas, Glaislael, Kir Kalithel, Arathaim, and Falas. Long may they prosper, and may the Immaculate God grant that that which is fallen shall rise again."

Some of the men looked confused, but most of the elves drank without hesitation and murmured approvingly among themselves. Marce glanced at Marcus and raised his eyebrows in question. Unsurprisingly, he had no idea what the bishop had done. King Mael, on the other hand, clearly did, as his face showed signs of both amusement and bitterness at the unlikely prospect of elven cities long dead rising once more.

"Claudo's just saying Amorr wishes the elf kingdoms well," Marcus explained to Marcipor. "There used to be seven where there are now only three."

The bishop's toast sparked an animated discussion between the bishop and the two elf lords at the main table, Marcus could hear. Earlier they had been discussing if the fall of Glaislael had always been inevitable or if the High King should have attempted to pursue an alliance with the kingdoms of man sooner than he had finally done. Marcus, having little interest in the subject at the moment, glanced back at the fifth table and was startled to see the pretty elvit with the white braids staring at him.

She raised her glass to him, the surprise of which caused him to choke on the wine he'd just imbibed and embark upon a violent fit of coughing. When it finally ended, he looked up, eyes streaming, to see that she was still laughing merrily, as were Marcipor and the elf maiden he'd been assiduously courting.

Fortunately, the High King happened to choose that moment to unveil the surprise he'd prepared for his guests. At his command, the huge green curtain rose from the far stage. It did so without ropes, Marcus noticed. These elves practically swam in an invisible sorcerous filth. It almost made him wish for the knucklebone of Saint Ansfrid of Tolanon, which was somewhere in his bags. Souls or no souls, they were most certainly damnable for all their wealth, magic, and beauty.

Speaking of which, he took advantage of the way everyone was looking at the stage to sneak another glance at the pretty elvit. She looked to be shorter than most of the other elves, and although it didn't seem possible, her features were even more delicate as well. She started to shift in her seat as if to turn toward the stage and thus toward Marcus, so he quickly returned his attention to the stage.

To his horror, he realized that the Ulfin was standing on the stage, devoid of any chains or clothing. Even the cord it had worn around its neck since they'd captured it was gone. Unbound, it looked every bit as deadly as Marcus knew it was. Its long, man-like hands were tipped with claws as long as a man's finger and teeth longer than a man's knuckle. But its eyes were wide, and it seemed to be breathing rapidly, which caused Marcus to conclude that the elven king had it somehow bound by his magic.

"Ikhiss stowbraahr rekksletnan . . . " the wolf-thing snarled at the seated crowd in its guttural tongue.

King Mael raised a finger and his queen murmured a word or two under her breath. Suddenly they could understand what the Ulfin was saying.

" . . . of Svangor Ironjaw's tenth pack. And you will release me, furless whiteskin, or I will crunch your skinny neck between my teeth."

"Amazing, is it not," said the High King, completely ignoring the beast's ravings. "The strength of an animal, the mind of a man, and the dark power of a demon, all bound together in delicate balance! Monstrous, to be sure, and yet a thing of perfect beauty all the same."

"I will take your wenches until they whine like lapdogs in heat! With my own jaws will I snap the heads off your pups and swallow them whole!"

King Mael did not appear to even notice the snarling threats. And yet, with a barely noticeable gesture, the beast suddenly fell silent, its jaws snapping shut as if an invisible iron band had been clamped around them. Its eyes bulged nearly out of their sockets, and the monster began to growl.

But its growls quickly turned into whines as it realized that not only had it been silenced, it was being suffocated. Marcus held his own breath, amazed and unsettled to realize that he was actually seeing true elvic wizardry on display! It was evil, to be sure. Clearly wrong. But it was also incredibly impressive.

King Mael watched impassively as the wolf-thing thrashed madly about, helpless in its chains both magical and material. Just as Marcus thought the beast was going to collapse, the king gestured again and was rewarded with a loud series of desperate, heaving gasps from his victim.

The beast's jaws yawned open wide, but its teeth did not seem quite so terrible now with the long red tongue lolling limply between them. The creature's raw vitality was such that it took only a few moments for it to recover, but when it did, the fire was gone from its eyes, replaced with a fearful wariness.

"In Elebrion, creature, we expect a certain amount of civility from lesser mortals who have ascended to our heights uninvited," the king said to the Ulfin. "If you cannot keep a civil tongue in your head, rest assured I shall see that it is removed."

"I came not by choice!" the Ulfin growled. "I was made prisoner and dragged to this place in bondage."

"That is true. And yet is it not also true that when you were made prisoner, it was while you and your companions were intruding upon my lands? Were you not engaged in hunting down and killing my subjects at that time?"

"They attacked us first!"

"If so, they were right to do so. You invaded my realm. Your lives were forfeit the moment you set foot upon Merithaimi soil without my leave."

The beast snarled, but it offered no defense of its actions. There was none to offer.

"Do you wish to attempt to purchase your life by telling me precisely what six Ulfin scouts are doing on the wrong side of the White Sea, hundreds of leagues away from the coast and deep inside the Shadowald?"

The only response was another contemptuous snarl.

"As you wish. Rest assured, your silence will avail your people nothing. Already my rangers are scouring the forest for others of your kind. My sorcerers are tracing your tracks. It will not be long before they discover the purpose of your expedition. But fear not, for your death shall serve a great and mighty purpose, one that your people will never forget should they dare to cross the sea and lift their hands against me."

"I am not afraid to die!"

"I said nothing of dying, wretched creature. Do you not know that there are fates far worse than death?"

Several of the elves laughed. It was a cold and merciless sound. Marcus exchanged a glance with Lodi, who merely shook his head and looked grim.

The elf king raised his hand, and a servitor approached the stage and mounted it from the left side. He bore a sword by its blade in both hands. When he reached the High King, he knelt, holding the blade over his head as if he were a squire. The king took the sword by its hilt and held it aloft, admiring it and turning it slightly to let the light reflect from it. It was covered with etched runes, not unlike Claudius Serranus's elf-sword, but it was longer and straighter, designed for two-hand use.

"This blade was named Wolfslayer, creature. It was forged two centuries ago at the order of my father, who was High King before me. At the time, he believed his armies would be joining those of the kings of men in order to wipe out the wolf-things that were threatening to conquer the Vargeyan Isles. As our guests tonight know all too well, his armies never sailed from

Kir Donas, which is why they did not drown in the winter passage across the White Sea.

"However, this is not the time for recriminations. Was it not this very afternoon that we laid those long-troubled ghosts to rest? I only mention the past to explain that for all this time, this blade has waited for a creature such as this to . . . activate . . . the spells that were placed upon it by High King Mondhryten and the *Custodas* of the Collegium Occludum." He twirled the heavy sword effortlessly in one hand and smiled. "Your gift was more precious than you know, my lord bishop."

Cassius Claudo's face was taut with tightly controlled emotion, but Marcus couldn't tell if he was angry or frightened. He didn't understand why the bishop would be upset about the elf king's theatrics, but he suddenly had a very bad feeling about what was about to happen. Most of the elves were smiling and looking as if they were anticipating something. The little elvit at the next table, however, appeared to be angry.

"You mean to torture this thing we presented to you as a gift?" Claudo asked, his careful articulation hinting at the depth of his feelings. "Is this intended to be an insult?"

"An insult? By no means! Think of this as an experiment of sorts. I am given to understand that your high priest has recently begun an extensive inquiry into the way in which diverse beings are animated. Whether or not they have, what is your word, souls. Well, tonight I mean to expand his knowledge. I promise, what you will see should prove most informative for him."

"You are speaking of foul sorcery," Claudo said, his cheeks flushed. "Such witchcraft is abhorrent of God. We will not stand by and permit this abomination to take place."

"Will you not?" The king smiled and pointed his sword at Claudius Serranus. "The famed Order of Saint Michael is here in force, are they not? The great anti-mages! Then I give them leave to interfere, so long as they do so without leaving their seats or lifting a material hand against me. We shall undertake two experiments in one. Magic against magic. I expect the latter will be of as much interest to Amorr's generals as to mine."

Cassias Claudo started to speak, but Captain Hezekius raised a hand and cut him off. He spoke to his men. "Take no action, Michaelines. No one interferes with the High King. Not a one! Do you hear me? We are guests here!"

"Captain," the warrior-priests barked as one.

"You are too kind, Captain," the king said. "Indeed, much too kind. I should have welcomed the test of your—what is your spellcraft called—*fidelie*? I should have welcomed a test of it against elven sorcery."

Perhaps you'll get the chance sooner than you think, Marcus thought to himself. And he doubted he was the only Amorran thinking that way.

"What is unusual about this sword is that it is a living blade," Mael said. "It is both weapon and vessel. There are not many of these swords, for they require an astonishing effort, and there are few indeed with the skill. But they are worth it, for they are of particular efficacy when used against that from which they have been born. Or perhaps 'drawn' would be the more precise word? I speak, of course, of the Law of Opposites, which is a core concept of our practical philosophy that you insist on calling magic."

The king paused and waited for Cassius Claudo to protest, but the bishop said nothing. His lips were firmly pressed together and his arms were folded, but he was clearly loathe to override the captain and risk causing an incident that would likely ruin all the objectives of the embassy, including the part about returning safely to Amorr.

"I agree with your silence, my lord bishop: this is no place for a philosophical lesson. Let us then proceed to more pragmatic concerns. Now, note the rage in this exquisite creature, the fury that animates it. Its anger is a craving for vengeance which, quite naturally, supersedes the compassionate desires. It is that lupine craving that, when harnessed, will give the weapon its unstoppable force against all Ulfin for all time.

"The key is to transfer that craving for vengeance into the blade. And not only transfer it, but transform it and redirect it toward the target we require. Even those sworn to chastity must know that love quite readily transforms into hate, even self-love. You see that the more proud and arrogant the subject, the better. And this one, I am pleased to see, has it to spare!"

The High King saluted the bound Ulfin with the sword. The man-wolf only snarled and spat at him. Then Mael glanced back at his queen, who began chanting quietly.

He turned one circle, then two, then three. As he completed the third turn he shouted something loud but unintelligible and hurled the sword at the beast like a shining spear.

The wolf-thing howled as the blade struck it. It stared down, transfixed at its breast, as an evil yellow smoke spilled from the wound. The Ulfin collapsed, its invisible bindings released.

"Lord Faelan," the king said, "as you are nearest the stage, would you please withdraw the sword from that which has tempered the spells of the sword?"

Looking uncharacteristically nervous, the elf lord climbed the stairs to the stage, gripped the hilt, and placed a booted foot upon the body of the Ulfin. With difficulty he wrested the blade from the corpse.

Everyone, including the jaded elves at their table, gasped. For the sword was moving, twitching and undulating like an arthritic serpent. To Marcus's horror, it suddenly screamed like damned souls were supposed to scream, and the appalling cry was in the voice of the dead Ulfin.

"Enough," declared the High King.

The runes on the blade suddenly flared bright red, the sword stiffened to its previous form, and the scream instantly stopped, much to everyone's relief.

The king held the blade aloft. "I give you Wolfslayer Ulfinsbane!"

Cassius Claudo rose to his feet, his face looking paler and more pinched than it ever had before throughout the course of the journey. "If you will excuse us, High King, we are exhausted. I thank you for the meal, and beg your leave to excuse me and my men from further festivities this evening. We are tired from our long ride up your mountain."

"You have it," Mael said, sounding disappointed, "although I demand your presence in my court on the morrow."

"Have you not already made too many demands on Amorr, your Majesty?" Claudo said.

"Your conceit is considerable, human. Perhaps you for-get—no, it is more likely you are ignorant of the fact—that my grandfather was ruling these very halls when your forefathers were roaming naked through the forests like animals."

"The angels too preceded the creation of man. And yet, as Paulus writes, 'Do you not know that you will judge the angels?'"

"Elfdom fears neither man nor angel. Nor judgment."

"Nor God?"

Marcus had risen to his feet, as had the entire embassy. But now they paused as the bishop and High King engaged in verbal battle.

The High King smiled coldly. "There are no gods, human, not in the sense you mean. There are only the higher Forms, of which we elves are the most perfect expressions on this particular plane. Of that which is good—beauty, time, wisdom, and talent—you must admit that we enjoy the greater portion. Clearly we most closely approach the ideal.

"If you insist on imagining that there is a God, my lord bishop, a singular and rational divine being who served out those portions with intent and purpose, why, then you and I must both be a part of Him. Only two of a thousand thousand thousand insignificant elements that, en masse, comprise the whole. But the notion of a single god is not only baseless, it is meaningless, immaterial. You worship a metaphor."

Claudo squared his shoulders toward the king. "We worship a God who became man. There is nothing less immaterial than that."

"You put much faith in an old text, human. If you value ancient writings so, I shall show you our library. We elves possess many such texts, some written by elf, some by man, some through demons, and some from gods. All of them are far older than those scribblings that give meaning to your fantasies and your dark dreams of slaughter."

The two stood locked in a deadly stare, seeming like titans of legend at war in the nether world.

Finally, the High King shrugged. "But it is late, and the entertainment planned is unlikely to be to your taste. So you have our leave to depart."

Marcus murmured some meaningless civilities to the elves at his table and turned to leave. But when he went to follow Lodi and the others, a hand caught his sleeve. He turned and was surprised to see the pretty elvit standing next to him . . . and that she was eye to eye with him.

They were green, he was surprised to see. He quite liked green eyes, especially when set nicely in such a lovely face.

"Are you the Valerian?" she demanded, her accent slurring the words slightly.

"You're not that tall for an elf," he blurted out, not knowing what to say in his confusion.

"Well, you're not that old for a man-priest," she retorted. "Are you the Valerian?"

"Yes, I'm called Marcus Valerius, son of Corvus. How are you called?"

"There's no time. Listen to me. Your life is in danger. You must not go to your chambers. As soon as you walk out of the building, jump up behind the statue on the steps, to the right. Wait for me there, and try not to move too much. I will see that no one notices you. And tell no one!"

"My life is in danger?" Marcus asked, alarmed, but already she had slipped away into the crowd of mingling elves and men moving toward the doors. In danger from whom?

Lodi, noticing that he hadn't followed them, had come back for him. "Are you coming?"

"Yes, yes, of course. Go on. I was just curious about something."

Lodi looked at him askance. "Are you feeling well? You look unsettled."

Marcus attempted a weak smile, but even he knew it was unconvincing. "I don't think the spice they used on the pork is sitting quite right with me. Let's go. I'll be right behind you."

Marcus yearned to find out what Lodi would think about the strange elf girl's warning. But she had said to tell no one, not to tell no one except his dwarven bodyguard, so he held his tongue. Was it a trap? No, that made no sense. If the elves had wanted him dead, he'd already be dead. They were in Elebrion, after all, and they could have simply poisoned his wine. The elf king certainly hadn't been shy about killing that Ulfin in front of everyone, and Marcus found it hard to imagine that he'd fear to do the same even to Cassius Claudo, let alone one of his lesser companions, if he felt the need.

He thought about Magnus's warning the morning of their departure. Was it possible that the magnates of Amorr who hoped for war had planted an assassin within the embassy? That was hard to believe. He'd gotten to know many of the men in the embassy over the last month, and while he didn't necessarily like all of them, he found it impossible to imagine any of them being willing to murder him.

He smiled ruefully. If it was so easy for a man to pick out another man willing to kill him, no king would have ever been murdered by his successor. When money and power were at stake, no man's life could be deemed entirely safe, not even his own. He came to his decision just as he walked through the door, only a step or two behind Lodi.

Glancing to his right, he saw the statue: a tall martial-looking elf holding a scroll and gesturing with his other hand. Feigning a cough, he doubled over and lurched to the right, pretending that he'd stumbled over his own feet. Seeing that Lodi and the priest who'd been right behind him weren't looking back, he took four quick steps and leaped up behind the statue, doing his best to press into the shadows it cast in the torchlight.

The moon was three-quarters full and reflected brightly off the stone steps and the building façade. But the statue was thick enough to block the view of anyone looking back from the lower steps, and one would have to turn one's head at nearly a ninety-degree angle immediately upon exiting the building to have any view of him at all.

It wasn't long before Cassius Claudo and Captain Hezekius strolled down the steps, flanked by four Michaelines and an honor guard of eight elves. The doors closed behind them, and the sound of their steps gradually died away.

Marcus found himself alone in the silent shadows. He began to feel very silly, crouching behind the tall statue, hiding from absolutely nothing. His legs were beginning to cramp, so he sat down and made himself as comfortable as he could on its broad stone base.

He amused himself by imagining who the hypothetical assassin might be. Perhaps Magnus had hired Lodi specifically in order to kill him. Except that Magnus couldn't have known which gladiator he and Sextus would choose. Zephanus had certainly made a fair attempt at talking him to death throughout their long ride. But it had been Barat, his own horse, that had done the only actual harm to him. He was surprised to realize that it wasn't hard to imagine Cassius Claudo ordering a murder. But it was impossible to think of the bishop taking orders from a merchant or caring about war profits. Father Aestus? No, if only because killing Marcus would rob him of a future interlocutor.

"Valerian," a female voice called softly.

Marcus jumped up, nearly hitting his head on the elf statue's protruding scabbard. He had the sense of something large nearby, but he couldn't see anything in the darkness. "Where are you? What's happening?"

"Take two steps back from the statue and relax. Don't move too much. You'll be perfectly safe, just don't struggle or make any noise."

What? Marcus obediently took two steps backward, but instead of holding still, turned around in a circle toward the voice. He didn't see anything, but there came a strange rushing sound as if a great wind had blown up. And then something impossibly big and strong grabbed him tightly around his arms and torso, and the ground began to rapidly fall away from him. He was suddenly above the rooftops of the palace, and he saw the moonlit mountains beyond.

He tried to scream, but the crushing force of the thing holding him had momentarily stolen his breath from him. He started to struggle, and then thought better of it when he looked at the stone streets of Elebrion flashing by beneath him. Relax, she'd said. He tried, but it was hard when the cold wind was making his eyes tear up.

The combination of the bright moon and the light from a great torch burning atop a watchtower they passed over gave him enough light to see what held him. He looked down at his chest and saw that he was being held in a pair of giant bird's claws.

Warhawk. Which meant that the elf girl was a sorceress, and probably a militarily trained one at that. He had no idea what an elven sorceress would want with him or why she'd want to save his life—unless that was a trick too—but he was quite sure that if they didn't get where they were going soon, he was going to freeze to death.

Then the words of his father that he'd thought he'd never need occurred to him. "Son, there are times when a battle isn't going well and you begin to think it will be your last. In those times, a man has two choices: curse God or praise Him. It's in those times that a man discovers who he is."

Marcus had no trouble thinking of a few choice curses at the moment, future bishop or not. He was pretty sure he would have used them all if he'd been able to get any words. Instead, as the icy winds tore cruelly at him, he found himself laughing. Laughing at the bizarre nature of his predicament and in the amusing irony of the words of the Psalmist raining down on the night-shrouded mountains.

"*Confitebor Domino secundum iustitiam eius et psallam nomini Domini altissimi!*"

I will give thanks to the Lord because of His righteousness and I will sing praise to the name of the Lord Most High.

Iᴬ Q. VII A. I AD I

Ad primum dicendum quod corpus non est de essentia animae, sed anima ex natura suae essentiae habet quod sit corpori unibilis. Unde nec proprie anima est in specie; sed compositum. Dicere animam esse de substantia Dei, manifestam improbabilitatem continet. Ut anima humana est quandoque intelligens in potentia, et scientiam quodammodo a rebus acquirit, et habet diversas potentias, quae omnia aliena sunt a Dei natura. Unde manifeste falsum est animam esse de substantia Dei. Ergo aelvi habent animae naturaliter unita.

THE GREAT BIRD finally released him from its claws onto a large projection jutting out from a mountainside. Marcus crumpled to the hard ground upon which it had deposited him. He closed his eyes and, despite his uncontrollable shivering, decided that nothing had ever felt better than the solid feeling of *terra firma* supporting his weight. Elves could rule the sky, because man was assuredly not meant to fly!

"Are you well?" asked the elf girl. She stood beside him on the cliffside terrace. A small hut nestled against the mountain cliff behind her.

"I d-d-don't know if I e-e-even know h-how to start answering that question."

"So, you're fine," she replied, sounding amused. "I'm sorry to have surprised you that way, but there was no other way to make sure that no one would loose a shaft at you or stab you in the shadows as you were walking with the others. Whatever is going to happen is going to happen tonight."

He looked up at her, still astonished by how pretty she was, despite the fact that she was almost surely insane, at least by human standards. And, in light of what he thought she was saying, quite possibly by elven standards too. She did, however, have the sense to be wearing a heavy fur-and-leather coat over the black dress she'd worn at the High King's feast—a coat that he could have very much used at the moment.

"Why are you so c-convinced that someone w-wants to kill me? And what sort of m-m-magic can tell you what is going to happen before time?"

"Wait here," she told him, and walked quickly toward a light that was flickering nearby.

Wait here? Marcus stared at her departing figure in disbelief, then rolled over onto his back and looked up at the warhawk looming over him.

It was nearly close enough for him to reach out and touch it. Or, more to the point, it was quite close enough to lurch forward and snap at him with its cruel and alarmingly powerful-looking beak. Its huge yellow eyes were larger than the golden plates upon which Marcus's dinner had been served, and they were regarding him with what he hoped was more curiosity than malice. He looked at the claws in which he'd so recently been held, and he shuddered. The bird could have easily ripped him to shreds if it had been so minded.

"Oh, Vengirasse won't harm you," the elf girl said when she finally returned. It had only been a short while, but in the freezing night, lying on a rock in front of a giant bird of war, it had seemed like a lot longer. She draped a thick blanket over him. "That should warm you up a little. He's very intelligent. Well, he knows the difference between portage and prey, anyway."

Marcus wrapped the blanket tightly around him. "Who are you, and why are you doing this to me?"

"*For* you," she corrected. "I am doing this, Valerian, because I'm told that it is in the interest of all elfdom that you survive long enough to inform the Sanctiff that, in your humble opinion, we elves are possessed of that nebulous substance you men call 'soul,' and that therefore there is no call for Amorr to direct its next holy war in the direction of Merithaim, Kir Donas, or Elebrion."

Marcus blinked. "So you captured me in order to force me to testify in your favor?"

"No, of course not! It's only that it would be difficult for you to do anything at all if you are dead. And I'm called Caitlys, Caitlys Shadowsong. Can you stand up yet?"

"I think so."

She reached out a hand and he took it. With some difficulty the two of them managed to get him to his feet. Despite her slender build, she was stronger than she looked and managed to hold him up when his left leg gave out on him.

He didn't realize he was so close to her until he found himself practically embracing her, with both arms around her shoulder.

Her breath smelled of honey, her hair of flowers, and his knees felt began to feel weak in a way that had nothing to do with the brutal cold he'd just endured.

He pushed himself away from her with a brusqueness that might have stemmed from pride, temptation, or fear. Or perhaps all three at once.

"Don't . . . I can walk on my own!"

"As you like." She seemed to take no offense, but kept one arm extended toward him in case he should lose his balance.

They walked toward a small stone dwelling that was rather more elegantly constructed than one would have imagined a hut perched on the side of a cliff to be.

"Come with me," she said. "There's someone here who can explain this to you better than I can."

"Who can explain it?" he asked as he followed her inside the hut. "Who lives here?"

Despite being made of stone, the hut was warm and well-lit by the fire burning at the hearth on the far side of the room. The walls were covered with wooden shelving covered entirely with scrolls and parchments. A wooden desk stood in one corner, a large wardrobe in the other. In front of the hearth was a tall form standing silhouetted by the flames. An elf, obviously, although Marcus couldn't make out much more than to note that he was wearing white robes.

The elf spoke. "*I* live here, and I welcome you to my humble home, Marcus Valerius of Amorr. Thank you for placing your trust in my emissary. I fear I am too feeble for such adventures of our faith anymore, but fortunately dear Caitlys is brave and her heart is true."

Marcus caught his breath, stunned literally speechless. The elf had not said, "your faith," but "our faith"!

Now that he was closer and his eyes had adjusted to the firelight, he could see that the elf was old, extremely old, judging by his thin white hair, the lines on his face, and the slight stooping of his shoulders. Yet even so, there was a sense of immense power inside him, as if the form of the ancient elf was merely a mask for the real being inside it. And incredibly, against all odds, he wore the sign of the tree around his neck on a silver necklace, something only one who worshipped the Immaculate would ever wear.

It seemed to Marcus that the ground spun. "Y-you are a brother? I don't understand! How can this be?"

The elf smiled. "I cannot tell you how delighted I am to greet you in the name of the Most Holy Immanuel, Marcus Valerius. Long indeed have I waited for this moment."

There was such an ethereal air of holiness about him that Marcus did not hesitate. He stepped forward and gave the Kiss of Peace to the old elf. The withered lips felt strangely soft and dry.

"Are you the only one?" he asked.

"In all elfdom, yes. You may call me Nomenlos. I chose that name for I have many deeds for which to repent, much pride for which to atone."

"You need repent nothing," Caitlys protested.

"Peace, child. You know naught of these things. In any event, it is not for you to judge. Marcus Valerius, the peril is great. For you, for your bishop, and for the elves. For months, the High King has known that the Sanctiff's investigation was proceeding and that your embassy was to be the final inquiry into the matter of the elven soul."

Marcus had thought the Sanctiff had hatched this idea just before summoning him to the palace. How did this elf know more than he did? "You have spies in Amorr?"

"Not me, but the High King. He has spies everywhere. There are few, man or orc, who cannot be purchased by one means or another. And everywhere a mouse or a crow can see, the High King's wizards may see also. The warhawks are not our only servitors among the animals, you know."

Caitlys brought wooden chairs for them to all sit down. "Most adepts can do transformations, of course," she said, "but that's rarely done simply to gather information. It's much too dangerous in enemy territory, and there's seldom anything that can be discovered that way that couldn't be learned simply by looking through the eyes of a familiar."

Nomenlos smiled at the unadulterated alarm in Marcus's eyes. "She does not share our faith, my young friend. And as it is not for her to pronounce my innocence, it is not for you to judge her guilty. We are all fallen short of the glory of God, my brother, even if some of us fall shorter than others."

Marcus sat in the chair heavily, glad for something remotely solid. He felt as if his knees would give at any moment, and this time it wasn't from the cold of his flight. "Fine, all right. Now can you please tell me who is trying to kill me?"

"We hoped that you might be able to tell us," Nomenlos said, taking a seat across from Marcus. "The High King's spies learned that a cabal of very wealthy men of the senatorial class had raised a significant sum in order to hire the killers. We even know their three targets: 'the two priests and the young Valerian.' They—you—were to be eliminated and the deaths blamed on the 'treachery' of the elves."

Hearing the words as they were spoken by the men planning to kill him frightened Marcus in a way that Caitlys telling him of the plot had not. He felt terribly vulnerable, even here on this hovel perched on a godforsaken rock clinging to the side of a mountain, and sought to find refuge in morbid humor.

"I wonder if they happen to be the same gentlemen who arranged for the War of the Human Alliance?"

Caitlys wrinkled her nose and looked at Nomenlos in confusion, but the elderly elf waved his nonsense aside. "Don't be afraid, Marcus Valerius. We will not permit them to harm you. You're safe with us."

"Why aren't I safe with the High King? You said his spies found out about all this, so why isn't he doing anything about it?"

"He didn't believe them," Caitlys answered. "Even if he did, it's hard to know if he would care, except in that the slaying of his royal guests would insult him as their host. He has no interest in pursuing another war with Amorr, but he wouldn't shirk from it either."

"The mighty are ever proud," Nomenlos murmured. "In any event, Mael's hands are tied. To intercede before the assassins strike would be to reveal the existence, perhaps even the extent, of his spy network. Even to watch the assassins closely enough to stop their wicked deeds would be a risk. Besides, his hosting cannot be faulted if one guest decides to slay another."

"The Senate would never believe that," Marcus told them.

"No, certainly not. Especially when only a few survivors manage to escape the massacre."

"Massacre? I thought only—"

"I suspect there are more than three deaths planned," Nomenlos said. "The sum reportedly given these men was improbably generous for a simple pair of assassins. How many are required to kill a novice, a fat priest, and an elderly bishop? Two? Surely no more than three!"

"I haven't actually taken my vows yet," Marcus said without thinking. "Improbably generous?"

"Seven hundred Savondese florins," Caitlys told him. "That's enough to buy the death of a king."

Despite the fire, Marcus suddenly felt even colder than he had when he'd been lying frozen on the rock outside. In his mind, he could hear Claudius Serranus's voice as they'd ridden under the hot afternoon sun. *It was a small consortio, only forty-five men . . . there's a fair number of captains who make a living turning foolish young farm boys into corpses every summer.*

"It's enough to hire a mercenary band," he said. A thought struck him. "There was an elf lord who was killed around twenty or thirty years ago in one of the mountain passes between Savonderum and the northern part of Merithaim. A lot of elves died there, but this one was the cousin—no, the nephew—of Lord Fáelán, who rode with us. I think he might have been related to the High King."

"Cathan u Treasach," Caitlys said immediately. "I remember he died when he was off raiding. Was it in the lands of men? I always thought it was on the steppes. I knew him well, of course. He was my cousin on my mother's side."

"He had a sword," Marcus said, "a particular sword with markings running down the blade. Runes, I suppose. Serranus has it now. Do the runes mean it was magicked somehow?"

"Most certainly," Nomenlos said. "Young Cathan was a most talented adept. Not enough skill to interest him in the Collegium, or it in him, but he would certainly not have borne a naked sword."

Marcus shook his head. It was hard to believe. It was impossible to believe! And yet, it must have been true. No true priest of Saint Michael would ever carry an ensorcelled sword, nor would a real Michaeline ever fail to detect one concealed in their midst.

He sat up tall in his chair. "I can tell you who your killers are."

"Can you?" Caitlys asked.

"Good," Nomenlos nodded with approval. "Who are they?"

"The Michaelines," he told them. "The warrior-priests with the blue cloaks. They must not be priests at all. Or if they are, they all knew about the ensorcelled blade, and they kept quiet about it. Their blasted Third Eye would've made it shine like a torch on a winter's night. It's all of them. Has to be. Every single, last, treacherous, blasphemous, cursed, hellbound one of them. They're hired killers, all right—only they're not the kind you were expecting."

Or that Magnus had anticipated, for that matter. How were Lodi and Marce supposed to protect him against thirty veteran wardogs? Oh, the Michaelines! It couldn't be. Marcus felt a slow fury building inside him at the thought of the men he'd thought had become, if not his friends, at least his companions. They'd smiled and joked and laughed with him for the last month, even as they planned to kill him.

"What will we do?" Caitlys asked Nomenlos, distress upon her pretty face. "Two or three, I could bespell. But so many? It's impossible, even with Fáelán's help! Bessarias, you cannot sit by and permit this to happen. You must act!"

"That," he said quietly, "is not my name. I am Nomenlos. I took a vow. I will not break it."

Caitlys turned to Marcus. "You worship his god. Tell him that he must!"

"Must what? I don't understand."

Caitlys pointed accusingly at the ancient elf, who stood calmly before her, unmoved by her temper. "He calls himself Nomenlos now, but once he was Bessarias, *Magistras Gnossi* of the Council. The greatest sorcerer the Collegium has ever known! Three thousand mercenaries could not stand against him!"

Marcus looked at the ancient elf, who returned his stare with a gentle smile.

"Is that true?"

The elf nodded. "Alas, it is true. But when I came to serve our Lord, I set my magic aside, as it is commanded. For nigh upon three hundred years I have not so much as scryed a pool nor spoken even a single word with the spirits. I fear my poor Mastema has been much aggrieved indeed."

To see Bessarius in his prime, read "Master of Cats" in Appendix Aelvi at the end of this book.

Marcus didn't know what to think. He didn't even know where to begin thinking. An elf who was not only an Immanuelite but a great and powerful sorcerer as well? Speaking with spirits? And an elf who claimed to serve the Lord Christ—did that not render the entire debate solved?

He shook his head. These strange and wonderful things would require much contemplation later, assuming he survived to contemplate them. For now, they would have to wait. The first thing, he decided, was to find a way to warn Cassius Claudo and Father Aestus of their impending assassinations . . . if they were still impending.

"Caitlys, there's no time for this. You have to fly me back to Elebrion. Nomenlos can't break his vow. It would be wrong. So it's up to us to warn my friends of their danger, and it may already be too late."

"Are you both mad?" she shouted. "By now they're probably dead! We must keep you far from there! At all costs, you must live! If you die too, there will be war on a scale that neither the kingdoms nor your cursed empire may survive intact! Amorr may have fifty legions but it has never faced the full might of the elves, before which even the Witchkings quailed!"

Marcus shook his head. "I can't simply run away. We have to at least try to warn them first. I am a Valerian, and a Valerian knows his duty."

Nomenlos—no, Bessarias—placed a wrinkled hand on Caitlys's shoulder. "Peace, child. We must have the courage to trust in the Immaculate One and pray that His will be done. I will not forswear myself, and you must listen to this man. He is young, but he has the strength of his fathers in him, and they were men who conquered many kings. Go, take him to the city. Warn the two priests of their false brethren if you can keep Marcus safe in doing so. Then fly to Kir Donas, where a ship may be found to take him to the lands of men."

"Madness!" Caitlys said, but even as she said it she appraised Marcus critically. "He'll freeze to death. We need more blankets or something."

Bessarias pointed to the wardrobe. "The bottom drawer, below the green robe. There are flying leathers I wore when I came here."

Marcus bowed to the ancient elf. "I only wish . . . I wish there was more time, sir. There is so much I want to ask you, so much you could teach me!"

Bessarias nodded back and smiled broadly. There was peace in his smile, and not a little pleasure. "There is indeed so much you have to learn, Marcus Valerius. That is why I envy you. So, be well, young man, my young brother-in-the-faith, and know that you have brought joy to an old elf's heart. And when you reach Amorr, I charge you to greet your High Priest for me in the Most Holy Name of our Lord!"

"And if he dies like a fool before he can get there?" snapped Caitlys as she shoved the bundle of heavy leathers into Marcus's arms.

He staggered, but Bessarias only laughed and lifted his right hand in blessing.

"Why then, one day we shall walk the streets of gold together and complete our conversation at our leisure. Fare you well, darling Caitlys. Fare you well, Marcus Valerius. And may the Immaculate Incarnate drive all darkness from you and shield you with blessing and light!"

Iᴬ Q. VII A. I AD II

Ad secundum dicendum licet creaturae non pertingant ad hoc quod sint similes Deo secundum suam naturam, similitudine speciei, ut homo genitus homini generanti; attingunt tamen ad eius similitudinem secundum repraesentationem rationis intellectae a Deo, ut domus quae est in materia, domui quae est in mente artificis. Non dicitur esse similitudo creaturae ad Deum propter communicantiam in forma secundum eandem rationem generis et speciei, sed secundum analogiam tantum; prout scilicet Deus est ens per essentiam, et alia per participationem. Ergo aelvi habent animae naturaliter unita.

THE LIGHTS OF Elebrion were few and far between as they broke through the clouds. Fog and cloud encircled the city on its mountaintop like a crown. Marcus greeted the sight with relief. The open sky was bitterly cold despite the protection of the oversized leathers he was wearing, but it scared him almost witless to fly sightless through the dampness of the clouds.

Still, if it was frightening to ride upon the back of the powerful warhawk with only a thin leather strap preventing him from plunging to his death, it was nevertheless much to be preferred over being carried dangling below it in its claws.

Caitlys was a warm, sweet-smelling presence in front of him, and he couldn't resist the urge to press more closely against her for warmth as she leaned back into him and pressed her cheek against his.

"Is there anyone you can trust?" she said over the wind.

"Yes!" he shouted back. "I have two slaves, a dwarf and a man."

"Are you sure of them?"

"Yes! One saved my life on the journey here. The other I've known all my life."

They soared low over the roofs, banking occasionally to avoid a spire or high facade that jutted inconveniently skyward. Marcus would have marveled at the warhawk's incredible ability to anticipate and avoid potential disaster at such speed, if only he wasn't terrified that every time they evaded an obstacle he was going to fall off. He gritted his teeth and fought the urge to tighten his grip on Caitlys's waist, which, he couldn't help noticing, was inhumanly slender even under her sky-riding coat.

"There!" she cried, pointing to a three-story building that looked vaguely familiar to him. "We have to get you inside without anyone noticing. We'll land on the roof. I hope your chamber has a window."

Marcus thought about the small room he'd been given to share with Marce and Lodi. It did have a window, he was sure. It had two windows, in fact, on either side of the corner . . .

It was a corner room! It would make it, and him, easier to find.

Now, if he could only remember which corner it was and which floor it was on. Unfortunately, he'd been to it only once, when they'd been shown there by the elven guards after their first appearance before the High King.

Lost in retracing his steps earlier that day, he didn't notice that Caitlys was landing the warhawk on the rooftop. As the bird lurched to an unexpected stop, his nose slammed into the back of her head and he cried out in pain.

"Pay attention!" she snapped. When he didn't answer right away, she turned in the saddle to look back at him. "You're bleeding."

"It's just my nose." He examined the blood on his hand. "I'll be all right. I think I know which room is ours. It's the one over there on the highest level."

She followed his pointing finger and nodded. "Good. It will be easiest if I lower a rope and you climb down. Can you manage that?"

"You have a rope?"

"Of course!" She pointed to a thick grey twine wrapped around the forward horn of the sky-saddle. "One never knows when someone will get hurt on a mountain or something needs to be moved quickly. And you're inexperienced with birds, so I don't think you'll have the balance to jump from Vengirasse's back to the window."

"No, I don't think I will. But you're not strong enough to hold me, are you?"

"The rope's tied to the saddle."

Marcus nodded, thoughtlessly wiped at his nose, then tried unsuccessfully to wipe the blood off onto the leathers he was

wearing. As he slid down from the bird's back, Caitlys played
out the rope to extend just past the top row of windows. "Two
more," he said. "You need to move him forward a little more."

The elf girl made a clucking sound, and Vengirasse indig-
nantly rose on his two legs and took a single step before ruf-
fling his feathers and making a protesting sound. "Enough,
lazy fowl." Caitlys scratched at his neck until he lowered his
feathers flat once more. "Will that do?"

"It should." Marcus gripped the rope with both hands and
slid slowly down the angled roof. The weathered stone was slip-
pery, and he had to steel himself to slide out over the edge,
bending at the waist so that he could get the rope below him
wrapped around his ankle to slow his descent a little more. "I'll
try not to be too long."

"Try not to fall or otherwise get yourself killed, Valerian. If
the rope's still there, I'm still here."

He nodded and waved, then turned his attention to the
task at hand. It was difficult but not impossible to hold his full
weight by his arms. His hands were the real problem, as they
felt as if they were burning because the rope was cutting into
them. Placing his feet against the building and walking himself
down helped a little. Happily for his hands, the window ledge
was only three body lengths from the roof, and it wasn't long
before he was crouched in the shelter of the lighted window
bay.

He peered into the room and saw Lodi, but no sign of
Marcipor. The dwarf, Marcus noticed, was no longer wearing
the bright red tunic he'd worn at the king's dinner. He banged
on the window glass. Once. Twice.

Alarmed, Lodi whirled around at the first sound, his arms
spread wide as if he was reaching out for weapons that weren't

there. Marcus almost called out to him, until he realized that to announce his name might well prove fatal if anyone else were listening nearby. He waited, therefore, as Lodi picked up his axe and peered closely at the glass, so close that his bulbous nose was nearly pressed against it. Then his expression changed, and he tossed the axe onto the closest bed before opening the window outward.

"Marcus, where the deep pits you been? What're you doing out the window? And what are you wearing?"

"Shhh!" Marcus whispered. "Keep quiet. There's an elvit on the roof. She's a friend. She lowered the rope for me. Now listen to me! The Michaelines aren't real. They're mercenaries, not real priests. They're planning to kill me and Bishop Claudo and Father Aestus, so we have to tell them and get them out of here somehow. And then get out of here ourselves!"

Lodi raised his thick eyebrows, but showed no other sign of surprise. "Can't say as they struck me as real priest-like, but then, they were supposed to be priest-warriors after all. Of course, man priests aren't much like dwarf priests, either."

The door to their room opened and they both whirled around to see Marcipor entering. He blinked with surprise. Unlike the dwarf, he hadn't changed and was still elegantly attired, if a bit disheveled.

"Shut the door," Marcus hissed.

"Did he hit you?" Marcipor asked Marcus as he closed the door. "Lodi, slaves don't get to punch their masters in the nose, even when they deserve it as richly as ours does. Marcus, what happened to you? Cassius Claudo has most of the Michaelines roaming all over Elebrion looking for you. I've almost lost my voice from running around calling out your name."

"I'll just bet they are," Marcus remarked sourly. He quickly explained the situation to Marcipor, who frowned, but otherwise took the news in stride.

"So, what do we do?"

Marcus wiped his nose. "I'll warn the bishop, and you tell Father Aestus what's going on. Lodi will get our gear together. Then we'll all climb onto the roof. I don't think the bird can carry more than three on its back, although maybe it can carry a fourth in its claws." He shuddered at the memory of the fear and cold. "Or perhaps Caitlys can ferry us to the stables. The bishop and Father Aestus should sneak out as soon as they can and meet us there. I don't think the treacherous false Michaelines will strike tonight as long as they don't know we know of their plan."

"Too dangerous," Lodi said, picking up his axe. "You're the target, boy. You stay here and pack. I'll go to the bishop. Marcipor, you go to the fat little priest, but don't tell him to sneak out. Have him keep his window open instead."

"Aestus can't climb the rope," Marcus said. "He's too fat. He probably couldn't even hang on while we pulled him up! And Cassius Claudo is too old."

"I'll climb down and carry them up," Lodi said. "No miner hasn't climbed up and down a shaft with twice the weight of that priestling on his back. And the roof is safer than trying to go out the stairs. If anyone sees either of them two sneaking about, they'll know somewhat's up and might just start their killing on the spot."

"Listen to the dwarf," Marcipor urged. "He's right. It's not safe for you to leave this room."

Reluctantly, Marcus agreed. Marcipor and Lodi departed on their separate missions, stealing silently out of the room and closing the door softly behind them.

Marcus looked around the room and saw that, fortunately, the habits of the road had not abandoned them upon their arrival in Elebrion: their packs remained largely unemptied. He shrugged off the overlong coat, slipped out of the too-long leather trousers with the legs rolled up, and removed the ruined remnants of his court finery. He felt a mild pang of regret for having worn them only once. But, since the fine fabrics were ruined anyhow, he scrubbed clean his hands on them and gingerly dabbed at his nose, which had almost, but not entirely, stopped bleeding.

It took him a moment to find his own riding leathers, which he'd previously left lying on the soft grey-feathered elven bed but were now missing. He located them in the bottom of the clothing chest, where Marce, or more likely Lodi, had put them. He wrinkled his nose as he drew them on. They were still filthy from the ride, but they would keep him warm.

His sword and the Merithaimi elvenblade were in there too, but he elected to stow the sword in his pack and content himself with slipping the scabbarded knife into his belt. If it came down to a fight with the wardogs, they were already dead. But one never knew when a sharp blade might be of value.

He stuffed Lodi's dress clothes into the dwarf's giant bag, which clanked ominously. Marcus gave it an experimental pull and found he could barely lift it. Marce's leathers, he laid out on the bed. The rest of their personal gear was packed away according to whom it belonged.

The door opened and he looked up, his hand dropping to his belt. But it was only Marce, who slipped into the room and closed the door behind him. Marcus nodded at him and knelt beside Lodi's pack to put away the long-tined metal comb the dwarf used on the rare occasions he unbraided his thick orange hair.

"You were faster than I expected. You told Father Aestus what he must do?"

"Father Aestus is dead, Marcus. They killed him."

There was something strange in Marce's voice. Marcus glanced back over his shoulder and saw that his bodyslave was moving toward him, holding his ludicrous gilded sword in hand.

For a moment, Marcus was too amazed to react. Or speak, or think at all. He simply stared at the tall figure with the familiar face and the eyes of a stranger, who barely seemed to even recognize him.

"Not you, Marce. It's not you. It can't be you!" His eyes dropped to the sword. The blade was bright and clean. "You didn't kill anyone. Why the sword?"

Marcipor stood over him, the blade hesitating in the air. "I'm not— This is . . . not what it seems."

He staggered a step and his sword arm dropped. "I can't do this. They told me I could, but I can't. I just can't." Marcipor's eyes were bright with tears now. "I can't kill you, Marcus. I'm supposed to, but I can't do it."

Marcus rose slowly to his feet and kept his hand well away from his knife. He could see Marcipor was struggling with something inside himself, and it was impossible to tell what might cause him to react one way or the other.

He wasn't afraid to fight the Marcipor he had known all his life, not even with a knife against a sword, for Marcus was the better-trained fighter by far.

But the Marcipor he'd known would never have raised a sword against him. Unless . . . unless he had been ordered to do so by someone he wouldn't dare disobey.

"Was it Magnus? Did Magnus hire the mercenaries?"

"Magnus? No. Not that I know of. It was after that night, the night the dwarf saved you from the wolf-thing. I was so glad you weren't hurt badly, but I was thinking about what it might have meant for me if you didn't . . . Please, you have to understand: I didn't want you to die! I'd never even thought about it, but after we talked, I thought perhaps it wouldn't be so bad to be free after all."

"I believe you," Marcus said, never taking his eyes away from Marcipor's face. "What happened? Who approached you?"

"The next day, I was riding ahead. Maybe you remember? With Zephanus and Captain Hezekius. I said something about you nearly getting killed and Zephanus laughed. He said it might have saved a lot of people a lot of trouble if you did and . . . they gave me gold, Marcus. Captain Hezekius himself gave me gold and told me I could ride with them if I wanted to join them. That I could be one of them. That I could be free like them—the lying devil! He should have given me thirty pieces of silver."

Marcipor looked at the sword and laughed bitterly. He cast it aside so it landed on the bed. "You should have whipped me when I asked, Master. Now you'll have to kill me. There's only one punishment for a slave who tries to kill his owner."

"You haven't tried to kill me, Marce, not yet. Who killed Aestus?"

"One of the Michaelines. Serranus probably. He's the real killer. Even the other Michaelines are afraid of him."

Not Zephanus, Marcus thought. He'd seemed so friendly. It must be that the smiling, laughing warrior-priest was an accomplished liar, and he was certainly intelligent. It occurred

to Marcus that he was probably the most dangerous mercenary of all, except possibly for the captain. Zephanas had
never served with Corvus, after all! But the lies had flowed as
smoothly off his tongue as a fine vintage wine being poured
from a crystal decanter by an expert servitor. Marcus had never
thought to doubt him for a moment.

There was a shout from somewhere inside the building, followed in quick succession by a wild scream and the bang of a
door being slammed shut. The screaming continued, inspiring
shouts and the sound of running feet.

"Lodi must have killed someone, or nearly killed them,
anyhow," Marcus said. "They'll be here as soon as they deal
with Lodi. Marce, we have to go."

"No," Marcipor shook his head. "There's only time for one
trip on the bird. You and the bishop have to go. And Claudo
needs Lodi to get him to the roof. That's three."

"So maybe it can carry four!"

"Too much risk. If they find me up there and you're gone,
they'll kill me."

"Marce, they'll kill you now!"

His slave, his childhood friend, shook his head. "They
might, but they probably won't. I'm just a slave who plays the
fool with a theatre sword. And they know it. You're a nobleman trained to fight by the best soldiers in the legions. They'll
expect you to be able to best me. But you'll have to hit me,
Marcus. You have to hit me hard enough to knock me out."

Marcus winced, but the rude plan made sense. Even when
Marce was standing before him with a sword to his undrawn
knife, he hadn't really been afraid.

They could hear a methodical slam-slamming vibrating
through the building as someone, probably the Michaelines,

sought to break down the door. There was the sound of more running feet, but all were heading away from them, presumably toward the bishop's chambers.

"Do it now. Quickly, please, it's the only way. They still might kill me to cover their tracks, but if they do, it's only what I deserve. Oh, Marcus, how could I be so stupid?"

"Well, you know, thinking was never your best attribute," Marcus said lightly, trying not to cry. "Here, maybe this will make things look more convincing."

He rubbed at his nose and came away with a little blood. It wasn't enough, so he grabbed his nose with two fingers and twisted. It hurt enough to make him gasp, but it had the desired effect, and as soon as he could feel blood trickling down his upper lip, he picked up the sword and smeared the tip with it. "You tried, okay? You managed to stab me in the shoulder, but before you could stab me again, I hit you. Okay?"

"Okay. Marcus, I don't know what to say. I'm sorry. Again."

Marcus pressed the bloodied sword into Marcipor's hand and kissed his forehead. Just then, there was a loud crashing sound and they heard the booming of a dwarven warcry. More screams erupted.

"*Ego te absolvo,* Marce. As often as you need it. Get away from those murderers as soon as you can and come back to Amorr. Come to House Valerius. It will wait for you. But if you can't, I free you now."

"No, Marcus—"

Marcus drew his dagger and hit his lifelong friend in the temple with the silver pommel.

Marcipor, a slave no more, never saw it coming. He crumpled instantly in an unwieldy heap. Marcus quickly leaned down to slash the side of Marcipor's head just above the right ear. The blade was wickedly sharp, and blood soaked through the golden curls almost immediately.

Marcus took one last look at the impromptu tableau. It would do. About the only thing that would have looked more convincing was if he'd actually cut Marcipor's throat. Poor Marce: freedom was even worse than he had feared.

God, You'll have to bring him back to Amorr, Marcus prayed silently. Because I can't.

He shouldered his pack and turned back to the window. The rope was still there, but it was bobbing up and down. It seemed Caitlys, quite rightly, was growing impatient. He gave the rope a tug, then climbed awkwardly over the wooden sill and wound the rope around his wrists to give himself a better grip for the climb upward.

"Valerian?"

"It's me, Caitlys," he called back.

"I heard screaming and I thought— Oh, never mind. Hold on," she ordered.

"Wait—" He swallowed his protests and concentrated on clinging to the rope as it jerked violently and began dragging him up the stone face of the building.

His arms felt as if they were being pulled out of their sockets, and he kicked his legs wildly, but somehow he managed to hold on. For a moment, the dark edge of the overhanging roof threatened to bash itself against his head, but then the rope pulled him away from the building, leaving him with his legs dangling uselessly and the sickening sense of empty air beneath him. But moments later, he could see the roof just beneath his feet again, and he let go before Caitlys had the chance to demonstrate any more insane avian tricks.

The bird landed next to him, and he looked up to see Caitlys leaning over the side of the bird, looking concerned. "Are you hurt? You're bleeding. If you let go of the rope, I'll throw it down for the others."

"Not there," he gasped, pushing himself up from the hard tiles. "Other side. Where all the noise is. Two more, but they come together. Maybe too late."

"Take my hand," she told him, and with that unnatural strength so at odds with her slenderness she all but pulled him up behind her, then urged the bird back into the air.

Lodi was still alive. Marcus could hear the shouts, curses, and weapons clashing from the open window below. They circled out away from the building, then swooped lower and slowed as they approached the window at which the bishop was standing with his back to them.

"Claudo!" Marcus shouted as he threw the rope. Cassius Claudo turned around, and his jaw dropped at the sight of Marcus and Caitlys on the back of the huge bird. But blind instinct caused him to catch the rope. It played out nearly to its full extent as Caitlys circled around again, and Marcus feared that the old man might try to hold on to it.

As they passed the window again, Marcus could see Lodi still battling to hold the broken doorway. He had the aid of the last of the bishop's servitors who were not already down.

"We need the dwarf," Marcus shouted. "The old priest can't hold the rope!"

"I know!" she shouted back. "When we go by again, tell him and the dwarf to fall on their faces on our next pass and hold on to the rope!"

"No, no magic!"

"Just do what I tell you, Valerian!"

"But we can't—"

"Do it!"

Appalled, but seeing no other way, he took a deep breath as they approached the window again. But before he could shout out her orders, Lodi hurled his axe in the face of one attacker, ducked the thrust of another, then turned and fled just as the sword of a third flashed down where he had been a moment before.

He swept something from a nearby table and tossed it over his shoulder without looking, then grabbed Cassius Claudo around the waist with his left arm and took the rope in his right hand. The grim look on the dwarf's face told Marcus what he was going to do.

"Go up, go up!" he screamed in Caitlys's ear.

She instantly leaned back and urged the bird higher. Vengirasse responded with four powerful beats of his wings. There was an immense roar, and the window belched out fire just behind Lodi as he dove over the window sill with the bishop in his arms. It was almost as if a huge dragon had found them unpalatable and vomited them forth, like a fiery Jonah being spat up on the beach.

For one horrible second, the rope grew taut, and the bird seemed to stagger in the sky. Marcus feared that Lodi had lost his hold on the rope.

But the dwarf had a grip like the iron in his mountain, and he held on to both priest and rope with stubborn dwarven determination until Caitlys managed to circle the bird back around to light upon the rooftop of the now-burning building.

Marcus couldn't resist hugging her in his excitement. She was laughing wildly, almost hysterically. Lodi and Cassius Claudo stood up unsteadily. Lodi was bleeding from four or five minor wounds, and both were half-covered from the black residue of the dwarf powder Lodi had used to effect their escape, but they were alive.

Then Marcus heard Caitlys catch her breath and say something softly in Elvic. He didn't know what it meant, but it didn't sound like anything salutary or edifying.

Then he saw what she was staring at, and he felt a sudden desire to learn what she had said in order that he might repeat it.

For out of the night sky, three dark shapes were sweeping down upon them from the direction of the royal citadel. The light of the fire burning below them cast golden-red reflections on the well-burnished helms and lance tips of the High King's skyriders.

I^A Q. VII A. I AD III

Ad tertium dicendum aliqui aelvi, etiam in statu viae, sunt maiores aliquibus homines, non quidem actu, sed virtute; inquantum scilicet habent caritatem tantae virtutis, ut possint mereri maiorem beatitudinis gradum quam quidam homines habeant. Sicut si dicamus semen alicuius magnae arboris esse maius virtute quam aliquam parvam arborem, cum tamen multo minus sit in actu. Ergo aelvi habent animae naturaliter unita.

MARCUS WAS MARCHED unceremoniously by two armored skyriders into a large room located two flights down from the avian stables at the top of the High Tower. Behind Marcus, other guards escorted Caitlys, Bishop Claudo, and Lodi. The procession made its way to the accompaniment of a litany of extensive verbal abuse to which Caitlys was subjecting their captors. He didn't understand a word of the elvish but was impressed by the effortless way it cascaded from her lips.

They entered a stone chamber. It was formed like a rectangle at the entrance with walls that angled out to meet the far side, which curved like a semicircle with the outside of the tower.

It was windowless, and the furniture looked comfortable but surprisingly shabby. Two couches and a chair were loosely arranged around a low wooden table. The table was marked by water stains, and four jeweled dice were scattered atop it. Three other cushioned chairs were arrayed as for a conference long complete. The stone walls were painted white and were unadorned but for a few lines of elvish scrawled upon the one to the left of the entrance. It was, Marcus thought, probably where the skyriders waited when they were on duty.

Upon one of the couches lounged King Mael, looking informal but still unmistakably regal in a purple silk robe. He also looked royally furious as he lounged on the overstuffed divan. He did not appear to have much appreciated being interrupted in whatever kingly duties he had previously been engaged.

To Marcus's surprise and dismay, in addition to a skyrider wearing leathers and a pair of elven guards, the king was accompanied by Zephanus, who was still wearing the rich yellow vestments and blue cloak he'd worn hours earlier. Marcus glared at the false priest. His earlier affection for the glib mercenary had been transformed by hurt and anger into something that almost approached hate. Zephanus wasn't the least bit abashed by the sight of Marcus. He actually had the gall to wink at him! The appearance of Cassius Claudo, however, seemed to throw him at least a little off balance.

Fury filled Marcus as he thought of how the brutish mercenaries had slain the brilliant, affable Jamite, who in his good cheer had seldom thought ill of anything, not even of those he had finally concluded were creatures without soul. It was, Aestus had argued, an intrinsic error to conclude that animation without *anima* was the result of a demonic heritage. The sparrow was equally unworthy of the Gospel, and yet it was loved by its Creator all the same. It was an outrage, an abomination, that such a brilliant mind should be forever silenced by stupid and greedy men so that other stupid and greedy men could hope to increase their wealth.

His silent lament for Aestus was interrupted by the elf king, however, as Mael pointed a languid, accusatory hand at Cassius Claudo and addressed him in a voice well laden with sardonic contempt. "My lord bishop, I must confess myself in awe. You are the first men to be permitted entry to Elebrion in the eighty-five years of my reign, and in less than twelve hours, you have managed to ruin the feast given in your honor, set your soldiers to disturbing the peace, and then, as some sort of piece de resistance, set fire to my city. Furthermore, I am informed by the captain of your guard that one of your companions here is plotting my death. And if that were not enough," he said, glancing at Caitlys, "he appears to have somehow seduced one of the noble flowers of my kingdom."

Caitlys, furious, started to open her mouth, but the king raised a hand in warning. "You will keep that pretty little mouth closed, my dear," he commanded. "Rest assured, I shall deal with you anon, and you shall have the opportunity to explain yourself in full, whether you will or no."

He turned back toward the disheveled bishop, who looked more like a scorched scarecrow than a lord of the Church. "Is there any explanation for these incredible actions—one that will be compelling enough to inspire me to depart from my natural inclination, which is to have the four of you beheaded, so that I may return to the rather more pleasurable discourse from whence I was summoned? And don't be so foolish as to make the mistake of telling me what I would or would not dare, inasmuch as I care not a warhawk's tail feather for Amorr and all its cursed legions!"

The elf king's ire was all the more frightening for the icily polite way in which he addressed them. It was entirely clear to Marcus that they would be missing their heads in a matter of minutes if Cassius Claudo did not handle the situation correctly. And it was the hardest thing he had ever done to keep his mouth shut, knowing that his fate rested entirely on another man's words.

Claudo bowed, not deeply, but merely to indicate a modicum of courtesy. His voice was calm and his demeanor was nearly as chilly as the king's. "I do regret, your High Majesty, that your royal repose should be disturbed. I may not apologize, however, as I was not the author of these disturbances. It took place by neither my order nor my knowledge. Neither was this most excellent dwarf involved, who risked his life in order to save mine from a band of assassins in the guise of churchmen, but more importantly, to save your kingdom and your nation from the misplaced wrath of the Republic. As for the young man and my lady elf, I can tell you little, except in that they were intimately involved in that same rescue, and for that I certainly owe them my life."

The High King seemed to take no offense at Cassius Claudo's insouciantly unapologetic response. Marcus breathed a sigh of relief. Instead, a hint of a twisted smile touched the king's lips as he turned to the dwarf. "So, you are the savior of my kingdoms, are you? In that case, perhaps I should reward you, dwarf. Is it true, what this priest says?"

"Most of it, your Majesty," Lodi answered directly. "Except for that setting of the fire bit. It was me that set it."

Mael blinked and shifted his weight forward to closer regard Lodi. "You are telling me that you set my city on fire?"

"I surely did, your Majesty."

The king glanced at his guards, then at Caitlys, as if to confirm that he'd truly heard what he thought he heard. "I see. Would it be an imposition to inquire as to wherefore?"

Lodi's heavy brow wrinkled. "What's that mean?"

"Just tell me why, dwarf." The king's voice was flat and deadly.

"Oh, sure. I had to throw some blow dust at the door to keep out the treacherous assassins working for the wardog captain of this one here who calls himself a priest." Lodi pointed to Zephanus. "They killed the fat little father before I could stop them, and then were going for the bishop here. I stood at the door and probably killed five or six of them with my axe there. But when Marcus threw a rope in and said it was time to run, I needed to cover my fallback. So, I covered it by roasting a few more of them."

Mael tilted his head. "To say nothing of 'roasting' what was once a fine residence and a stellar example of the Bondonassian school of the sixth century. I shudder to think what you might accomplish had pyromancy been your intent. But we shall overlook the fire for the nonce. It occurs to me, however, that in the future we shall have to search our dwarven guests a little more thoroughly than has previously been our custom."

Lodi didn't look as if he'd followed everything the king had said, but he caught enough of the gist of it to understand that he wasn't going to lose his head immediately as punishment for starting the fire. It was, Marcus considered, a good start, and the situation appeared to continue improving as the king turned his attention to Zephanus, who, despite not being a prisoner, had remained silent throughout.

"There appears to be some divergence between your version of events and theirs, Zephanus," the king said with an apparent disinterest that fooled no one in the room.

"In appearances only," the mercenary calmly replied. "As a matter of actual fact, the details of their story entirely support what I'd told you before."

"Enlighten us, for I fear I do not follow."

Marcus had spent enough time with Zephanus in the last month to know that they were dealing with a wicked and devious foe who, despite his lack of scholarly learning, was quite cunning in a low but effective way. The false priest spread his hands and expressed a sense of mild regret as he gestured toward Cassius Claudo.

"Your Majesty, the Order of Saint Michael, in which I have the honor of serving as humble priest, was given the honor of escorting Bishop Claudo to your great city. We did so at the request of the Sanctiff. Our captain gave us to understand that an embassy of reconciliation was in the works. We did not know, your High Majesty, that in truth, a small cabal of merchants and powers within the church were conspiring to compel your people into war with the Republic by assassinating your Majesty."

"That's a lie!" Marcus shouted, and the guards on either side of him grabbed him tightly. "He's no priest!"

"If he speaks out of turn again, cut his tongue out," the king instructed a guard, then returned his attention to Zephanus. "Pray continue, good sir priest. A cabal of traders and churchmen—surely an exotic combination!"

"It happens they share a common interest, High Majesty. The traders seek the usual war and military contracts, while the churchmen are fanatics who seek the abolition of those they view as the spawn of devils. You are not, after all, created in the image and likeness of God, or so they say. If I may ask a pertinent question, when your High Majesty first received our delegation, did you not make comments indicating your Majesty was aware of the elvish controversy that has riven the scholars of the Church?"

"A tedious and specious matter, but necessarily of some interest given the potential ramifications. Yes, I am informed."

"Then perhaps you are aware that the two scholars in the delegation, Bishop Claudo and Father Aestus, are supposed to have reached opposing conclusions in the matter. What you surely do not know is that they were secretly in agreement with the anti-elven fanatics, and their rivalry was intended for public consumption, and more importantly, the Sanctiff."

Marcus almost couldn't restrain himself from contradicting the traitor on this point. But he managed to, quite literally, hold his tongue.

"When the Sanctiff chose a representative of each view for his embassy," Zephanus said, "he unwittingly chose two elf-hating clerics. The Knight-General of my Order, who knew Cassius Claudo well from the days of their youth, also knew that he did not in fact hold the positions he argued so famously in his *Summa Spiritus,* and therefore offered our company as guards. Guard them we did, but we were also charged with watching them, which we have done throughout."

"And the other scholar, Aestus—is he dead, as they say?"

"I don't know, your Majesty. I fear yes. You may perhaps recall that when Aestus and Claudo were overheard discussing their plans, my captain sent me to you at once with word of their imminent attempt on your life. That was before any of this had happened, except for the absence of the young Valerian there. When he disappeared, it was assumed that he was to be the assassin and that he was in the process of preparing to assault you."

Marcus felt his face flush. Would he be given a rebuttal?

The High King regarded Marcus neutrally. "How, Zephanus, would my death convince your Sanctiff of their philosophical point?"

"According to my captain, their goal was to provoke a violent reaction from your heir," Zephanus said. "They hoped he would react in a way that would justify their assertion of intrinsic elven malfeasance. With the delegation dead, news of how your death took place could easily be suppressed."

The king looked dubious. Again he gazed at Marcus. "But these men are members of the delegation themselves."

"They are fanatics, High Majesty. Such men glory in their martyrdom."

King Mael's eyes turned to Caitlys. "And the involvement of the High Lady Shadowsong?"

Zephanus shrugged. "I couldn't possibly tell you, your Majesty. I am no scholar. I am merely a priest and warrior, and naturally my ignorance of elven politics is complete."

Despite himself, Marcus had to feel a momentary admiration for the way in which the false Michaeline planted his devious seeds of doubt. No doubt there were plots against the throne, perhaps even some that had involved Caitlys's family in the past. He saw the king glance at Caitlys before turning the royal gaze on Cassius Claudo. In his current disheveled state, with his half-burned clothes and his thin, hawkish face, the bishop did look convincingly like the sort of fanatic who believed it to be God's will to strike down a soulless, inhuman king. Marcus desperately wanted to speak, to puncture Zephanus's lies, but the hands still gripping his arms reminded him of what the cost would be.

"What do you say for yourself, emissary? Are you a fanatic? Is your *Summa* nothing more than a charade?"

"As the author, it is hardly for me to judge, your Majesty." Claudo smiled thinly. "I will confess that I admire the young man's ability to speak so inventively without prior notice of a need to explain the actions of others. He must be formidable in the field, where such animal cunning has great utility. What he said, however, is little more than a concoction of unadulterated lies, insinuations piled upon inveracities, and, fortunately, a construction that I imagine might be readily penetrated by one such as yourself."

Zephanus was indeed a quick-thinking man, Marcus thought, for he began to perspire almost immediately when Cassius Claudo coolly spoke the word "penetrated." His hand twitched, and for a moment Marcus thought the mercenary might attempt to draw a dagger hidden somewhere on his body.

"Yes," said the elf king slowly. "I scryed the scene prior to your arrival, and, improbably as it seems, both of your wild tales are essentially congruent with what I saw. The bodies, the fire, and so forth." He looked squarely at Zephanus. "But it occurs to me that earlier this evening I suggested a battle of magics, a trial of Amorran fidelie contra elven sorcery. Will you consent to such a trial now, on behalf of your Order?"

Cassius Claudo caught Zephanus's eyes and smiled coldly. "Yes, High Majesty. Such a test might well be pertinent right now."

Caitlys shrugged herself out of the slackened grip of the guard at her side and stepped toward the false Michaeline. "Allow me, your Majesty," she demanded, her fierce green eyes blazing. "Let me try the man magic!"

"As you like," the elf king said with a shrug. "It will save the time of finding another adept. The sooner we're done here, the better. Sir priest, are you ready?"

"No," shouted Marcus, wondering at his own actions. "He's got no magic. This would be murder!" He shrugged free of the surprised guards and threw himself in front of Zephanus. Even a traitor deserved to be given a—

Zephanus used Marcus's body as a shield to step around and elbow the nearest guard in the face, breaking his fine elven nose. Zephanus pushed Marcus toward the guards, attempting to buy himself a fraction more time before the guards could draw their swords and reach him. A dagger appeared in his hand, and he drew his arm back over King Mael.

But before it even began to move forward, Caitlys cried out in elvish, and a silver storm of thirty knives appeared out of nowhere and slammed into both Zephanus and Marcus.

A crimson spray of blood flew into the air as the force of the blades hurled Zephanus back into the white walls, nearly cut in half.

Marcus looked down at his unmarked body in confusion. The deadly blades had passed right through him as if they were nothing more than illusions, while Zephanus's eyes were already beginning to glaze over in death.

Despite the unexpected violence, High King Mael hadn't moved from his seat. He looked more irritated than alarmed despite the spatters of blood that stained the right side of his robe. "Blade Rain, Caitlys? Was that really necessary?"

The pretty elf girl was still facing the remnants of the erstwhile mercenary, holding out her left hand with her fingers splayed. She grinned mischievously and flexed her fingers twice, then lowered her arm. "Merely a show of appreciation for the great wisdom of your adjudication, Majesty. Yours was a test worthy of . . . What was the name of that human king? I've forgotten."

"Solomon," Marcus said as if in a dream, stunned by Caitlys's casual violence and his lack of injury. He couldn't take his eyes off the blood of the shredded thing that only moments before had been a living man. One he had once thought to be a friend. The dark power of elven sorcery was terrible indeed.

He found himself thinking of Nomenlos, his elvish brother in faith. What had Nomenlos—or rather, Bessarias—done with magic so long ago that he should still feel his remorse so bitterly?

Back to Solomon. "How is this like Solomon's adjudication in the least? His wisdom entailed avoiding any division."

"We should all be grateful that the little darling didn't elect to throw a Flame Wind and incinerate us all," the king said sourly. "I am curious, though. Why did your spell only affect the one and not the other here?"

"I don't know," Caitlys said, looking at Marcus. "Are you a wizard, Valerian?"

Marcus frowned and felt the relic he'd been keeping in his pocket. The gift that Magnus's client had given him, Saint Ansfrid's knucklebone, was hot to the touch. Had it really just saved his life? He didn't quite know if he should feel guilty or grateful, but he was entirely sure that it would not be a good idea to let the elves know what appeared to have happened. "No, I'm no wizard, Lady Shadowsong."

He looked down at the bloody remains of Zephanus. His gorge rose, but he managed to suppress it. For all that the mercenary had been a treacherous, murderous killer, it seemed impossible to accept that such a friendly, charming man could be no more. He forced himself to look away from the corpse. When he did, he realized the king was addressing Cassius Claudo.

"My lord bishop, are we agreed that there are two possible conclusions? Either the priestly order is helpless against elven magic in general—and mad young sorceresses in particular—or the young mercenary was not, in fact, a priest of the order as he claimed, rendering the rest of his story suspect. I suggest that the latter is the more useful conclusion."

"I concur," Claudo agreed somberly. Unlike the elves, he appeared grieved by Zephanus's death. It occurred to Marcus that the bishop too may have come to like the vibrant young mercenary. "But more of the false priests remain."

The king smiled cruelly. "Leave them to me."

"No, your Majesty," Claudo said. "Their crime is against the Order of Saint Michael. The Knight-General alone must judge them."

"He may judge what remains of them."

"I have seen what passes for elven justice. It is nothing of the kind."

The High King's eyes narrowed dangerously. "Perhaps I dare not permit you to return to Amorr after all, emissary. Is your influence with the Sanctiff to be as pernicious as the late captain claimed?"

"The Sanctiff speaks with God's voice, not mine. I am merely his eyes here in Elebrion." He gestured toward Marcus. "And not the only eyes."

"I see." The king stared at them, stroking his hairless chin with his thumb and forefinger. "Very well. Then hear my voice, which in this place is as good as a god's. Get you gone from my city tonight, bishop, and speak good or ill of the elves as you must. Four hawks will fly you to Kir Donas. From there, you will take ship. Caitlys, you will lead the portage wing. That shall be your punishment, though there may well be more once I have the chance to ask further questions and discover what other havoc you have wrought."

Caitlys rolled her eyes. Marcus flushed, trying not to look at her as he realized how happy he was that he could see her for a little while longer. If only he could fly with her and not one of the others.

"The brass eagles," Cassius Claudo said. "And the dwarf and the men. Further, this boy has a young slave. He, at least, bears no guilt."

The elf king waved an indifferent hand. "I care nothing for any of them. They shall be returned to Amorr under guard, alive and well, and you may dispose of them as you see fit. Mark you, Amorr will bear the cost—if it wants them, it can pay for them. I'll send the eagles with them, assuming your cursed dwarf-fire didn't melt them down. And never again shall man set foot in Elebrion. Oh, I suppose there may be the need for the occasional emissary, won't there? Very well." The king rose from the divan. "It's late, I'm tired, and I'm in no mood to pontificate. Now go away, Cassius Claudo, and be damned or blessed as you please."

"It shall be even as you command, High King." Claudo actually smiled as he bowed, deeply, to the king of the elves. "*Farae thutoth genel naraeparan.*"

"And also with you," the king said. "An admirable sentiment. Now go, before I change my mind and blade storm you all—including you, Lady Shadowsong."

Without delay, they all made haste to obey the elf king's command.

I^A Q. VII A. I AD IV

Ad quartum dicendum quod vivificare effective simpliciter perfectionis est. Unde et Deo convenit secundum illud I Reg. II, dominus mortificat et vivificat. Productio horum animalium ordinatur secundum ordinem corporum quae eis ornantur, magis quam secundum propriam dignitatem. Praeterea, perfectior est vita in aelvis quam in hominem quantum ad anima vivificat corpus. Quandoquidem aetas hominum solum septuaginta, sed aetas aelvorum plusquam quingenti. Ergo aelvi habent animae naturaliter unita.

DEAD LEAVES CRACKLED under Barat's hooves as Marcus approached the Pontus Rossus River, the division between Amorr the city and Amorr the empire. The cool October breeze seemed to grow chillier the closer he came to the rushing water, and he pulled his red cloak closer around him to keep warm. The two guards at the bridgehead waved him through without stopping him, most likely due to the two columns of Redeemed that were riding in formation behind him, or perhaps only because they were lazy.

It was good to be astride his own horse again. The elf king had been true to his word and sent all of the Amorran possessions, from the legionary eagles to the captive mercenaries to Marcus's own horse, to the Civitavecchia. He'd met Lord Fáelán at the seaport and was surprised to have the chance to welcome not only Marcipor but also two of Cassius Claudo's guards who had somehow survived both the mercenary attack and the dwarf's unintentional attempt to set fire to Elebrion.

The sight of the city gates made Marcus think of Lodi, and he smiled. He'd freed the dwarf the morning after their arrival at Kir Donas. Inexplicably loyal, the dwarf protested, insisting that it was his duty to see Marcus safely back to House Valerius. But once Cassius Claudo had arrived at their ship with ten Petrine monks fortified by a squad of Church troops, Lodi allowed that, barring shipwreck, he needn't fear for Marcus. In addition to confirming the dwarf's manumission with his personal seal, the bishop had given Lodi a handsome purse of gold at Marcus's request. Then of his own volition Claudo presented the dwarf with a necklace from which dangled a gilded phalange from the foot of Saint Saturus.

Marcus knew that Lodi harbored little trust in the saint's ability to protect him against future imprisonment or poverty. Still, as Claudo pointed out with the customary haughtiness that Marcus was beginning to suspect might actually conceal a sense of humor, even so intrepid a dwarf as Lodi might find a token that proclaimed him to be a friend of the Church to be useful. Especially, the bishop noted, in the event that the Sanctiff determined that it was not only the elves but all ahomum that did not, in fact, possess souls.

On that same morning, Marcus had had to part with Caitlys. They had spoken but little during the journey, though each conversation had been sweet and imbued with something Marcus did not properly understand. Sextus could've explained it, though, he was certain. Marcus knew he must be parted from her, whether because of race or distance or the vows of the Church. Nevertheless, he felt . . . incomplete. And then there had been the matter of the kiss. He felt his cheeks blush furiously at the memory.

Marcipor, for his part, had been subdued upon his return. This was partly due to his feelings of guilt, but it was mostly from witnessing the death and degradation of so many men he'd come to like and even admire. Zephanus, Ecclesiastus, and Captain Hezekius were dead, while Claudius Serranus and Habbakus had been turned over to the Order of Saint Michael, along with their nineteen surviving comrades.

Marcipor refused to discuss his freedom with Marcus but insisted on claiming responsibility for his previous duties. For the present Marcus was inclined to leave the subject alone if that was his friend's wish. Marcipor hadn't accompanied him to the Michaeline's great citadel at Mount Cassanus, from which Marcus was now returning with the Redeemed. The trip there had been to bring the mercenaries to the Michaeline's Knight-General for judgment, and Marcipor wanted no part in that.

The captives had acquitted themselves well for the most part. They showed no fear, but only a little uncertainty when they first encountered the true warrior-priests in all their blue-and-gold splendor.

Claudius Serranus, catching Marcus's eye, gestured with his chained hands. "I don't suppose you'd spare the condemned one last draught?" The scarred mercenary winked.

"I surely would, Claudius Serranus, if I only I had it. Will you answer a question?"

"I don't see why not. Although I'll be disappointed in you if it involves the word 'why'."

Marcus laughed. "Oh, I know why, Serranus. You're mercenaries. You kill for gold. And seven hundred florins is an excellent price for three deaths. I'm honored that my head should have commanded such a bounty."

"Well, it wasn't you as such, Marcus Valerius," Serranus said drily. "Not that there aren't those who wouldn't like to see you dead now. Best watch your back now that you're in the city. The captain's dead, but there might be some sign of them who hired us in his papers."

"The bishop thinks so too. He's got men looking into that now. No, Serranus, what I wanted to know is how you knew so much about the Michaelines. How did you manage to impersonate them so successfully?"

Claudius Serranus stared at him for a second, then threw his head back and laughed. He lifted his iron-bound hands and wiped first at one eye, then the other. "You're the bloody scholar, Valerius. You of all men should know. When we got the contract, the captain sent Zephanus out to find every scratching and scroll concerning those cursed priests that we could find. *De Munitionibus Castrorum* was the most useful. Those of us that can read took turns reading it out loud to those that couldn't."

"Hyginus?"

"Precisely. When the captain found out you were a scholar, I thought I'd have to kill you that first day."

"I never got around to reading him."

"So I noticed. Lucky for you, lad. Unlucky for me." Serranus shrugged indifferently. "Lady Fortune is a whore. Trust in your sword or trust in your God, but don't put your faith in her. Now, do you think this Knight-General might be persuaded to sell us to the stables? Or even the salt mines? Not much profit in killing us now. The elves could have taken care of that business."

"I don't know, Claudius Serranus," Marcus had replied with a smile. It was impossible to dislike the man's indomitable spirit. "But I rather suspect he knows a good fighting man when he sees one. If there's to be crusade, he'll need all the fighters he can find. Try trusting in God for once, Serranus, instead of your sword, and I shall pray that one day the Immaculate One will wash that blackened soul of yours as white as a Sanctiff's beard."

The Sanctiff received Marcus in the same poorly lit chamber as before. Cassius Claudo was with him, wearing his usual black robes. But this time the ambience in the small room felt small and petty rather than intimidating. Had everything else gotten smaller, or was it possible that he had grown? And of course, Aestus was not there.

He bowed to the two churchmen, thinking how well they would serve as icons of the two species of virtues. The bishop would stand in for the intellectual, and the Sanctiff himself would stand as the moral.

"Holiness. Excellency," Marcus said. "Knight-General Francescus Centurionus conveys his warmest regards from Mount Cassanus. He wished me to extend his particular gratitude to you, Excellency, for the gift of the imposters."

"Impudence," sniffed Claudo. He had been more offended by the false Michaelines than any of the Michaelines themselves. "Did Centurionus tell you what he intended for them?"

"Yes, Excellency. They shall be slaves of the Order for seven years and a day, and they shall serve Saint Michael as their skills best dictate." Serranus, at least, would be content with his lot. The warrior would live to fight another day, but now he would fight in God's name, not Mammon's.

"A judicious decision, and wise," remarked the Sanctiff. He looked older since Marcus had seen him last. The creases under his eyes had grown deeper. It was as if he had borne the heavy weight of his contemplations as a physical burden. "And have you reached your own decision, Marcus Valerius?"

Marcus took a deep breath, knowing that this was the moment toward which he felt God had been leading everything. Not that his own opinion would carry more weight than the bishop's, much less the Sanctiff's. But it was no less than his duty before God to render a sober and well-reasoned conclusion. He squared his shoulders and met the Sanctiff's eyes.

"I have indeed, Holiness. It is my considered opinion that the elves do indeed possess immortal souls."

Both men's eyebrows rose unexpectedly, making him nervous. He rushed to support his statement.

"Yes, I believe that logic conclusively dictates that elves do possess souls which are naturally united to them. And I would even assert the possibility that many more so-called 'sub-human' species of Selenoth may possess the spark of the eternal, depending of course upon how one precisely defines the 'Imago Dei.' I have presented this logic in a philosophical text I have entitled *Summa Elvetica*. It is modeled on Oxonus, and of course, His Excellency's own . . . Why are you laughing?"

"My dear boy," the Sanctiff said, shaking his head as he smiled gently, "I meant what decision you have come to about whether or not you are going to take your priestly vows as a servant servant of the Church."

Marcus sputtered. "I . . . You . . . "

"Alas, Marcus," Claudo said, himself still chuckling, "I'm sure His Holiness would have been delighted to take your *Summa* into consideration when he composed his bull on the matter."

Marcus was chagined. Why had they sent him on this journey if they did not care for his findings? Why had he spent hours assembling his thoughts and agonizing over the wording in his *Summa*? He bowed to them, more from anger and shame than reverence. "I sought only to serve."

"And well you have served, Marcus Valerius," the Sanctiff said. "I shall indeed read your findings, and with great interest. But at this moment I still await your vocational decision."

Marcus straightened, no longer afraid to look either man in the eye. "I have decided to serve God, Holiness." He let the statement hang in the air. They could interpret it as they liked. Then he finished. "But I believe I may serve Him best by remaining outside the Church."

The Sanctiff surprised him by smiling. "I am pleased to hear that, Marcus Valerius. Well pleased! The Excellency said, and I concur, that despite your immense love for the Immaculate, your vocation is essentially intellectual, not spiritual. Do not ever confuse the Church with the God it serves, young man."

"Nor God's voice on Earth with the still, small voice that speaks after the wind, the earthquake, and the fire," Cassius Claudo added.

The Sanctiff shot an irritated glance at him, but the bishop's face did not so much as hint at a smile.

"Even so," the Sanctiff allowed after an uncomfortable moment of silence. "Tell me then, Marcus—if you will not take vows, what do you intend to do?"

Marcus felt light. Immensely relieved. He had just broken out from under what felt like a holy but heavy burden, and the Sanctiff had praised him for it. "After consulting with my uncle, Lucius Valerius Magnus, I have decided to put myself forward for tribunus plebis in two years, when I am of age. And in the interim I hope to join my father on campaign. If I have learned one thing since we last spoke, it is that not all knowledge can be gleaned from texts."

"Indeed." The Sanctiff distractedly stroked his beard. "Your ambitions appear to be as consequential as your advisors. I wish you well in them. But first, I would know if you would be willing to accept one more charge from the Church before you begin your career outside it." It seemed that a great weight had settled on the Sanctiff's shoulders. What was this new development?

"I hope you consider me always to be at your service, Holiness."

"Well said!" The Sanctiff glanced at Cassius Claudo, who nodded, then went to a shelf and retrieved two scrolls. One was larger than the other and was capped with engraved gold over the red wax seals. "Like you in your many thoughts, Marcus Valerius, I too have made a decision. I require you to bear this," he said, gripping the larger scroll, "to Elebrion as Amorr's formal and inviolate emissary, and present this document to the elf king. It contains the text of a sanctal bull that will be published in one month's time. You must deliver it to the elf on that same day—the first of November. The Immaculate preserve you."

Marcus bit his lip and bowed obediently to mask the emotion that rushed through his body. So it was to be war. Holy war based on one man's word and death on both sides.

One month would give the legions time to assemble and the generals time to make their plans. The winter would be used to set the pieces in place—of which he, if he was then serving on his father's staff, might well be one—and then in the spring they would strike.

All of his desperate efforts in the elven city had been for naught. The end result was no different than if they had never gone. Indeed, this was the very result the false Michaelines had meant to achieve by striking him down.

At the thought, he was finally free of the doubt that had lingered when he'd decided to spurn ordination. The Church wanted war, and war it was going to get. He would have none of the hypocrisy of the supposed investigation. His anger swelled. If he'd had his *Summa* with him at the moment, he would've cast it into the fire on the spot. Though he felt obliged to serve the Sanctiff one more time, he would do so in the knowledge that he would not be oathbound to do so ever again.

Nevertheless, despite his rage, it did occur to him that the trip would allow him to see Caitlys again.

"I shall be honored to do precisely as you command, Holiness." If there was just the slightest stress on the last word, neither the Sanctiff nor Cassius Claudo deigned to notice.

"Then go with God, Marcus Valerius. Our blessing is upon you. Give the other scroll to Father Cornelius at the Proeliatum, and he will see that you are properly outfitted and escorted for the journey."

"Yes, Holiness."

The two great men of the Church watched the newly appointed young ambassador to the elves walk quickly out of the chamber. They saw his flashing eyes and stiffly erect back, which betrayed his despairing anger.

Cassius Claudo shook his head. "This verges on cruel, Ahenobarbus. At least you might have left the scroll unsealed."

"I doubt he'd look anyhow. It is a penance, after all. The discipline will serve him well. He is young still, with all the proud judgment and arrogant short-sightedness that youth entails. Even now, after all he has learned, he has not yet taken to heart the lesson that things are not always as they seem *a priori*."

"Particularly where princes and prelates are concerned." Cassius Claudo laughed, a short, hard bark of a laugh. "It is a loss for the Church, though."

"You were the one who saw the elf maid kiss him just before she left you at Kir Donas, were you not? Marcus is not temperamentally suited for the Church, dear friend. It would be a torture where it should be joy. Our desire for talent must never be used to overshadow an absence of calling. That way lie madness and material empire."

The bishop shrugged. "That may be true, but why give him penance? He did no wrong in receiving the kiss. He could have pursued more, had he wished, because he did not know I was there. It was a temptation perhaps, but manfully resisted, if not conquered. And, Ahenobarbus, they truly are as beautiful as angels."

"Did wrong? No, far from it—he did very well indeed! Or perhaps she did. Do you know, Caecilus Cassius, that it was she who made my decision for me?"

Claudo blinked. "Your Grace?"

The Sanctiff laughed heartily. "It is true! It was not your flawless reason that did the trick, nor all of poor Aestus's flowery rhetoric. It was the elf girl! You caught her kissing our dear Marcus, and when she saw you, she blushed. Blushed, Claudo! That, beyond all the intellectual arguments that might ever be raised, convinced me that elves have souls."

"You don't say," Claudo's voice dripped sarcasm. "The blush of an elf girl? So why should we use the minds that God has given us, when we can let our hearts reason for us?"

"Come, Excellency. Does not Augustinus say 'Purity is a virtue of the soul'? Think, Caecilus Cassius. To blush as she did is to be impassioned by an offense against that which is immaculate. Don't you see it? Only a creature with a soul could possibly be cognizant of offending such virtue."

The bishop was silent for a splendidly long moment. Then he nodded and arched an eyebrow at the Sanctiff. "You have been delving deep, haven't you? No wonder you look as if you've been wrestling with all the devils in hell."

"I have! I usually have scholars like you and Aestus and young Valerius to do my digging for me. But I felt this matter called for a more comprehensive inquiry on my part than relying solely upon prayer and counsel."

"It did, truly." The bishop shook his head. "I still think it's a real loss to the Church to lose that young Valerian to the field or the Senate."

But the Sanctiff only laughed. His was a droll, cheerful laugh. It made even the dour bishop's lips twitch into a smile.

"The Church's loss, perhaps, but not God's. My very dear Caecilus Cassius, have you never perused the list of true saints? Have you never seen how very few of them happened to be men of the cloth?"

IMMACULATUS DEI

1 Novembre 1043

His Sanctified Holiness Charity IV

THE IMMACULATE GOD

so loved man that He created him in such wise that he might participate, not only in the good that other creatures enjoy, but endowed him with capacity to attain to the inaccessible and invisible Supreme Good and behold it face to face; and since man, according to the testimony of the sacred Scriptures, has been created to enjoy eternal life and happiness, which none may obtain save through faith in our sublime Lord Immanuel, it is necessary that he should possess the nature and faculties enabling him to receive that faith; and that whoever is thus endowed should be capable of receiving that same faith. Nor is it credible that any one should possess so little understanding as to desire the faith and yet be destitute of the most necessary faculty to enable him to receive it.

Hence Christ, who is the Truth itself, that has never failed and can never fail, said to the preachers of the faith whom He chose for that office, 'Go ye and teach all nations.'

He said all, without exception, for all are capable of receiving the doctrines of the faith.

The enemy of the human race, who opposes all good deeds in order to bring men to destruction, beholding and envying this, invented a means never before heard of, by which he might hinder the preaching of God's word of salvation to the people: he inspired his satellites who, to please him, have not hesitated to assert that the elves of the west, the orcs, goblins and trolls of the east, the dwarves, jotun and ulfin of the north and the diverse creatures of south that bear the shapes of both man and beast, and other people of whom should be treated as dumb brutes whose creation was inspired by that enemy and are therefore incapable, by virtue of their intrinsic nature, of receiving the true and immaculate Faith.

We have certain knowledge that in some cases, these various races have entered into this world through the wickedness of man and other beings. We acknowledge that the existence of these demonic races, spawned from the lusts of spirits and the evil will of fallen men, a willful and malevolent perversion of God's creation and we deny and rebuke the unseemly notion that these beings are a form of man or can be deemed to possess an immortal soul.

We, who, though unworthy, exercise on earth the power of the Purified and seek with all our might to bring those sheep of His flock who are outside into the fold committed to our charge, consider, however, that the elves are a people truly possessed of souls which are naturally united to them through the act of Creation by the Most High God and that they are not only capable of understanding the true and holy faith but, according to our information, they desire exceedingly to receive it. Desiring to provide ample remedy for these evils, We define and declare by these Our letters, or by any translation thereof signed by any notary public and sealed with the seal of any ecclesiastical dignitary, to which the same credit shall be given as to the originals, that, notwithstanding whatever may have been or may be said to the contrary, the said elves and all other people who may later be determined to be similarly ensouled by Us, are by no means to be deprived of their liberty or the possession of their property, even though they be outside the faith of the Most Holy Lord Immanuel; and that they may and should, freely and legitimately, enjoy their liberty and the possession of their property; nor should they be in any way enslaved; should the contrary happen, it shall be null and have no effect.

By virtue of Our apostolic authority We define and declare by these present letters, or by any translation thereof signed by any notary public and sealed with the seal of any ecclesiastical dignitary, which shall thus command the same obedience as the originals, that the said elves, should be converted to the faith of Our Lord Immanuel by preaching the Immaculate Word of God and by the example of good, holy, and peaceable living.

SUMMA ELVETICA

BY MARCUS VALERIUS

ARTICLE I, QUESTION VII.
WHETHER THE ELVES HAVE SOULS NATURALLY UNITED TO THEM.

Objection 1. It would seem that elves do not have souls naturally united to them. For it is written: "God formed man of the slime of the earth and breathed into his face the breath of life, and man was made a living soul." But he who breathes sends forth something of himself. Therefore the soul is of the divine substance. Elves, created subsistent and distinct from man, did not receive the divine substance from God. Therefore the elves do not have souls naturally united to them.

Objection 2. Further, man is created in the image of God, after the likeness of God. The elves are not created in the image and likeness of God. Therefore the elves do not have souls naturally united to them.

Objection 3. Further, the psalmist asks of God: "What is man that you are mindful of him?" In answer to which question he writes: "You made him a little lower than the heavenly beings and crowned him with glory and honor. You made him ruler over the works of your hands; you put everything under his feet": whereby we discern that man is foremost among all creation that is materially subsistent. Therefore the elves do not have souls naturally united to them.

Objection 4. Further, Man was created on the sixth day. The more perfect has precedence in the order of nature as given in the account of Creation, therefore man is more perfect than the elves. Now the most perfect state of the soul is to be separated from the body, since in that state it is more similar to God and the angels, and is more pure, as being separated from any extraneous nature. Inasmuch as they are less perfect than man, the elves are still further removed from the most perfect state of the soul. Therefore the elves do not have souls naturally united to them.

On the contrary, Oxonus said: "In rational animals the sensitive appetite obeys reason." Therefore, in so far as they are led by a kind of estimative power, which is subject to a higher reason, that is to say the Divine, there is a certain likeness of moral good in them, in regard to the soul.

I answer that: On this question there have been various opinions. First, if the soul by its nature were a complete species, so that it might be created as to itself, this would prove that the soul was neither man nor elf. But as the soul is naturally a partaker of the form of the body, it was necessarily created, not separately, but in the body. For if the soul had a species of itself it would have something still more in common with the angels. But, as the form of the body, the question of the soul belongs to the animal genus, as a formal principle, and therefore it may not be settled on that basis but must be answered with regards to the particular nature of the elven species.

Second, the condition of man in the state of innocence was not more exalted than the condition of the angels. But among the angels some rule over others; and so one order is called that of "Dominations." Therefore it was not beneath the dignity of the state of innocence that one man should be subject to another. Forasmuch as one man can be subject to another without imputing significance to his soul, the elves can be subject to the mastership of man without significance to theirs.

Third, while in all creatures there is some kind of likeness to God, in the rational creature alone we find a likeness of "image"; whereas in other creatures we find a likeness by way of a "trace." Now the intellect or mind is that whereby the rational creature excels other creatures; wherefore this image of God is not found even in the rational creature except in the mind. Gregory (Hom. x in Ev.) calls an elf a rational animal, therefore the elves are more properly likened to men and angels instead of the irrational creatures.

Reply to objection 1. The body is not of the essence of the soul; but the soul by the nature of its essence can be united to the body, so that, properly speaking, not the soul alone, but the "composite," is the species. To say that the soul is of the divine substance involves a manifest improbability. For the human soul is sometimes in a state of potentiality to the act of intelligence—acquires its knowledge somehow from things—and thus has various powers; all of which are incompatible with the Divine Nature, wherefore it is evidently false that the soul is of the substance of God. Therefore the elves have souls which are naturally united to them.

Reply to objection 2. Although creatures do not attain to a natural likeness to God according to similitude of species, as a man begotten is like to the man begetting, still they do attain to likeness to Him, forasmuch as they represent the divine idea, as a material house is like to the house in the architect's mind. Likeness of creatures to God is not affirmed on account of agreement in form according to the formality of the same genus or species, but solely according to analogy, inasmuch as God is essential being, whereas other things are beings by participation. Therefore the elves have souls which are naturally united to them.

Reply to objection 3. Certain elves in this state of life are greater than certain men, not actually, but virtually; forasmuch as they have such great charity that they can merit a higher degree of beatitude than that possessed by certain men. In the same way we might say that the seed of a great tree is virtually greater than a small tree, though actually it is much smaller. Therefore the elves have souls naturally united to them.

Reply to objection 4. To give life effectively is a perfection simply speaking; hence it belongs to God, as is said (1 Samuel 2:6): "The Lord killeth, and maketh alive." The order in which the production of the animals is given has reference to the order of those bodies which they are set to adorn, rather than to the superiority of the animals themselves. Further, it is said that life is more perfect in the elves than in man inasmuch as it is the soul that gives life to the body. Whereas the span of man is but threescore and seven, the span of the elves is in excess of five centuries. Therefore the elves have souls naturally united to them.

AUTHOR'S NOTE

This novel did not proceed according to plan. It was originally conceived as a epic philosophical trilogy, in which the reader would be immersed in medieval scholastic thought and explore various facets of some of the great philosophical debates that took place both within and without the Catholic Church.

Misunderstood by most modern intellectuals and ignored by the irreligious authors of modern fantasy fiction, the great scholars of the church were no close-minded ideologues, but rather brilliant men who conceived and refined many of the rational mechanisms that we today take for granted. It is not a coincidence that William of Ockham, author of the *Summa Logicae* and known for the logical principle that bears his name, was a Franciscan monk.

While the logic of churchmen such as William of Ockham, Aurelius Augustinus Hipponensis, and Thomas Aquinas most certainly has its flaws, the fair-minded reader must admit that their philosophical methods, however alien they may appear to modern eyes, are rather more reasonable and straightforward than the shamelessly manipulative Socratic method made famous by Plato. Unfortunately, my initial goal of assigning roles for the diverse schools of philosophical thought to each of the conventional fantasy races foundered on my inability to meaningfully connect it to the story of the prospective young priest traveling to the elflands.

Fortunately, I had long been fascinated with the problem of a medieval Church-dominated society forced to come to terms with the existence of traditional fantasy concepts such as elves, orcs, dragons, and dwarves.

It has long been my contention that the superficial medievalism of fantasy fiction has crippled the genre, rendering its settings incoherent and its characters shallow and unconvincing even in the hands of writers much more talented than I can ever hope to be. It is absurd, for instance, to base a plot that turns on a nominal Divine Right of Kings where there is no Divine from which the right is derived, and modern fantasy is littered with nonsensical priests without gods, who might as well be white wizards.

So, the part of the original story that concerned the conflict between medieval Church and medievalesque fantasy not only survived intact, it became the central point of the plot. Needless to say, this notion of centering a story around primarily philosophical action would have rendered the book all but unpublishable, were it not for the fortuitous emergence of Marcher Lord Press.

I had originally planned to title the book *Sublimus Dei*, which is the name of the papal bull issued in 1537 by Pope Paul III that declared the primitive people of the Americas to be rational beings with souls. Its text, somewhat altered, appears in the final chapter. The original translation of the Latin encyclical can be found at Papal Encyclicals Online as well as the Catholic Encyclopedia at New Advent.

One day it struck me, however, that while the book could be presented as a metaphorical argument for the ensoulment of the elves, the structure of most philosophical arguments tend to be inordinately one-sided. There was, however, an exception.

Thomas Aquinas in his *Summa Theologica* makes use of a particular method that provides, or at least appears to provide, the opposing side with a fair hearing.

Happily, this provided me not only with an obvious title for the book, but also a useful means of structuring the story in a manner that was at least tangentially connected to the argument. In the unlikely event one has not noticed, each "step" in this book has a Latin section header. Each header is a part of the single question presented in its entirety—and in English—at the end of the story.

Here I must once again express my gratitude to Meredith Dixon, whose Latin expertise filled in the gaps where I could not simply lift the text from Saint Thomas himself. For the reader who happens to be curious about where various concepts were derived, note that Questions 51, 71 and 90–96 of the *Prima Pars* were particularly useful.

The argument presented is nonsensical, of course, but it is nonsensical in very much the same manner that so many of the philosophical and theological arguments presented by the great minds of the medieval ages were. But we should not scoff; it is deeply ironic that the leading atheists of our day happen to subscribe to this same method of argument, wherein empirical facts are ignored in favor of specious rationalizations that appear to be convincing so long as the logic is never weighed against the observable evidence.

Hence the description of the book as a "casuistry" [pronounced ka-ZOO-iss-tree], which can mean either "oversubtle and fallacious reasoning" or "the application of general ethical principles to particular cases of conscience." One could reasonably argue for either definition, and I gladly leave it to the reader to decide which is the more fitting.

Luckily for the elves, man is in little possession of any evidence against which to balance the reasoned argument of the *Summa Elvetica* made on their eternal behalf. Therefore, we have no choice but to conclude with Marcus Valerius that *aelvi habent animae naturaliter unita.*

16 September, 2008
Zürich, Switzerland

APPENDIX AELVI

TALES FROM THE WORLD OF SUMMA ELVETICA

Master of Cats

ESSARIAS CAREFULLY HELD the *calengalad* balanced a half-hand above his palm, studying it closely as the delicate structure rotated slowly widdershins, its blue-green lattice of light sparkling like a precious jewel. The tiny *giloi* were flowing rapidly in, around, and through the dark center of the structure, and occasionally he could see a glowing red streak as the sequence he'd marked happened to flash past his eyes.

He whispered a word, and the rotation slowed, almost imperceptibly. He frowned, still unable to properly track the tiny ruby-red lights that whirled about inside the luminescent spider's web. Then he found them, but, infuriatingly, not where they should be. In fact, if his eyes did not lie, they were precisely somewhere they could not possibly be. It was hopeless!

The temptation to hurl the wretched construction from his high window overlooking the river was almost overwhelming, but he resisted the urge despite his great frustration. A mere physical smashing couldn't harm the calengalad itself, but any force inadvertently released from it could endanger anyone passing by. Furthermore, such an incident would attract far too much unwanted attention.

"*Darro,* be gone!"

The calengalad disappeared, safely banished into the aether from whence it had been summoned. Arilon, his legendary master, dead these past two hundred years, taught that everything in the material plane was constructed of miniature grains, far too small for the eye to see, and yet large enough to contain all the secrets of the universe just as the seed of an animal carries within itself the secret of life. Grains upon grains, bound together by a magic beyond magic, everything was made of it: the stone walls surrounding the great keep, the dancing flames ensconced in the stairwells, even the flesh that had long ago rotted from the bones of an elven archmage.

"They are like the dots of the Ponschule," Arilon explained to him once, referring to an artistic style that had reached the height of its brief popularity when Bessarias was still a young apprentice. "One dot, in itself, is nothing. But thousands upon thousands of dots, placed in a particular order by the hand of a creative adept, can be a truly meaningful construction indeed."

"And who is the creative adept, in this case?"

The archmage had frowned at his impertinence, properly recognizing it as such.

"This silliness does not become you, Bessarias. If you would amuse yourself with debates of gods and origins and forms, there are masters who will be delighted to indulge you. I am not one of them."

So chastened, the great one's student had ducked his head in apologetic submission. And now, centuries later, Bessarias found himself smiling at the thought that his question, however silly at the time, had perhaps not been so far adrift.

In twelve hundred years, the Collegium Occludum had never known a mind so great as Arilon's. Less accomplished masters of magic had left behind legacies of greater fame in the outside world, but although demon lords, masters of the Deep, and *vauderistes* cast terrible magics that annihilated armies, sank mighty fleets, and otherwise decided the fate of nations, there was not one that did more than make skilled use of the Who, the What and the Where. Arilon had been the first to plumb the secret depths of the Why and the How.

Even so, his fantastic conception had been an errant one. Seventy-six years ago, Bessarias proved it false, beyond any shadow of a doubt. It was not entirely wrong, for the calengalad, as his master had named his hypothetical grain, was real enough. The problem was that it was more truly a seed than Arilon had ever imagined, for it was not so much an object in its own right as a little world containing worlds of its own. It was an accumulation of other, smaller elements, ethereal sparks of light that danced and whirled like maddened fairies intoxicated on the bacchanal blood of a toadstool. It could even be broken, as Bessarias learned to his horror when he accidentally created the Glass Desert.

It was a dreadful mistake, but a significant one. In more ways than one. Indeed, the ghastly cataclysm brought about by his experiments marked only the third time in recorded history that Elebrion's High King had dared to intervene in the affairs of the Collegium. But on this occasion, there were no protests from the proudly independent college of magicians. Indeed, open relief was expressed throughout the college. A royal decree was made—there would be no more experiments involving the shattering of the sphere—as was Bessarias's fame.

Or perhaps infamy would be a more accurate term. His name was known throughout all Selenoth now, and feared, as if he had meant to call up devils from that unknown plane of unthinkable power and knowingly penetrated the veil that should have at all costs remained inviolate.

But fear had brought him more than fame. It brought him power too. Now he was of the Seven, a member of the college's ruling council. He was only the fifty-third archmage to hold mastery in two of the eight formal disciplines of the Octovium, and the fifth to do so in three. Arilon had been the fourth. He lacked for nothing. And yet, at this very moment, would he not trade everything for a simple answer that would tell him why the cursed giloi were behaving so strangely?

He had tried everything, drawn upon every single one of the Collegium's vast resources. He had lashed demons with whips of celestial fire, mercilessly ripped speech from the lips of the dead, sent scores of apprentices digging through the college's most ancient archives, and still he had learned nothing. The truth, whatever it was, would have to be found some other way.

There was a soft knock on the door. He waved a hand, and the door opened in obedience to his will.

"Greetings, *Magistras*." The hooded elf bowed respectfully as a large grey cat leaped out from his arms. "Mastema suggested you might be finishing soon. I trust I do not disturb you?"

"Ah, Kilios. Come in, come in. I am already disturbed, though not by you." He sighed heavily. "I wrestle with the pillars of the universe, and they are less forthcoming than your visions."

"Such is the burden of greatness, Bessarias." The cat's yellow eyes were mocking. "Pillars aren't generally known for their elocution. Perhaps that's your problem."

"Silence, Mastema," Kilios rebuked his friend's familiar. He was a gaunt wizard of great height, with eerie pupilless eyes set deeply in their sockets. He was a seer, a powerful one, and not all of his visions were pleasant. The knowledge of evil yet to come is perhaps the hardest wisdom of all, and over the years it had left its bitter mark on his haggard face. Blind, but not without sight, he walked the winding corridors of the great tower as easily as any other mage possessing more conventional vision.

"He tells me you have been holed up in here for three days. Will you eat?"

"Soon, I think. I am not yet hungry."

"Of course. It is always hard to return to the world of carnate concerns."

"It is indeed. Now tell me of the latest gossip. I remember there were rumors of an incipient battle in Nordfall."

"Were there? I did not know. I was meditating alone yesterday, until Mastema did me the honor of paying his respects."

"Don't flatter yourself, seer." The cat looked up from the paw it was washing. "There was a rat on your corridor."

Bessarias smiled affectionately at the large feline. The demon had been with him for nearly two centuries, always inhabiting the body of a grey cat with black markings. How he managed to find them on such a regular basis, Bessarias didn't know and was not inclined to ask.

"He is too proud to admit it, but I suspect he gets rather lonely when I'm occupied with my studies."

The cat snorted loudly.

"I wasn't lonely. I was hungry because you hadn't fed me for two days. And in answer to your question, yes, there was a battle yesterday, and the Red Prince's knights crushed the wolf-breed. Ethaleas set his students to scrying it as an exercise, and I watched them. I imagine the wolves had never seen cavalry before, because the Savondese rode them down like unarmed peasants."

"It is said they are of unnatural origin," Kilios commented.

"The wolfbreed?" Bessarias scoffed. "I've heard the rumors, but I find them hard to credit. If no one in this tower has created a viable form of being in more than a millennia, who else could hope to succeed? Those pathetic bunglers in Savondir? They flatter us, to be sure, but they do not even dream of approaching our skills. If nothing else, their lives are too short."

"I say it was the Witchkings," hissed Mastema.

"Perhaps," Bessarias admitted the possibility. "Who can know the bounds of their perversions? But again, they were human. Fifty or even sixty years is too short a span for proper mastery."

"Of course," Kilios agreed. "I myself am glad to hear of the Savondese triumph. They may envy us, even hate us at times, but they are civilized. To a degree, you understand."

"To a degree, yes. Is there anything else of interest?"

"Not particularly. Mmm perhaps there is one thing. We have the dubious honor of hosting a human visitor, an Amorran, if you can believe it."

"Really? How did that come to pass?"

The seer shrugged and glanced at Mastema, who appeared to have lost interest in the conversation and was carefully licking his left paw.

"I don't know. I heard that he arrived two days ago under the aegis of the High King, but he doesn't seem to be a messenger. Some sort of religious, I recall."

"How very curious!"

Bessarias was intrigued. A human, an Amorran no less, hailing from the Court of Elebrion? Humans had a very different view of magic than his own people. They tended to view it mistrustfully at best, but those of the Empire were downright fanatics in their distaste for anything that smacked of the metaphysical. No, not anything, he corrected himself, for they were rigid monotheists who worshipped a slain god who was somehow not dead. Dead or not dead, though, this god had favored them, for their armies were strong and their rich empire now encompassed nearly a third of the land of Selenoth. It was an altogether curious thing.

He made an impromptu decision to seek out this strange human. If nothing else, the Amorran promised to be an interesting distraction from his recent failures. In a lifespan that was now approaching its fourth century, Bessarias had learned to appreciate the pleasure of the unexpected and to seek out the unusual. It refreshed the mind, which otherwise grew stagnant and eventually decayed. And this visit qualified on both counts, as the Amorran empire was less than a hundred years old, but in that time not one of its citizens had ever requested a single audience with the members of the Collegium, for any reason.

"Has anyone spoken with him yet?"

"Other than welcoming him for the ten-day, I can't imagine anyone was interested." Kilios raised his pale eyebrows. "You want to speak with him?"

"Yes, strangely enough, I do."

Bessarias laughed suddenly.

"I think I'd sit down for a nice chat with a sun-stoned troll if I thought it might take my mind off those cursed giloi. Let me ask you, what do you do when the impossible happens before your very eyes?"

A faint smile flickered past the blind seer's lips.

"I hold my silence and hope I was mistaken, until events prove otherwise. Which they inevitably do. Thus am I thought a poor visionary, but a sane one. It is better that way."

"Ah, your mind is sharper than the proverbial razor of Ockham, old friend." Bessarias clapped his colleague on the shoulder. "Now come, walk with me, and we shall go in search of our exotic guest. Mastema, will you join us?"

"To see a human?" The cat's rasping voice was scornful. "Why would I want to do that?"

The Amorran had been installed in a small, elegant guest building which was separated from the great tower by a splendid garden, the centerpiece of which was a cunningly constructed maze. Bessarias, not in the mood for puzzle games, easily made his way through the tortuous hedgerows by the simple virtue of a navigational spell. Left . . . right . . . left . . . left . . . right . . . he followed the little crimson spark as it leaped inerrantly from one nexus to the next.

"I will leave you here, Magistras," Kilios told him as they reached the intricately carved doors of the building. "I feel a vision descending upon me, and I think it would be best if I did not risk polluting my sight with the presence of the human. I must go now and meditate."

"Very well. But if what you see has anything to do with the calengalad, anything at all, you must let me know at once."

"I will do so," the seer promised, but for a moment, his unearthly eyes seemed to glow with amusement. "Nevertheless, I fear the likelihood is small. Be well, Magistras."

"Be well, my friend."

Bessarias raised his hand, and the two doors swung open silently. The entryway was grandiose, for all that the guest building was small in comparison with the great tower of sorcery. It was palatial and literally fit for a king. It had to be, for it was often occupied by visiting royalty hailing from one land or another who came to pay their respects or, more usually, to beg for favors.

"Magistras."

Two elven guards bowed respectfully to him. He did not know them, but they had the look of Kir Donas. That breezy maritime kingdom lacked both the regal tradition of Elebrion as well as the martial prowess of Merithaim, but it was wealthier than either and was even said to be richer than mighty Æmor itself.

"Take me to the human, the Amorran," he ordered.

The guards led him up the grand marble stairway to a small apartment on the second floor. It was small compared to the other apartments here and was usually used to lodge a minor courtier or a squadron of royal bodyguards. For a single religious, though, it was ludicrously spacious, especially if their guest happened to be a member of one of the more ascetic orders and was accustomed to a simple cell.

Bessarias nodded his thanks to the guards and politely refrained from opening the door with his magic, instead choosing to knock softly with his fist. He waited patiently until the door opened inward and revealed the lined face of an aged human monk, with closely cropped grey hair and a bland, harmless expression. He was short, even by human standards, as the top of his tonsured head did not quite reach Bessarias' chest, and he was wearing the orange robe of a third-day guest with the cowl thrown back upon his shoulders.

"I greet you, good sir, in the name of whatever god you worship. My name is Bessarias. May I enter this room in peace?"

The left side of the Amorran's mouth twitched in what might have been a grin.

"In peace, you may enter. In the name of my Lord Immanuel, you may enter and be welcome. My name is Herwaldus."

"I thank you, Herwaldus."

Bessarias inclined his head briefly and entered the apartment. It was richly decorated with thick carpets and gossamer-thin silk wall hangings, in a green-and-yellow springtime theme of new life.

"May I offer you any refreshments?" Herwaldus offered. "My kind hosts have provided me with every kind of luxury here, three different kinds of wine, many fruits and vegetables, and enough cakes and bread to feed an army."

"I shall have a glass of wine, thank you."

Bessarias lifted his hand, and one of the wine decanters began to pour itself into a nearby glass of crystal. Herwaldus, to his credit, did not flinch, or even appear to notice. Bessarias also saw that with the exception of a half-empty carafe of spring water, the well-stocked table appeared untouched. The monk must be from one of the ascetic orders after all, he decided. No ordinary human would have passed up the opportunity to sample the exquisite delights of elven fare, so much more delicate and sophisticated than the cruder foods upon which humans normally subsided.

"May I ask what brings you here?" he asked the monk, after sipping delicately at the Savondese red. It was an acceptable vintage, if not a particularly good one.

"The truth. I come to share it with your people."

"How interesting." Bessarias smiled inwardly. Now he understood why the High King had foisted this man off on the Collegium. Mondrythen would have no wish to have the plea-sure-seeking chaos of his court interrupted by what he could only see as dreary human moralizing. The surprise was that the king hadn't simply slain the man outright, or at least sent him back to Æmor with stripes upon his back. "As I, like many of my colleagues here, flatter myself in aspiring to be a seeker after truth, I shall be most interested to hear what you have to share with us. You are a monk, I see. Of what order?"

"Tertullian."

"I am not familiar with it. What distinguishes your broth-erhood from the others of which I have heard, the Alessians, for example?"

Herwaldus nodded.

"A good question. We all serve the Lord Immanuel, of course, but whereas our Alessian brothers seek to withdraw from the world to further their pursuit of righteous holiness and purity, we are charged with embracing it in all its foulness."

Bessarias lifted an eyebrow.

"Ah, foulness. That would be my people, yes? If my memory serves me correctly, 'children of demons' is the specific appella-tion favored by your priest-king, is it not?"

"Æmor knows no king," Herwaldus answered, unper-turbed. "The Sanctiff is only the head of the Church, the first among equals, and he is not infallible, though some wish to believe him so. Please understand that I do not consider any of the elven folk to be foul in their essence, I only refer to the state of sin in which your people, like every other race on this fallen world, are imprisoned by the foe."

"The foe? Ah, yes, your Lord Sathanas. I have never had the honor of speaking with him directly, but I am acquainted with a few of his lesser servitors."

The human looked confused. Bessarias smiled again, but this time, he allowed a touch of cruelty to enter his voice.

"I am not a child of demons, but among other things, human, I am a master of them. If I should so desire, I could summon one here and command it to burn the skin from your body without harming the robe you wear. Or I could have you borne through the air to a deserted isle, and leave you there to contemplate your so-called truth until you died of thirst."

"If you wish," the monk acceded politely.

"You do not believe me?"

"I believe that you have the knowledge, yes. The power, certainly. Beneath your beauty and your courteous manner, I see great arrogance, the terrible pride that comes only from the possession of great power. I think that if Raphaelus were to paint an image of Lucifer before the fall, he could do no better than to use you as his model. But I also know that you will not harm me, because it is not permitted at this time. My mission is not yet finished."

"Permitted? By whom?"

"My Lord Immanuel, of course."

Bessarias studied the human. The elderly monk did not seem to be afraid of him, but his eyes held no hint of madness either, only calm determination and, just possibly, a small spark of defiance. The magician decided that he rather liked this little old man, who was undaunted in the face of one whose very name was enough to cause kings and warlords alike to shake with fear.

He fluttered the fingers of his left hand, and Herwaldus's robe changed colors, from orange to spotless white. The monk looked down, startled, then up again at Bessarias.

"What's this?"

"An invitation." Bessarias made a circle with two fingers, and a sigil in red was magically stitched onto the robe's left breast. "This will demonstrate to all that you are my guest, and you may stay beyond the ten-day for as long as you wish or until I withdraw my invitation."

"Thank you . . . I thank you, Bessarias. May I ask why?"

The magician smiled, and lifted a warning finger.

"Do not think I am inclined to accept your so-called truth. I am three hundred and twenty-two years old, and I have seen more of this world in all its foulness than you can possibly imagine. Before Fabian rejected the crown and founded your empire, I was numbered among the greatest masters here. But in my wisdom, such as it is, I have learned to always listen first and to judge later. You shall have your chance to speak, and then you will leave, in peace."

The monk nodded humbly.

"That is all I seek. You are courteous indeed, and I thank you for your consideration, Bessarias."

"We shall talk again soon," Bessarias promised the little man, and after wishing him good health, walked from the chambers. Before he had even reached the bottom of the stairs, he was already filing away their conversation to a corner of his mind as a new approach occurred to him.

"What about an impenetrable barrier?" he mused aloud. "If the giloi were forcibly reflected, then tracking their vector might provide some interesting information . . ."

Neither of the two guards betrayed any sign of anything but respect as the Magistras walked past them, unnoticing.

"I hate it when they mumble," the taller guard remarked to his companion as they watched Bessarias disappear into the maze.

"I know. I'm always afraid they'll turn me into a newt or something, and not even notice."

"He's the one that made the Glass Desert, you know."

"Did you really need to tell me that? Pox, but I cannot wait to get back to Kir Donas and away from these mad wizards!"

"Six months, sergeant, only six more months . . ."

Over the course of the next several weeks, Bessarias was pleased to make the discovery that the monk was not only possessed of a degree of intelligence, but a surprisingly literate education as well. In addition to any number of human philosophers, Herwaldus knew his Khonnus, his Tithanas, and, as became any sentient being with pretensions to intellectual distinction, his Lathas. The breadth of his knowledge was remarkable, considering his scanty years, and Bessarias found that he was forced to revise some of his less flattering opinions of humanity.

It was a brisk autumn evening, but the fire in the hearth kept the chill at bay as the elven magician prepared another verbal sally at the human he was beginning to consider a friendly adversary.

"I cannot find logic in your wholesale condemnation of our magic. Diablerie, I will concede, could be considered evil by its own measure. Perhaps also some forms of blood magic, and from your monotheistic point of view, I will even concede the possibility of deep magic as well. But as for other disciplines, such as vauderie, for example, wherein the action springs solely from the exertion of the practitioner's will, that I cannot accept. Surely in cases such as these, any good or evil to be found lies solely in the ends, not the means!"

"I am heartened to hear that you are, at last, willing to contemplate the possibility of such things!"

"Good and evil? Certainly, if only for the purpose of this particular discussion."

The monk sighed.

"As Stagirus writes, one is forced to wonder if it is possible to distinguish between you and a vegetable, if you yourself are incapable of distinguishing between the two. Good and evil, that is."

"Ah, but I believe that Lathas had the right of it when he declared that there is only a better, and also a worse principle. When the better has the worse under control, then one is said to be master of himself; but when the better principle is overwhelmed by the worse, then he is a slave."

"But you are speaking of slavery and mastery, not good and evil."

"Exactly! What you call good and evil are only daimons, influences, outside factors which may help or hinder the proper development of the self. When one has mastered one's self, by exerting control over one's baser instincts, then one does what is right through the approach to a higher form of being. The nature of the self is not unlike the nature of magic; both are there to be conquered by the higher mind, through the exertion of the will. Some succeed, most cannot."

"It is not hard to understand why you hold Lathas in high regard. Do you see yourselves as guardians, then, of your lessers?"

Bessarias spread his hands, as if to indicate all the world around them.

"Are we not? Without its masters, a community soon falls into ignominy and despair, as the meaner desires of the many must be held down by the virtuous desires and wisdom of the few. It is our responsibility to preserve and protect not only the bodies but also the minds of those we serve."

"Hmmm . . . You deny good and evil, but uphold virtue?"

"Virtue is service to the greater community. The truly virtuous individual, having mastered himself, makes careful use of his skills, not for the sake of his own momentary desires, but for the sake of being able to perform his duty to the community."

"I do not understand. What is this duty?"

"For the master, to command. For the slave, to obey."

"I see, I see." Herwaldus stifled a smile. "Does it fall to the individual, then, this vital decision as to which group he rightfully belongs?"

"No, that is a task for the community, or rather, the wise in their midst, although the potential for mastery is not difficult to detect. There is such a thing as a will to power, which can seldom be concealed, either from the self or from others. Certainly it cannot be hidden from us here in the Collegium; indeed one of our primary purposes is to find and guide those individuals with the potential, those who possess the will to master not only themselves but also the world around them."

The monk nodded, and a look of triumph brightened his eyes.

"And that, I fear, is where you fall into error, my friend, so wise and yet so foolish. Not my will, but thine, that is the essence of the good. It is not the act but the motive alone that matters. That which is in accordance with God's will is good. That which is not is evil. It is a question of means, not ends."

Bessarias chuckled, but he betrayed no hint of mockery when he replied dryly, "I imagine it falls to the individual then, to make this decision as to motive?"

"Yes, for who else can know the truth? Otherwise, there is only the truth of appearances. Still, it is written that by their fruits ye shall know them . . . and, of course, God always knows the truth of the heart."

"I cannot argue with you. You speak of things beyond reason, beyond rationality. Things I have not seen, not in more than three centuries. Nor, I imagine, has anyone else."

The monk smiled at the magician. He looked almost complacent, as if they were playing cards and he was holding an unbeatable hand.

"I believe you will see, Bessarias, in the fullness of time. But for now, I will only say that in my humble opinion, your great college is well named. It is occluded indeed."

The monk's insufferable and judgmental certitude was often infuriating, but Bessarias also found it delightful. He had no doubt that he would win in the end, as all the human's arguments held together only as long as their dialogue remained in the realm of the hypothetical. Eventually, the discussion would move from the ideal to the real, and in that realm, Bessarias knew he was a master without equal.

The game had been entertaining, but now, with the onset of winter only six weeks away, the time had come to bring the matter to a close. Bessarias had developed a certain affection for the stubborn human, and while he had no intention of allowing the man to remain and pose a distraction all winter, he also did not want to force the fragile old monk to return to his brethren amidst the throes of that harsh season. Thus he had invited Herwaldus to his own chambers that night, and since he was vain enough to enjoy witnesses to his victories, he had also invited Kilios as well as Lacellas and Amitlya, two of the Collegium's greatest practitioners of vauderie and deep magic. Mastema, of course, was there as well.

The two archmages were seated on either side of the fire, studying the human with varying degrees of curiosity and disdain, when Bessarias gestured grandly and revealed a large crystal scryglass he had borrowed from one of the Collegium's farspeakers. Inside the glass was the image of a hilly, wooded land, unmarked by signs of civilized habitation, but alive with the flutter of birds' wings and the gentle rustling of green leaves in the wind.

"Fra Herwaldus, I have enjoyed our conversations. But I must tell you, for all your eloquence I remain unmoved. Your arguments are learned and internally consistent, for which you must be congratulated, but I have seen that they bear less relation to the world in which we live than do the idyllic reflections of Lathas on the perfect kingdom. That is why I have asked you here tonight, that you might see that my arguments are based, not on theory, but in the material, and to give you the opportunity to prove, in front of these reputable witnesses, the validity of your own."

Bessarias gestured to the scryglass.

"Behold the land of Shimra, as it was. When I was new to my mastery of the fifth discipline, I was perhaps more reckless than wise. But I was pure in motive, seeking only the truth, when in pursuit of that knowledge I shattered one of the myriad spheres that serve as the invisible bricks in the mortar of the material world."

The image changed abruptly, revealing a vast and lifeless desert, flat, and devoid of form. The unnaturally smooth ground had a glossy sheen, as if it was made of glass, which it was. It was the Glass Desert, the site of his most notorious and yet glorious accomplishment. Or was it a failure? He still wasn't sure.

"God have mercy!" he heard Herwaldus mutter.

"You have seen me use my powers on a number of occasions, but without seeing this, you could not possibly understand the extent of them. Only now are you capable of understanding that I tell you truly when I say that those of us here who are known by the name Magistras are not only beyond your concepts of good and evil, but we may well exceed the very concept of your god!"

The monk seemed shaken, almost as much by his words as by the terrible display of his power, still reflected in the glass. He couldn't seem to take his eyes away from the terrible image. Bessarias, noticing this, waved his left hand and the utter desolation disappeared. He didn't particularly enjoy looking at it it himself.

"I trust that is an adequate demonstration?"

"More than adequate! My sweet Savior, how we must grieve You!" Herwaldus shook his head and looked up at Bessarias in disbelief. "And that was a virtuous act, by your reckoning?"

"Virtuous, yes. Unfortunate, costly, and misguided also. I would undo it if I could, but the act was a worthy end to justify an unlucky and regrettable means. The calamity was integral to my understanding of the calengalad."

"Don't break it, that's the main thing," Lacellas whispered across the hearth to Amityla, and the golden-haired sorceress laughed as she held Mastema in her lap and stroked his thick grey fur.

The human's face wrinkled even more than usual as he peered at the beautiful elf. Her presence seemed to discomfit him a little. Or was he staring at the familiar? It seemed there was something about the cat that fascinated the elderly human.

"My own demonstration must needs be less dramatic, I'm afraid," he said finally. "But I can think of one that would be fitting, under the circumstances. There are no sick here, but my Lord was ever one for warring against the demons that pollute this fallen world."

He turned back to face Mastema, and the cat, sensing his hostility, hissed angrily. Unperturbed, Herwaldus pointed a knobby-knuckled finger at the cat and rebuked him.

"You are a creature of filth and shadow, feeding off the souls of the mortals you despise! Name yourself, demon!"

"I am Mastema, you wretchedly stupid human, as any here might have told you if you'd troubled to ask!" retorted the cat. "Now leave me alone and —"

"Begone, Mastema, in the most holy and sacred name of my Lord Immanuel!"

The gathered magicians gasped as one, for when the monk shouted the name of his god, Mastema suddenly slumped, apparently lifeless, in Amityla's arms.

"You killed him," she cried. "What have you done?"

Herwaldus stared at the dead cat, his jaw agape and his horror apparent to all. He reached out a hand, slowly, to touch the cat's throat and confirm Amityla's fateful pronouncement.

"I am so very sorry, Bessarias," he began to apologize. "I only meant to banish the demon from your dear pet. I did not think to kill it."

Bessarias shouted with laughter.

"Oh, the blood that stains your hands, Herwaldus! Will you ever wash them clean?"

He chuckled at the shock on the old human's face and waved away his attempts to express his regrets.

"This is not the first, nor the fortieth body Mastema has shed. I fear you misunderstand the nature of my pet, my friend. The demon does not possess my pet. He is the pet."

The monk stared at the magician for a long moment, clearly at a complete loss for words, until he finally shook his head.

"If the Son of Man rebuked his own followers as a perverse and unbelieving race, what must he think of you elves? Making pets of demons? Faugh! But then, my Lord did not come to bring justice. He came that all might know mercy and grace. And since He was known for helping the blind to see, then perhaps there is a more apt exhibition of His power."

He turned toward Kilios and met the seer's blind eyes unflinchingly.

Bessarias frowned. Healing was one of the most difficult disciplines, and one of the most notoriously unsuccessful. Even at the Collegium, no one had ever attempted to restore the seer's natural sight, since he had obviously been blind since birth. He wondered at the monk's daring in attempting a demonstration so fraught with peril.

"With your permission?" Herwaldus approached Kilios.

The blind seer nodded his acquiescence, and the human gently placed his small hands over the strange, sightless eyes.

"Heavenly Father, Almighty God, in the name of Thy son Immanuel, who lives and reigns with Thee, I pray Thee heal the eyes of this, Thy child, that these others might bear witness to Thy power and honor Thy great name. Amen."

He withdrew his age-spotted hands from the seer, and Bessarias gasped, incredulous at the sight. Nor was he alone in his astonishment. Amityla was sitting in stunned consternation, while Lacellas had leaped to his feet, his mouth working in awed silence. Kilios, meanwhile, was staring levelly at the human, and in the center of his formerly empty whites were black pupils surrounded by a ring of green.

"Amazing," the seer whispered. "Your power is great indeed!"

"The power is not mine, but Him I serve."

Kilios nodded, then smiled sadly.

"I must warn you that you have struck a spark here that may set alight your own pyre."

"I am prepared."

Bessarias found himself entirely confounded, confused not only by the human's tremendous working, but his friend's strange comments too. The monk and the seer seemed to be communing in a language untelligible to the rest of them.

"What is this? I don't understand!" Lacellas protested.

"Explain yourself, Kilios," urged Amitlya.

The seer glanced at Bessarias, and for the first time in an acquaintance that spanned centuries, their eyes met knowingly. It was strange, like being struck with a powerful jolt of static, but it was wonderful too. Until Kilios opened his mouth, and

Bessarias suddenly realized that in welcoming the seemingly harmless old human inside the Collegium's high walls, he had made a bad mistake, one that could have deadly ramifications for the magicians of the College, if not the entire elven race.

"I can see, but my vision is gone," the seer declared, in a soft voice full of wonder. "My second sight. I cannot feel it; it has been taken away!"

Bessarias was displeased to receive the Council's summons, but not surprised. In the three days since Herwaldus had "healed" Kilios, wild rumors had been circulating through the entire Collegium, to such an extent that some of them had even reached him despite his self-imposed seclusion. Elves were little prone to panic, least of all the powerful magicians of this college, but the incident was a disturbing one, especially due to the human element.

The magic of the elves, after all, was the protective shield that preserved their three small kingdoms, caught as they were between the hammer of Savondir and the anvil of Æmor. And in keeping with the metaphor, there was always the unpredictable danger posed by the raging furnace of the savage orc tribes and their terrible ogre kings.

"I'm glad you could join us, Magistras."

Bessarias bowed respectfully to the only magician who outranked him here, the *Custodas Occulti,* Grandmaster of the College. The other five masters sitting around the semi-circular stone table were his equals, for all that some were glaring at him as if he were a prisoner and they the jury. Gilthalon particularly looked as if he would like to play the part of the executioner;

the *Magistras Daimonae* was a handsome but cold-mannered *diableriste* with golden eyes that burned like coals.

He took the last remaining chair, its back carved with the sigil of the unblinking eye that indicated his own position, *Magistras Gnossi*. As Arilon had been before him, Bessarias was the Master of Hidden Knowledge.

"I understand my guest has created somewhat of a stir."

"A stir? You might say that!" Alisiassa was the only female Master, and the most hot-tempered of the Seven. "Do you know what is being whispered among the acolytes? They are terrified, they think that the *Malfermathas* has come, that the death of magic approaches, and the End of Ages is at hand!"

"The End of Ages is always at hand," wheezed the ancient *Magistras Vitae.*

"This is ridiculous." Bessarias laughed aloud. "The human is an old religious, nothing more. He serves a god of which we know little, one possibly of greater power than I had first considered. But the discovery of a new god is hardly cause for a commotion, much less this meeting!"

"It amuses you?" Gilthalon spoke for the first time, in a voice that was deceptively soft. "Not since the days of the Witchkings has the gift been stilled in another. When this new human empire arose, I thought it would be harmless, not only harmless, but helpless, fearing magic as they do. Now Æmor is rich, their legions many. And with the power of this god at their disposal, what is to stop them from becoming another Vingaara?"

The demonlord's point was a sobering one, Bessarias was forced to acknowledge, if only to himself. Since the dawn of history, only the magic of the ancient Vingaaran Witchkings, the long-dead fathers of diablerie, had ever exceeded that of the Collegium. They were long gone, but more than a trace of their evil legacy remained, and it was in this very chamber that the last Witchking had died, boiled in his own blood eight centuries ago.

"I do not see the Amorrans as a threat to us. This particular human seeks only to help us, in his strange, misguided way. We don't need his help, of course, or that of his god, but his sentiments are genuine, if misplaced, I assure you."

"So you say," Gilthalon sneered rudely. "Your familiar says otherwise. He says if we do not stamp out this new human abomination, they will seek to destroy us."

"I did not know my fellow councillors were in the habit of consulting with my pets. Do not put too much credence in Mastema's words, Magistras. He is a demon, after all, and they are a prideful, touchy lot. Mastema, I'm afraid, is rather pettier than most, and this religious has offended him."

"As he should! Æmor's very religion is offensive! Do they not dare to call us the children of demons?"

"That is a lie, and far from the truth, as you know better than most," Bessarias chided Gilthalon. "Like all humans, the Amorrans fear what they do not know. What is done is done. Kilios has lost his vision for the nonce. Perhaps it will return, perhaps it will not. But what would you have us do? The human has broken no law, neither of Elebrion nor this college. Do you forget that he has done what none of us, despite our great powers, could do, in restoring sight to the blind? He and his god must be cherished and studied, not castigated and feared!"

"So speaks the Master of Cats," muttered the Magistras Vitae, sparking an amused grunt from the Keeper.

"If his curiosity gets him killed, so much the better." Alisiassa, uncharacteristically, took Gilthalon's part. "The problem is that Bessarias thinks nothing of sacrificing us all on the altar of his vanity. Not only us of the Collegium, but the Three Kingdoms besides!"

"One almost hesitates to remind this Council of the origins of a certain well-known desert," agreed Magistras Vitae, with a disagreeable smile.

There was a long moment of uncomfortable silence, which Bessarias, despite his irritation, did not dare to break. Finally, the Custodas Occulti spoke.

"There is too little information on which to proceed. We must know more. Bessarias, I do not question your judgment of this man's character, but if he may call upon the power of this unknown god, then others may do so as well, others who seek to do us harm. Now, I hope that we of this council are all agreed that in this case we must seek justice beyond the mere interest of the stronger, namely, ourselves, but at the same time, it must be said that we simply cannot allow this man to depart and leave us ignorant of what might be a potential danger."

"Give him to me," Gilthalon requested politely, but his voice held a dangerous edge. "He will hold nothing back from me."

"Indeed, I think your arts may indeed be useful in this matter, Magistras." The Grandmaster shook his head and irritatedly waved off Bessarias' outraged protest. "Silence, Bessarias. I have no intention of allowing your guest to come to needless harm. I have in mind a test, wherein the human shall set the power of his god against the arts of one of our own."

"Custodas, I beg—"

"Yes, yes, Gilthalon, I can think of none better to uphold the honor of the Collegium. Unless of course, there are any objections . . ." The Grandmaster glanced about the table. "With one caveat, of course. You will take the proper precautions so that our guest shall come to no harm if he cannot, as we must expect, stand against your spirits."

Gilthalon growled under his breath, but he nodded reluctantly. Bessarias had no concerns on that score, as the fiery Magistras was most vain about his honor. He did have another consideration, though, which he brought to the Grandmaster's attention.

"Galamiras, what if the impossible occurs? What if, by some strange chance, the illustrious Magistras Daemonae is defeated?"

Gilthalon made an incredulous face, and Alisiassa laughed outright. The remainder of the Seven looked amused; only the Grandmaster's expression did not change.

"In that case," he said solemnly, "we will kill him. Assuming, of course, that we can."

As soon as the council meeting was closed, Bessarias stormed out of the tower and toward the guest palace. He had been outvoted, five to one, with his only support being the abstention of the *Magistras Morte*. Furious and in no mood for mindgames, he summoned a vortex of negation to surround him and blasted an elf-sized path through the magical greenery of the maze. The startled guards were barely able to get out of his way as he banished the vortex just in time to spare the marble steps. He marched upstairs to the room that

Herwaldus had first occupied as a guest, which now served as his jail.

The young guard standing outside the chamber started to raise his spear to block the entryway, but he reconsidered quickly and adroitly stepped aside upon catching sight of the thunderous expression on the Magistras' face. Dereliction of duty was a serious offense in the High King's army, but the punishment, harsh though it might be, paled in comparison with provoking the wrath of an already irritated Master.

The table laden with delicacies was gone, he saw, but the room was otherwise exactly the same as he had last seen it. Herwaldus looked none the worse for wear as he rose quickly to his feet, alarmed by Bessarias' precipitous entrance. Kilios was there too, seated by the fire, and his eyes, so recently restored, were troubled.

"You come from the Seven," the former seer stated. "What have they decided?"

"To put him to the test. The loss of your vision has frightened them, like children hearing their first tales of the Witchkings. My blasted cat must have his revenge, and Gilthalon has fallen for his wheedling manipulations with no more thought than a lovelorn elfling promised a witch's philtre."

"The Witchkings?" asked Herwaldus, sounding more curious than concerned.

"Never mind them," Bessarias snapped. "Tomorrow, before the full Assembly, the Council has decided, in its wisdom, to set Herwaldus against one of our own. The objective is to learn the extent of this strange god's power, so that we may determine if it might pose a threat to us."

"Wonderful," Herwaldus exclaimed.

"Who will it be?" asked Kilios.

"Gilthalon, of course."

The seer whistled and shook his head. Herwaldus noticed his reaction and looked curiously at Bessarias, who tried to explain.

"Like myself, he is one of the Seven. He is a master of demons, supremely skilled, and he is not well-disposed toward your kind. Fortunately, Galamiras has ordered him to ensure your safety, so you will not be harmed."

"I have no fear of that." The little monk smiled. "He is a master of demons, you say? So too am I, through the authority of my Savior. Though this magician raise a thousand against me, the power of my Llord's name shall send them fleeing in every direction!"

"You don't understand. That's absolutely the last thing you must do. If you somehow manage to defeat Gilthalon, it will be your doom. The problem is almost certainly academic, since I don't believe you can beat him, but at all costs, you must lose. You don't want to die, do you?"

"I am prepared. I do not seek death, but neither do I fear it."

"But what about your god? Surely he wouldn't want you dead."

"He said, 'Follow Me,' and He was not one to despise a criminal's death. And is it not written, 'Then shall they deliver you up to be afflicted, and shall kill you, and ye shall be hated of all nations for My name's sake'?"

"I am really beginning to suspect that you are senile," Bessarias snapped. He turned to Kilios. "What if we get him out of here instead? Tonight!"

"You would defy the Council?"

"I am the Council! And I'm not defying anything. He's my guest, isn't he? If I revoke his guesting, then he's not allowed to stay the night. We can escort him to the Amorran border, and from there, I'm sure he'll be fine."

"I won't go." Herwaldus shook his head.

"You have to! Gilthalon won't kill you, but the experience will not be a pleasant one, I guarantee it. Do you have any idea what even a fairly minor demon can do to you?"

He snapped his fingers and the flames in the hearth were suddenly filled with horrific images.

"Please, make them go away," Herwaldus begged, obviously upset by the fiery scenes of pain and torment.

"You see? And that's what could happen to you if things go well! We elves are civilized, yes, but we can be cruel, you must understand that. If the Custodas Occulti decides you must die, it is quite possible that he may not grant you the kindness of an easy death."

The human swallowed hard. His eyes closed, he took a deep breath, and then shook his head.

"No. I am not ashamed of Him, and I will not have Him be ashamed of me. I will not go. And if you force me, I shall return."

"Can't you talk some sense into him?" Bessarias asked Kilios.

"I doubt it. Nor would I, even if I could."

Bessarias scowled suspiciously at the seer.

"Don't tell me you've embraced this human lunacy! Herwaldus has been wronged, yes, and he does not deserve what the Council has in store for him, but this . . . this discipline of his—and I admit, there appear to be some aspects of it that may deserve closer inspection—but it is only a very, very small part of the pattern in its totality!"

"I have seen more than you know, Bessarias. For eighty-five years, I have borne witness to many things which were not, and were yet to be. Never once was my vision errant, but now, only now and in the light of this man's truth, do I see clearly."

The two elves locked gazes, and Bessarias had to look away from the passionate intensity in the other's frighteningly normal eyes.

"Fine, fine. Hold your tongue, if you must. I am disappointed, though. You must know what Gilthalon has in mind. He doesn't like humans at the best of times. So be it. But Herwaldus, if you can, will you please do me the favor of explaining why you are so determined to go through with this?"

The monk nodded. He was smiling, although he was still pale from the terrible sights Bessarias had shown him in the fire.

"There is no mystery. When I was young, newly sworn to my vows, I read of a man who was convinced that every being of every race was, in fact, a child of God. Now, you must understand that this view is not held universally by all who worship our Lord. In fact, it is espoused by only a few, and in the Church's considered opinion, the belief treads perilously near to heresy. Nevertheless, this man held firmly to this belief, as did his friend Tertullis, the founder of the order to which I belong.

"His name was Diaspelian, and it was his heart's desire to go forth unto the nations, preaching to all who would listen the good news of the Lord Immanuel's death and resurrection, urging repentance from sin and telling of the life beyond death that awaits us all. He traveled throughout the barbaric lands that were eventually to become the kingdom of Savondir, and many came to know the Lord Immanuel and were baptized as a result of his efforts. He founded as many as thirty churches, and still he knew his work was incomplete. Then, ten years after Diaspelian's departure, his friend Tertullis received a letter."

Bessarias watched as Herwaldus opened the precious brass-bound book that was, aside from his staff and robe, the monk's only apparent possession. The human withdrew a single unbound piece of paper and handed it to him. The elven mage scanned it and saw that it was lovingly scripted in a primitive human language.

> The strang people called here Orkks are a cruell
> and unlovlie people, near unto the hyghte of a
> manne, but of stature broade and myghtie. Theyre
> skin is of a greenish colour, and upon theyre faces
> is set a countenanse most bestial. Theyre black
> haire is long and coarse, like unto the maine of a
> horse. They weare it tyed into a brade, encircled
> bye a ring carved from the bone of an enemye
> slane. They know no kinge, nor do they fear noght
> but theyre savage demon-gods, whome they
> worshippe with rytes too terrible and bloodee to
> record herein.
>
> The stoute people of Albysse war most
> bravlee against thes savages, who do not subsist
> uponne the lande, but instaed are content to rob
> and plunder the fields of theyre naebors. They
> eat the flesh of manne, and I have been tolde of
> how they will dessend upon a village in greate
> number, seeking to devourre all they fynd therein.
> Whether they be demonspawn or not, I cannot

saye, for they know noght of theyre historie,
lacking alle knoweledge of wryting excepting
onlie the groteske rune-scratches of theyre
magickians.

And stille I believe it maye well be that
they too are childrenne of the Living God. Are not
we not allso fallen short of the grace Devyne and
the glorie of Heavens Son? Soon I goe to humblee
preach His Truthe to the chiefs of the great clanne
of Grimwalde…

Bessarias shook his head, and a faint smile crossed his lips.

"I can't imagine the orcs were particularly receptive to his message."

"No, it is said that he was killed and eaten less than a week after he entered the Grimwalde."

"And this is your inspiration? You truly are insane!"

Herwaldus smiled tightly, shaking his head.

"Twenty-five years ago, a traveller came to our chapter house in Bruscato. He asked for permission to take holy vows and join our number, and after some discussion, he was welcomed into our brotherhood with thanksgiving and much praise for the name of our Lord Immanuel."

Bessarias nodded, impressed with the tale's conclusion despite himself.

"I take it his skin was a greenish color, with a countenance most bestial?"

"Exactly. Brother Grimfang was an orc, from a small body of believers who are descended from the three individuals baptized in the name of our Lord by Saint Diaspelian before his death. I came to know the brother well before he died, and despite his fearsome appearance he was a gentle spirit of uncommon wisdom and faith. So you see, if Diaspelian did not fear to go and speak the truth before that terrible people, how then should I despise the opportunity to do the same before yours?"

Bessarias sighed, both saddened and confused. Somewhere, there was truth in all of this, but the gist of it eluded him. He had no idea if Herwaldus was truly a madman, a masochist, or a wise and holy prophet. But he was sure of one thing. Events had moved far beyond his ability to control them. He glanced at Kilios and shrugged.

"As you will, Herwaldus. I admire your bravery, if not your judgment. May your god be with you tomorrow."

The aged monk smiled and placed a hand on his shoulder.

"Thank you, Bessarias. You have been a gracious host, and I am grateful. But my fate will be as it will. Do not trouble yourself over it."

"Very well, I will not. Besides, I have a cat to hunt down. And may the seven hundred bastard spawn of Belial curse me if I don't beat another nine lives out of him!"

The Great Hall was more crowded than Bessarias had ever seen it. Acolytes rubbed elbows with stooped, creaking adepts, all eager to witness what promised to be an epochal duel. Not since Moldar the Dire's infamous challenge of Ulandir Brighthand had the whole assembly shown such interest in a challenge, although the crowd of spectators was much larger today.

Only four witless acolytes had shown up on that occasion to watch the celebrated necromancer extinguish his brilliant young rival; three, accidentally caught up in Moldar's evil working, shared Ulandir's untimely doom, while the fourth, his reason shattered by the terrible cries of his companions, wandered outside the following winter and froze to death.

Mastema, unsurprisingly, was nowhere to be found. Bessarias had made only a half-hearted search for the little beast, knowing full well that his pet knew him well enough to lie low until the first flush of his anger had passed. Still, he kept his eyes open for a glimpse of grey fur or a pair of supercilious yellow eyes.

At the Grandmaster's gesture, Bessarias reluctantly joined the other Magistres on the central dais. Together, the Seven formed a loose circle around the human, who looked tiny, frail, and ugly in the midst of all these elves. Galamiras had already prepared the working that would protect them and the crowd should anything go awry with Gilthalon's summonings; it was something he had personally developed after the debacle of Moldar's cruel victory.

"Shams!" cried the Custodas Occulti, and in response there was a faint shimmering in the air above the dais. It was barely visible, but it sparked an outburst of excitement in the watching crowd.

"Fakre!" shouted Alisiassa.

"Nasre!" "Sij!" "Eism!"

Bessarias sighed, fuming inwardly, but powerless to intervene.

"Bakra," he muttered dutifully.

The crowd buzzed at his obvious reluctance, but the working did not require enthusiasm, only proper form. The shimmering solidified into a transparent but palpable shield of pure power forming a large cylinder that fit within the larger circle of the ringed Masters. Gilthalon, wearing a striking black robe edged with gold, stepped confidently into the magic shield and dramatically raised his hands to complete the spell.

"Kadir!"

The Assembly clapped and roared with approval as the handsome *Magistras Daemonae* acknowledged their cheers, then turned to face his opponent. The shimmering shield could only be broken by the Custodas Occulti in conjunction with at least three of the participating Masters, and if anything should happen to him, then both Gilthalon and Herwaldus would be trapped inside for the six days it would take for the powerful working to expire.

With elaborate courtesy, Gilthalon quickly sketched a protective circle around Herwaldus, then himself. Bessarias nodded, satisfied that the diableriste was content to obey the strictures laid out for him. It was not long before there was a popping sound, and a small imp, only knee-high to the human, appeared inside the shield. It had blue skin and tiny horns that were barely more than buds.

As the crowd of magicians exploded with laughter, Gilthalon gleefully gestured toward Herwaldus, inviting him to respond. The monk did not seem to know he was being mocked, for his face was grave as he dropped to one knee to examine the miniscule demon.

"What is your name?"

The imp glanced back at Gilthalon, who nodded.

"Bromphethskagsruinmela," it answered in a high, piping voice.

"Well, Brom . . . Bromphim . . . whatever your name is. Begone, I say, in the name of my Lord Immanuel."

The imp shrugged helplessly and with another brief pop, vanished from sight. Gilthalon's eyebrows seemed to rise of their own accord, but he did salute the human's achievement with applause that was not entirely derisive.

"Well done, human," he called. "Now how about this?"

The Magistras summoned a much larger demon this time, with massive black wings and the head of a bull, armed with a pair of sharp tusks that jutted dangerously upward from its lower jaw. Whereas the first spirit had appeared almost harmless, this brute looked anxious for violence.

"I am here . . . " it rumbled in a low voice that reeked of evil.

"Have a go at the gentleman in that circle there, will you? There's a good fellow."

Bessarias shot an angry look at Galamiras, but the Grandmaster only smiled and pointed to the circle of flames that sprang up around Herwaldus each time the bull-headed demon attempted to strike at him. Gilthalon was playing fair. The malignant spirit roared in anguish, then turned on its summoner, only to be driven back by a whip of silver fire that suddenly appeared in the Magistras' hand.

"I wouldn't recommend stepping out of that circle there," the demon master told the monk as he lashed the howling spirit." "Our friend is more than a little agitated, I'm afraid."

"Begone, by the blood of the Lamb," Herwaldus ignored the demonlord. "Begone, in the name of my Lord Immanuel I command you!"

Vast silence filled the hall as the angry spirit disappeared with a furious scream. Gilthalon dropped his whip, which lay crackling and hissing as his feet as consternation filled his face.

"You didn't even know his name!"

"I don't need it. My Lord is the Alpha and the Omega."

Herwaldus bowed politely, but not before Bessarias saw his lips twitch with a small smile of satisfaction. Gilthalon saw it too, and it fanned the flames of his ire. His cheeks reddened, and the gold of his eyes darkened to a furious bronze as he began a third summoning.

"I don't like the sound of that," the Magistras Morte commented, as Gilthalon's chanting continued for an ominously long time. "Think the shield will hold?"

"Nothing can break it," Bessarias heard Galamiras answer confidently.

"I do hope you're right."

Bessarias hoped so too, as upon the cessation of the demon-lord's chant, a noxious golden fog began to coalesce and swirl inside the magic shield only ten feet in front of him. As it solidified, it became quickly apparent that there was something very large writhing and thrashing about inside of it, and out of the corner of his eye, he saw that some of the more cautious spectators in the back were beginning to slip quietly out of the Great Hall.

If Herwaldus was having second thoughts about this whole venture, Bessarias couldn't blame him. Even from the safety of his position outside of the impenetrable shield, he felt as if his insides were turning to water. Next to him, he could feel Galamiras gathering his power. Swallowing hard, he did the same.

Gilthalon looked confident, though, and his expression was initially one of savage delight. But his composure was shaken, along with the Great Hall itself, when a vast thunderclap boomed and echoed repeatedly off the stone walls and he found himself on his knees before a terrible six-armed being, twice the height of an elf, all fire and metallic flesh, with a serrated sword in every hand except for the one pointing at the Magistras Daemonae. Its beautiful, androgynous face was distorted with affronted outrage.

"Who are you?" it demanded as four silver wings unfurled behind its back and almost touched the gilded timbers of the ceiling.

The diableriste pushed himself to his feet, and in anger found his courage as he stared up at the tall angelic creature. He gestured threateningly with the whip of arcane fire.

"What concern is that of yours? I have summoned you, and you will obey me!"

For a moment, Bessarias thought the great archdemon might test the power of Gilthalon's circle, but something in Gilthalon's determined face must have dissuaded it, for its wings abruptly descended and its blazing radiance dimmed a little. The Magistras nodded slowly.

"You fear to try me? Then you are wise. But if you would test yourself, you may try him. He claims that he can master you, that you shall flee at his command."

As the demon turned around, it shot a last, withering glare at Gilthalon, but saved its most scornful sneer for Herwaldus, who was eyeing the great being with an unreadable expression.

"Then come out of the circle, if you think yourself equal to the task, human."

Slowly, deliberately, the old monk scuffed the protective chalk with his left foot. His eyes locked on the demon's, he took a single step forward, accompanied by a chorus of gasps from the watching magicians. Bessarias looked away, not wishing to witness the human's violent end. He was surprised when he heard nothing but the old monk's high-pitched voice.

"You have no power over me," Herwaldus announced. He folded his arms and seemed to grow in stature, in authority. "Nor will you harm me. You know who I am, and you know the one I serve."

The demon said nothing. It only growled low in its throat.

"What is your name?" the human demanded.

"Vashyash," it answered in an imperious voice.

"Go then, Vashyash, leave here and return no more. In the name of my Lord Immanuel, who lives and reigns at the right hand of the Father, I command you!"

"I hear. I obey."

Gilthalon shrieked in protest, but to no avail. Swifter than it had come, the demon dissolved into the golden cloud, which rapidly disintegrated, leaving only the bittersweet scent of myrrh behind. Then Herwaldus turned to face Bessarias, and with a sad smile, bowed respectfully.

"I trust the demonstration was satisfactory?"

Then he reached out, and to the great horror of every magician present, stuck his arm right through the magical shield. Its translucent shimmering immediately became opaque, then, with a blinding flash brighter than the noonday sun, exploded into a myriad of colors that rapidly faded into nothingness.

The little monk bowed his head humbly and made the sign of the cross on his chest. But because all eyes were fixed upon him, no one saw a grey flash leap onto the pavilion and spring at the man's spindly legs while he was still giving thanks to his god.

"Glory to Your great name, Almighty Father . . . "

"I warned you, you idiots!" Bessarias started at the sound of his familiar's voice. "Mmmph!"

Herwaldus shrieked and clutched at his leg, almost toppling over on top of his attacker. It was Mastema, and he had buried his sharp feline fangs into the soft muscle of the human's calf.

"Bind him!" Gilthalon screamed furiously, taking advantage of the human's distraction, and the *Magistras Materiale* was quick to obey. Herwaldus suddenly flew backward through the air, and smashed into the stone wall behind the dais. He hung there, stunned, suspended by invisible chains that the Magistras rapidly wove out of the air itself as Mastema smiled in bloody satisfaction.

"Pah!" he theatrically spat out a small chunk of withered manflesh. "I'd rather eat swamp goblin."

"What are you doing?" Bessarias shouted at Gilthalon. "He has done no wrong!"

"No? You saw what he just did. We cannot permit him to live!"

"So what are you going to do, kill him now?" Bessarias appealed to the Grandmaster. "Look at him, Custodas. He's helpless!"

"I hope so. If I thought he could escape those binds, I'd let Gilthalon kill him right now." The Grandmaster's eyes were dark with worry. "But we really must learn more about the source of his power. We must have it from him, one way or another."

"What, you're going to torture him?"

"If we must. Though I hope it won't come to that."

Gilthalon, however, was not interested in the source of the human's power. Humiliated in front of his peers, the demon-master was intent on revenge. Even as the two magistres spoke, he was approaching Herwaldus with his golden eyes filled with hate. Twirling his fiery whip in his left hand, the diableriste smiled cruelly as he came to a halt in front of the monk.

"I can't say that I was not impressed. But you should have let Vashyash kill you. He can be untidy, but at least he is quick. I, on the other hand, am not so inclined to mercy."

He flicked his wrist, and the magical whip slashed across the human's face. Herwaldus did not cry out, but his eyes bulged out and five blistering burns appeared instantly on his left cheek. The watching crowd cheered and shouted insults at the suspended human. One enthusiastic young mage hurled a fireball high over the monk's head, sending sparks raining down upon his white robe when it splattered on the stone wall.

"Galamiras, stop them," Bessarias said grimly. "You'll learn nothing from a dead man."

"I imagine there are a few necromancers here who might disagree with you, my dear Magistras."

"Silence, Mastema!"

Bessarias angrily kicked at his pet, but it easily avoided the blow.

"You came to tell us of your god?" Gilthalon was mocking the monk as he struck him a second time. "We, who are ourselves gods?"

Herwaldus lifted his head and started to respond, but the words never left his mouth. Bessarias, sickened by the barbaric spectacle, had had enough. He lifted his hand. A blast of soul-fire erupted from his open palm, burning through the monk's heart and severing the mystic silver chain that linked every mortal soul to its body. There would be no necromancy here today.

Gilthalon whirled around, furious at being cheated of his victim, as a shocked silence descended upon the hall so fast one would have thought a mute spell had been cast. Galamiras, his face full of consternation, clutched at his sleeve, but Bessarias angrily pushed the Custodas away. Rage filled his heart, and it was all he could do to refrain from sending another blast or two at his erstwhile colleagues, not to mention Mastema. Lesser magicians scrambled to get out of his way as he stalked from the hall in search of Kilios.

"I thought you might come. Is he dead yet?"

"Yes," Bessarias nodded. "I killed him."

Kilios raised his eyebrows but did not rebuke him. He only frowned and looked off into the distance, before returning his gaze to Bessarias.

"You seem perturbed," the former seer said.

"I am. He was a good man, but they were angry, and afraid. I did not want to see him suffer."

"I know. Do you think they will seek to chastise you?"

Bessarias scoffed at the thought.

"Over a human? Even if they cared, they wouldn't dare. No, I am not troubled by my actions, but by what I saw today. It is as if my eyes have suddenly been opened, and what I see of the world no longer fits my previous understanding."

The former seer nodded, a faint smile playing across his lips.

"I understand."

"Kilios, for my entire life, I have been seeking power, knowledge, wisdom. But to what end? Today, I saw the wisest, most powerful elves in all of Selenoth acting exactly like a barbarous gang of orcs! They saw something that they did not understand, they were forced to confront something they feared, and so they reacted in exactly the same manner as an illiterate, devil-worshipping, mud-rooting swamp goblin! But what is the point of all this painstakingly gathered knowledge if in the end we reap naught but a harvest of death?

"When I first began my studies, I sought nothing more than the truth behind all things. Today, I learned that I have found nothing of that truth here, nothing of beauty, nothing but a thousand thousand means of creating the utmost devastation and destruction!"

"I am sorry," answered the seer. "What would you do?"

"If I cannot find the truth here, I must go elsewhere. I will follow in the footsteps of that orc of whom Herwaldus told us, and go to the brothers of the Tertullian Order. I don't know if their truth is the one I seek, but I am certain that Herwaldus knew more of it than me."

Kilios smiled, and he placed a hand on Bessarias' shoulder.

"Then we shall travel together, my friend. And that your troubled heart may know some peace, let me tell you of the last vision I saw before my sight was taken from me. I saw a man with blood on his hands touch my eyes, and the dark cloud which surrounded me disappeared, replaced by a shining ray of brilliant light. I saw you striking down a white lamb with an iron dagger, then hurl the dagger from you, far beyond the horizon. And finally, I saw the two of us, standing side by side before the walls of a great city."

"I will never give up my magic!" Bessarias growled at his friend. "If that is your interpretation, then your vision is a false one, and it comforts me not at all."

"Who can say what the future will bring?" Kilios spread his hands. "But Herwaldus is dead, is he not, and by your hand. My friend, I do not tell you what you must do, I can only tell you what I have seen. For myself, I am glad to be freed of the prison of my visions."

"I rejoice to hear it. But I will not give up my magic, I don't care what you have seen."

"The choice is always yours, Magistras. Shall we seek that great city together nevertheless?"

Bessarias nodded.

"We will do that, Kilios, and we will leave immediately. First we travel to Æmor, and if what we seek cannot be found there, we shall go to lands and cities yet unknown."

"You would leave today?"

"At once," answered Bessarias without hesitation. "I have wasted three centuries here. I would not squander another night!"

Kilios nodded sagaciously. "I expected as much, and so I have already arranged for supplies and clothing to be prepared for both of us, as well as four horses for the journey. Go and fetch whatever else you would bring, and I will await you at the front gate."

Bessarias laughed aloud. He was amazed at how his frothing anger had suddenly been transformed somehow into something approaching joy. Herwaldus had spoken often of dying that others might live, and for the first time, Bessarias felt some inkling of understanding what the little human might have meant by that.

• • •

It took him little time to gather those possessions he felt he could not do without. Where he was headed, he would have very little need of anything. He packed up a few of his most precious belongings, among them an old manuscript enscribed in the hand of his master, the scryglass, and a small gold-and-silver working of the calengalad. He took it for remembrance's sake; as for the calengalad itself, it was a conundrum that would have to await some other inquisitor. He had other, more important riddles to solve. He took one last look back at the well-appointed room in which he had spent so many decades, then softly closed the door and began to make his way down the countless stairs of the broadly twisting staircase.

He had just turned the corner of the tower's final landing when he heard someone call his name.

"Bessarias!"

It was the Custodas, Galamiras. The Grandmaster was waiting in the shadows at the bottom of the dark granite steps.

"I heard that you were leaving. It's true, then?"

"It is true," Bessarias said, in a firm, but friendly manner. He held up a small bag of jewels, which held centuries-old Vingaaran rubies of such quality that they would do honor to the High King's crown. "Kilios and I are going to Æmor. Do you think these will pay for a month's worth of inns along the road?"

"Don't use those. If those happen to be the stones I think they are, someone will burn down the inn around you in hopes of getting at them. Take the eastern route, and I'll arrange for Mondrythen to provide you with a bag of Amorran coin before you reach the border. But the human city? Why there, and why so suddenly? Because of your guest? I do not understand. What is a human to the likes of you and me?"

Bessarias stared at Galamiras for a long moment. He wasn't sure he could properly explain himself, not in a manner the other elf would comprehend.

"It has little to do with the human. He was only the catalyst. I think the reason I must leave is that I'm beginning to suspect that the truth I'm seeking is one which cannot be found here."

Galamiras frowned, but finally, he nodded in sympathy if not understanding.

"I hope you find your truth, Bessarias. Will you return to the College?"

"Someday. I think so. But, Custodas, I must tell you, I do not think it will be the same Bessarias you see before you now.

The Grandmaster laughed.

"I am not entirely sure I know the Bessarias who stands before me now. But you will always be numbered among us, old friend, whatever truth you find and however far you travel. Be safe, and be well."

Bessarias bowed deeply and respectfully. He raised a hand in farewell and turned to leave. Then a thought occurred to him, and he lifted his head.

"Galamiras, will you do me a favor?"

"Of course."

Bessarias reached into his robes and drew out the intricate model of the calengalad. He studied the precious metal for a moment, almost wistfully, then sighed and handed it to Galamiras.

"I don't need this anymore, but I suppose someone will someday. Give this to them, with my regards, will you? And my sympathies."

"I will do that," the Custodas Occulti agreed, but he had a suspicious look on his face. "You've given up on that particular line of inquiry, then?"

"Do you know, I think I might have."

Galamiras smiled wryly.

"So the door to that particular abyss shall remain locked for a while longer. I imagine that's something that I really should regret given my position, but somehow, I find that I cannot. Hark, is that the world I hear, breathing a deep sigh of relief? Fare you well, Bessarias."

Bessarias only chuckled and raised his hand in benediction. He started to leave, then paused as he sensed someone watching him. He turned around and saw that Mastema was staring at him, unblinking, from the shadows underneath the circular stairwell. The cat's yellow eyes seemed to radiate contempt, but there was a hint of distress in its harsh voice as it called out to him.

"You leave without so much as a word for me, Magistras?"

Bessarias tried to think of something, anything, to say to his longtime companion, who had served him so faithlessly and well, but he found himself at a loss for words. As he stared back at the cat, a question Herwaldus had asked him once before entered his mind, unbidden. It was a question, but it was also an answer.

What fellowship can light have with darkness?

And so without a word, without even a final gesture of farewell, Bessarias turned his back on the demon that had once been his pet, and it was as if a burdensome weight was suddenly lifted from his shoulders. The great iron doors of the Collegium Occludum opened before him, spilling warm autumn sunlight onto the cold stone of the ancient hall, and he strode resolutely forward, out of the shadows and into the blinding embrace of the light.

FINIS

Birth of an Order

865 Anno Salutis Humanae

QUINTUS TULLIUS WAS exhausted. His thighs were chafed raw, his entire body ached and he had neither slept nor eaten much in the last three days. Nevertheless, he held his head high and sat erect on his horse despite what the effort cost him. General Varus was determined to bring the Merethaimi army to battle, and every man in his three legions knew he would march them straight into hell itself before he'd give up the pursuit.

Miserable as he was, Quintus couldn't feel sorry for himself. At least he was on horseback. Varus was driving the men mercilessly; yesterday, Quintus heard they'd marched almost twenty-two miles overland. That was nothing special for a legion traveling along a well-constructed road, but here, in the hilly roadless wilds of the Ippolese borderlands, it was a brutal pace.

And yet, Varus had little choice. The elf king's army was half cavalry, and its infantry consisted mostly of long-legged archers. For the last month, the cursed elves had marched circles around Varus's three legions, maddening the general with their tantalizing proximity. Twice, King Everbright had even drawn up his forces as if to offer battle, only to melt away silently in the deep of the night.

Quintus smiled wryly as he recalled the curses that had echoed throughout the camp when the general emerged from his tent only to discover that the enemy had again disappeared. That was three mornings ago, and it seemed as if they'd been rushing headlong in mad pursuit ever since. Quintus didn't even want to think about how many miles behind them trailed their supply wagons and the artillery; it would be half-burned polentus and no meat again tonight. Even the most desperate camp followers had been left in their dust for more than two days.

His horse staggered wearily over the top of a steep rise, and as he surveyed the long lines of troops below, he felt an unexpected burst of energy at the sight of two Vezian outriders galloping toward the head of the first column, directly toward the general's eagle. With luck, they'd have news of the enemy's precise whereabouts, not far off, he hoped. He wheeled his horse about and made his way carefully back down the slope he'd just climbed, looking for his legatus, who, as was his wont, was riding with the legion's rearguard.

"Sir, a party of scouts returns! They ride hard!"

The legatus, Flavius Mamercus, was a stout old soldier, bitter and cynical from more than thirty years on the campaign trail. He received the welcome news with little more than a scowl. A plebian, he was as apolitical a man as had ever marched a mile with sandals, shield, and sword. Quintus, whose patrician family had seen better days, was at first grievously disappointed when he learned that he'd been assigned to the man as a tribune of the Seventh—serving a Flavian would do nothing for him in the circles that mattered back in Æmor—but he'd since learned that if Flavius Mamercus could do him no political favors, he was a treasure trove of martial experience.

"Did they come from the east or west?" Flavius asked. He nodded thoughtfully at the answer. "Demmed demonspawn ran into the horse Varus sent off two days ago. If they declined the engagement, they'll head for the ford at that little village. What's it called?"

"Rovina," Quintus answered immediately. Mamercus expected his tribunes to read their maps and read them well. So, he was surprised when, without warning, the legate frowned and spat contemptuously.

"Varus is a demmed fool. Lad, you'd better pray the elf king is stupid enough to tie himself down with Tertio's horse, because mark my words, we're in for it if he doesn't."

We are? Quintus didn't understand the legate's reasoning, but before he had the chance to ask Mamercus to explain himself, a horn sounded, signaling that they would make camp for the night. He saluted quickly and rode off, for as the senior tribune, it was his duty to see to the disposal of the legion's ten cohorts as they prepared their nightly fortifications.

The legate's words worried him, though, as the plan was to catch the elf king between here and the great river Angusa. A fast and treacherous river, Angusa could only be forded in two places. Rovina was one of them, and Tertio's five hundred mounted spears stood between Everbright and the other ford.

Two hours later, in the general's command tent, Quintus learned precisely why Mamercus was looking even more sour than usual. The grizzled legate was jabbing a sausage-like finger at the map that had been unrolled in the center of the tent.

"They turned away from Tertio here. They're marching north now, toward Rovina, here."

"Exactly as I hoped," General Varus answered, his deep voice rich with anticipation. He was a tall, handsome man from one of Æmor's richest families, if not its most respected. At forty-three, he was already a curator, and rumor held him to be a serious candidate for one of the three Consulships next year. And Varus, along with every officer in the camp, knew that returning to the city with an elf king in tow would suffice to ensure that the rumor became reality.

"You see, Flavius Mamercus, your pessimism was misplaced and our gamble is paying off in most handsome returns. The elf made his fatal mistake in fleeing from our horse, because the advantage now lies with us. We outnumber him four to one, and regardless of whether he tries to hold the pass against us or runs for the river, he is lost. In the mountains, he cannot bring his horse to bear, and the greater part of his army is therefore useless. We are too close for him to risk the river crossing, so he will have to stand and fight with the river at his back or lose the greater part of his army. And so, finally, we have him!"

"Or does he have us?" muttered Flavius dourly. "Blasted blighters always got tricks up their sleeves. Turn us all into glass."

"Legend and lore, old sourpuss." The legate of the Tenth Legion was another up-and-comer, a mere equestrian, not a senator, but one known to be a rising star of the popolares. His name was Maurus Gallus, and he was Varus's strongest supporter. "Their mages can't do much more than throw fire at us. They might as well be made of wood and twine. I'd fear them more if they had twenty onagers instead. Although 'tis true, unless we can wait to bring up the artillery, we shall have to advance naked in the face of their archers as well as that accursed magery."

"Fire holds no fear for a man behind a shield." Varus snorted. "Everbright has not been running from us for the last four weeks out of confidence. He is a coward. A bolder man would have smashed through Tertio and used the southern ford, but of course, he is no man! Now he is caught between iron and water, too proud to flee and save himself. They say he has lived more than five hundred years; I say it is time to put an end to him!"

Quintus saw Mamercus roll his eyes as his fellow officers cheered their commander's bold words. That did not, however, stop him from adding his own voice to the acclamation. For who could stand against the might of the Amorran legions when God Himself marched with them against the evil spawned of demon loins?

Still, he knew a sliver of doubt when, as he left the general's tent and began to make his way through the thousands of small fires lighting up the night, he saw the stocky silhoutte of Flavius Mamercus facing the looming darkness of the mountains. He waited silently as the veteran legate cursed under his breath then turned around to lay a heavy hand on his shoulder.

"We'll reach the pass by noon, lad. Keep your eyes open and your wits about you as we go through. That's where I'd hit us, was I the elf. The first will march in the rear with the horse; I want the sixth in the middle with you, and I'll give you twenty extra horse. The eighth will take the fore, and I'll give them to Brutus. If anyone can extricate them from this whoreson's chamber pot, it's him."

"You truly think the elf will try to ambush us?" Quintus couldn't see the legate's face in the night's shadow, but the grim tone of his voice was unmistakable.

"If he doesn't, he's a bigger fool than Varus. Now, you've the makings of a good soldier, Quintus Tullius, don't forget that. When all hell breaks loose, take a deep breath, look around you and remember that telling your men to do something, anything, is always better than doing nothing."

The legate squeezed his shoulder once and walked away into the night. Quintus shook his head and smiled after the crotchety old man, and yet he could not quite shake the discomfiting notion that no one who had seen the tail end of five centuries was likely to be a fool.

General Varus might not have the benefit of his opponent's five hundred years' experience, but neither was he a military novice. Well aware of the potential danger posed by the pass through which they must cross, marked by wooded ridges on either side, he sent two turmai of thirty riders to sweep the ridges on either side before the great column began to march through. The sun had reached its zenith by the time the eighth of the Seventh passed the giant boulder that marked the start of the pass, which Quintus learned was called Ardus Wald.

Soon after, the sixth cohort marched in, and Quintus thought that the forward elements of the Tenth Legion were likely clear through to the other side. It seemed that Flavius Mamercus's fears were misplaced, as on either ridge he could see an Ippolese horseman stationed in a position of overwatch. He was wondering if Varus might push on to Rovina tonight, and had just reluctantly resigned himself to another long day's march when Marius, the cohort's centurion, pointed at something high in the clear sky above them.

"That's a bloody big bird there."

Quintus leaned back in his saddle and shaded his eyes. It was large, sure enough, but it soared so high that Quintus could not determine its size. It was clearly a raptor of some kind, however, as it soared effortlessly on the mountain winds.

"Must be an eagle. Too big for a hawk."

Quintus shrugged and returned his attention to the men marching in front of him. But when Marius inhaled sharply, he glanced back at the centurion, then back up at the great wash of blue. What he saw bid fair to take his breath away too.

For he suddenly realized that the great bird was higher up than he'd thought, and much larger. Worse, he saw that someone rode upon its back. War eagle! He watched, frozen with awe, as the tiny rider raised an arm, and a moment later, there was a flash of purple lightning followed by a thunderclap that ripped through the empty sky.

The earth responded with a thunder of its own. There was a terrible rumbling on every side, and battle-hardened soldiers shrieked in terror as the ground shook beneath their feet. Quintus was thrown from his horse as the animal panicked, and terrible screams began erupting from the column behind and before him.

Stunned, he pushed himself up from the rocky ground and through to draw his sword. It would be a useless gesture, perhaps even stupid, and yet it might give him sense of purpose. What had Mamercus told him? Take a deep breath and look around you.

He looked around and saw that if all hell had not broken loose, certainly its close cousin had been unleashed. Arrows were hissing from the heights above, and he stared in disbelief as the Ippolese horseman who had been guarding the north ridge knocked arrow to bow and loosed it into the chaotic midst of his cohort before melting back into the trees. Treachery!

Or perhaps not. Think . . . think! Something was wrong. Something was terribly wrong, for the Ippolese were no more horse archers than were the Amorran legions. They were lancers. Elf magic, then? As if to confirm his thought, a massive green fireball was hurled down from the heights and whizzed just over his head to explode harmlessly behind him. Or perhaps not so harmlessly. Someone was screaming, and he smelled the stink of burning flesh. He saw a man on a horse and scrambled toward him. It was Marius.

The centurion had somehow managed to keep the men in a semblance of order. They had their shields out, and Marius was cursing like a demon-possessed madman as he ordered each contubernium into a series of eight-man tetsudos. Praise the Lord for centurions, Quintus thought as he scrambled toward the man.

"You're alive, sir!" Marius shouted. "I saw you go down and I feared the worst! But sir, we can't stay here, sir! What do we do, sir?"

Quintus blinked dumbly at the veteran centurion. What do we do? You're asking me? The realization that the men were looking to him for direction hit him like a physical blow. Wounded men were screaming on every side, and whether he looked to the front of the pass or the rear, he could see arrows and fireballs smashing into the helpless mass of men. They seemed to come from nowhere. Something, anything, is better than nothing. He could almost hear the old legate's voice echoing through his mind.

"Give me your horse," he shouted. "Tell the men to seek what cover they can find and stay in turtle-formation until I see if we can go forward or if we have to retreat. The slopes are too steep, we can't attack."

"Sir," Marius thumped his chest and slid from his horse. Quintus caught up the reins and leaped into the saddle. Urging the beast forward with some difficulty, he pushed his way out from amidst the Eighth, and, as soon as he was clear, dug in his heels and galloped madly forward along the rock wall.

He leaned as low over the horse's neck as he could as he rode past the confused and noisome swarm of trapped and frightened soldiers. He saw the Fifth's centurion was leading a group of ten or twelve men up the steep northern slope, but a fireball flew from the woods on the south ridge and burned the man alive along with the two soldiers nearest him. The survivors, shouting with fear and horror, tumbled down the slope and fled back to the meager shelter of the trapped column. Quintus fought off the sudden urge to vomit. You don't have time for that, he told himself.

He was just reaching the third cohort when he saw Brutus, the veteran primus pilus, riding toward him. At the sight of Quintus, the centurion brought up his horse and slid from its back before his mount had even stopped.

"Down, Quintus Tullius, get down!"

Quintus quickly complied, just in time, as an arrow split the horsehair plume on his helm. "Can we go forward?"

"No, it's blocked! Their mages brought down a landslide on top of the Twelfth's rearguard. Curse the hellspawn! We have to back out of the pass. I don't think they have many archers up there on the heights, but we can't see them. No one's spotted a single one yet! It's not just the trees. I think it's a sorcery of some kind."

His borrowed mount suddenly screamed horribly and reared, nearly pulling Quintus off his feet before he remembered to let go of the reins. Despair threatened to overpower him as the horse ran off, an arrow protruding from its flank.

"That's Marcus's mare. Is he dead?"

"No, I left him in command of my cohort. You've the horn, why haven't you sounded the retreat?"

The centurion grinned unexpectedly, exposing worn, yellow teeth. "Not yet, lad. Who's to say we can retreat? Think, Quintus Tullius. If they've the mages for one landslide, odds are they cut us off from behind as well. If those rocks they dropped on the Twelfth's rear were the last bit, then why are they hitting us here?"

Quintus groaned. Brutus was surely right. In fact, Flavius Mamercus was quite possibly buried under an avalanche of stone already. Still, they could assume nothing; it was their duty to see if the legate survived and had orders for them.

"Give me your horse, then. I'll go."

Brutus laughed and shook his head. The centurion almost seemed to be enjoying the madness engulfing them on every side. "No, lad, you've done for two already. You're bad luck. Take the horn instead; if you don't get orders in a quarter-hour, blow the retreat. We can't take much more of this before we break, and then we're all dead."

Quintus accepted the horn and slung it around his neck. Brutus didn't salute; the older man simply slapped him on the shoulder before remounting and riding off. Quintus nodded, trying to find courage within his heart, and for a moment he almost believed they might survive this disaster. But his heart quailed when he saw an arrow take the primus pilus in the side before he had ridden twenty paces. Brutus swayed but did not fall as he continued riding, although the way in which he slumped in the saddle made Quintus think that the tough centurion might have received his death wound. God Almighty, fifteen thousand men, trapped by the mountains and beset from above, was it possible they were all going to die here? But he was too young, far too young to die. Surely, it was impossible!

He raised the horn to his lips, then lowered it. Too soon. Brutus was wounded, not dead. He might yet make his way through. Once the retreat was sounded, what little discipline remained would disappear as the legion dissolved into a mob of five thousand frightened, desperate men.

"Where's Licius Julius?" he shouted to a pair of soldiers crouching back to back behind their shields. The youngest of the tribunes had been with the third.

"Dead!" one shouted, pointing to a charred mass of bones and half-molten iron. "They got him and the centurion at the same time!" Fewer fireballs were now arcing down from the heights, but those that did were larger and aimed more selectively at the iron-shielded tetsudos protecting small groups of men gathered together for protection. The deadly hail of arrows continued too, finding even the smallest gaps in a soldier's armor. It was a loser's choice between fire and fletched arrow, and death either way.

Quintus was suddenly possessed of an irrational anger. He shook his fist and shouted at the cloudless sky, not at the enemy but at his faithless God. "Where are You now, Immaculate One? Are You with us no more? Have You abandoned us? Will You leave Your servants to die, blind and helpless, at the hands of Your enemies? Just give us a chance, Lord, at least give us the eyes to see those who strike us down!"

He blinked. As if in answer to his cry, his vision suddenly went awry. Strange colors filled it as the entire sky seemed to warp and swell above him. Half-expecting to be struck down by lightning for his near-blasphemous diatribe, he wondered if perhaps he was already dead, smitten by the fist of a vengeful Divine. But no, he looked at his hands. They were cracked and calloused as always. He glanced up at the southern ridge and saw, to his amazement, a strange purple glow was emanating from the woods. There was something in the middle of it, and when it moved, he realized that it was an arm. An arm that belonged to one of their wizards, he realized, as a fireball resulted from the motion.

Close to the eerie glow, perhaps twenty paces, he noticed a pair of arrows flying out from the trees. They seemed to come from nowhere; he wondered if perhaps Brutus was right and the elf mage was cloaking the archers with a spell of invisibility. Were such things possible? Quintus fell to his knees in sudden and grateful awe. "Oh, Lord Almighty, thank You, thank You, oh mighty God!" If only they had their artillery with them, he realized, they could strike back. And the elven mage was out of range for pilum, but slings, now, that was another matter.

"Velites, to me!" he roared in a voice that carried over the shouts and cries of the wounded. Five Caslani emerged reluctantly from the makeshift shelter of their dead horses and sprinted toward him. "Do you see that tree, there, with the crooked branch? Count ten trees to the right and give me five volleys. I don't care if you don't see anything. Just give me five unless I tell you to stop!"

"Sir," they saluted despite their obvious bewilderment and began to load stone pellets into their slings while still crouching as close to the ground as possible. "What's the use," grumbled one of them in his rough Ippolese accent.

"Because I can see through the wizard's spells," Quintus snarled. "Now give me those volleys or I'll strangle you with your own bloody sling!" The recalcitrant man's eyes narrowed, and although his companions betrayed similar skepticism in varying degrees, all five obediently began whirling the thin leather straps over their heads. "There we go!" Quintus cried as he heard the snap of leather and saw the wizard's glowing arm suddenly disappear, shattered, he hoped, by one of the small missiles. The purple glow remained.

"That's it, that's it," he shouted. "That's it, don't stop!" The Caslani, inspired by his enthusiasm, stood taller and slung their deadly slings with the fury born of a release from helplessness. Quintus could not see if any stones struck home, but after the third volley, the purple glow abruptly disappeared, and a roar, half-frightened and half-angry, went up from the nearby soldiers behind him as ten archers appeared out of nowhere on the ridge above them. A flurry of spears were launched, uselessly, at the now-visible enemy, but a dozen more Caslani rose up and joined the first group of slingers in driving the archers back into the woods before a hail of stones.

Quintus looked back over his shoulder and saw that the archers on the northern ridge were now visible too, although only he could see the two unearthly-colored glows in among them, one red and one green. This time, he was able pick out one mage clearly as the elf lifted his hand, pointed, and caused another lethal fireball to explode within the Amorran ranks. But Quintus quickly indicated both locations to the slingers, and by the fifth volley, the wizards were gone, presumably in retreat, leaving more archers visible to the naked eye.

He was surprised at how few there seemed to be; from the number of dead and wounded lying about he would have guessed three times as many.

He could still hear shouts and explosions to the east and west, and it occurred to him that without the terrible magic fire to drive them back, this cohort could easily take the ridge, then sweep through the woods clearing the heights. Off to his right, he saw the southern slope even had a small gully that would offer them a modicum of protection from the archers as they climbed. He smiled, and, for the first time since the battle began, drew his sword. "Take heart, men of Æmor, take heart," he cried to those nearby. "The wizards are gone! Their spell is broken! Follow me or die!"

Once again, he raised the horn, but it was the charge he sounded. The Caslanis cheered and sent up another storm of stones, one of which caught an unlucky archer squarely in the forehead. The unconscious elf collapsed and tumbled from the ridge to the savage roars of the angry soldiers. Before Quintus could even begin to make his way toward the slope, the elf had been dispatched and two dozen men were swarming up the gully.

The archers on the northern side began directing their volleys into the backs of the climbers, but the Amorrans were well-armored, and the Caslani below were quick to turn about and drive back the elves with a series of furious volleys. Five or six men fell, stricken, but the raging iron tide rose inexorably up the slope, heedless of the elven arrows.

The shouting above him and ring of metal on metal spurred Quintus on, but by the time he reached the top, the only elves that remained were dead ones. Most had run away, but nine lay in their strange blue blood. Two of the nine were unarmed, mages, by the look of their robes, and the soldiers gave those bodies a wide berth. It was said that devils came to claim those who wielded unclean powers when they died, and even the most hard-bitten legionary in the cohort was leery of such things.

The men cheered at the sight of him standing in their midst, horn in hand. But then they fell silent, and he realized they were waiting for orders. His orders. But this time the thought did not daunt him. This time he knew what had to be done.

That first lot, he immediately sent west with orders to clear the heights and find Flavius Mamercus, if possible. As more of the cohort clambered over the top, he directed the next group to the east, then sent more to the west. Every twenty men, he changed directions. He counted more than three hundred forty; the Third had been bled, to be sure, but it hadn't lost quite as many as he feared. But when he saw the first Caslani begin to reach the heights—they'd stayed behind to cover the infantry's ascent—Quintus stopped them.

"Stay below!" he shouted at the slingers still climbing. It looked as if only twenty or so of the cohort's forty lightly armored missileers had survived, including three of those first five, but they would suffice. "Stay in the pass, all of you from him on, go west and tell the Fourth they can escape this way."

"And the rest of us?" asked the slinger standing beside him. Quintus recognized him as the first man to join him earlier. No coward, this one. Quintus grinned at him and brandished the horn.

"We'll climb back down and run east to spread the word, friend. As far as we can. Are you with me?"

The slinger grinned and thumped his chest. His face was bloody, his armor was nothing but the indifferent protection of leather, and he didn't even wear a sword. But he was game, even so. "To hell or to Elebrion, sir!"

The baths were an almost unbelievable luxury following more than nine months in the field. When Quintus closed his eyes and sipped at his glass of chilled wine, he could easily almost imagine that he too had died on the rocky field of slaughter and was now in paradise.

The retreat had been nightmarish, as the elves kept up their barrage of arrows and balefire from the southern ridge until the last soldier had been extricated from the deathtrap. Flavius Mamercus had survived the rockslide intended to seal them to their fate—as the primus pilus correctly guessed, the canny elves had used their cursed sorcery to unleash avalanches fore and aft—only to take his death wound from an arrow that found its way to his unarmoured armpit.

"I knew you were a soldier, boy!" Mamercus had coughed up blood as Quintus had knelt next to him. Reaching out, he'd placed the wooden rod of command in the younger man's hand. "Knew it from the start. You saved the legion. Now you must get them home."

"But what about the Tenth and Twelfth?" he'd asked the dying legate.

"Not your concern. Just get the lads home. Æmor may have need of them once word of this disaster gets out."

Flavius Mamercus died that night in the rude encampment the survivors constructed a half-day's march from the pass. But it was an orderly retreat, not a rout, and that evening, Brutus, the tough old primus pilus who'd somehow survived his wound, presented Quintus with a crown woven of grass before the assembled legion. Of the 5,240 men of the Seventh who'd marched from their winter quarters last spring, they counted 4,195 survivors; almost a quarter were wounded. The eighth, ninth, and tenth cohorts had taken the worst of it, but by the grace of Immaculatus, the fifth, sixth, and seventh were mostly unscathed.

A month later, Quintus handed the Seventh's rod over to a hard-faced general at the bridge that marked the city limits, who glared at him as if he were personally responsible for the Amorran defeat. Quintus only smiled to himself; no doubt the man's demeanor would be rather different had he known about the grass crown. Eager to get back to Æmor and break the news to his father, Quintus had taken his leave of the men and ridden ahead of the marching legion, but as always, bad news had flown on crow's wings.

The ultimate fate of the other two legions was still unknown, but common wisdom, always optimistic in Æmor, currently held it that General Varus had escaped the elven trap on the other side, and, in his fury, chased King Everbright across the border. As to that, Quintus was not so sure, but he held his tongue. Nor had he told anyone except the primus pilus, Marius, and his fellow tribunes about the miraculous ability to see the elven mages that had saved them all.

The clamor of the great city was startling after months in the wilderness, even months spent in the close vicinity of twenty thousand men. The women, in particular, drove him nearly to distraction with their flowery perfumes that somehow managed to penetrate the stink of his long-unwashed body. As he rode past the Archalean baths, he suddenly decided that he couldn't possibly go to his father looking—and more to the point, smelling—like a peasant who hadn't bathed since the new year.

The attendants were taken aback by his jangling armor, but they showed no hesitation to take his coin, and one of the slave boys even offered to clean and polish it for him. Quintus had gratefully accepted the service, and even more gratefully accepted the flagon of chilled wine offered to him. The warm water was even better than a woman, he thought with satisfaction. Lying back against the side of the pool, he placed his head in one of the rests and closed his eyes. He lay there, gently rocking with the water's movement, at peace with the world.

Or so he thought. He was more than a little startled when his arms were seized roughly by two strong pairs of hands and he was dragged violently from the pool. His wine glass shattered on the ceramic tile and the dark wine poured into the water like blood as he was left sprawled naked on the cold tile. He rolled over and gasped as he saw that the men standing behind those accosting him bore the bound axes of Amorran authority. But what could the lictors want with him?

"Quintus Tullius, you are summoned, by order of the Urban Praetor." The head lictor was a tall man, and his cold grey eyes were hard. "Put your toga on, sir. My orders are to bring you to the Praetor at once!"

"Am I under arrest?"

"My orders are to bring you to Gaius Aufinius."

"Why?"

"My orders are to bring you to Gaius Aufinius."

Clearly, the lictor was not inclined to be forthcoming. So be it. Quintus couldn't put on his toga; he didn't have one. But the wide-eyed slaveboy brought him his armor, still uncleaned, and, with some distaste, Quintus slid his stinking tunic over his head, followed by his armor. He did not attempt to strap and buckle it, though, for the lictors had the authority to unbind those axes and behead him if they so chose, and Quintus had no intention of providing them with an excuse. There must be some mistake! Varus had surely returned. But was the news for good or ill?

The lictors, impassive, gave nothing away, but Quintus soon knew the truth from the long faces and unfriendly glances of the senators they passed even as the lictors marched him up the steps of the Rostrum. Whatever fate had befallen the two legions was not good.

"Quintus Tullius, son of Virius Tullius." The praetor called out his name in a deep, sonorous voice, and it echoed ominously across the open square. Not many people were about at the moment, but those few who were turned their heads. "Tribune of the Seventh Legion, in service to the late Legatus Flavius Mamercus."

"Yes, Gaius Aufinius," Quintus answered, his voice breaking a little. His uncertainty as to whether he was under arrest or not was making him nervous. He could feel the sweat beginning to form under his arms already, and cleared his throat. "That is me."

The praetor nodded acknowledgment, barely glancing at him before turning to the group of twelve or so men standing together to Quintus's left. Quintus had not noticed them at first, but as soon as he saw them he realized he was in serious trouble. Some of Æmor's leading popolares were in the midst of that group, and to a man, they were allies of Lucius Valerius, whose head, Quintus assumed, was very likely adorning a lance belonging to King Caerwyn Everbright.

"Who lays the charges?"

"I do," answered a tall man with a red beard and a purple stripe on his toga. He was a curator, and worse, a Lucian, the cousin of Lucius Varus.

"Then speak, Lucius Ahenobarbus."

"I accuse Quintus Tullius of treachery! I accuse Quintus Tullius of cowardice in the face of the enemy! I accuse Quintus Tullius of fleeing the battlefield!" The man's voice was a loud one, a deep professional speaker's bass that projected throughout the square and beyond, and curious onlookers began to enter the square. "I accuse Quintus Tullius of sorcery, of complicity in the murder of his legate, Flavius Mamercus, and in the betrayal of the legions of Æmor!"

Quintus blinked, struck dumb by the outlandish monstrosity of the accusations against him. Had there been treachery? It was possible. They had surely stuck their necks in the noose at the pass. But what could it possibly have to do with him? He was no commander. He was only a lowly tribune!

"How say you, Quintus Tullius?" The praetor sounded almost bored and did not even bother to look at Quintus.

"Innocent! I am innocent!" he shouted. He stared wildly about the crowd gathering beneath him. "I have done no wrong!"

"Then you have nothing to fear," said the praetor, but in such an off-handed, unconcerned manner that Quintus suddenly felt almost as frightened as he had at Ardus Wald.

"I am no traitor," he shouted. "Not a month ago, I was given the grass crown by the centurion Brutus, first spear of the Seventh!"

"Liar!" The cry rose from the group of men behind his accuser and they quickly drowned out his protests. Neither the praetor nor the lictors saw fit to quiet them until one of the lictors moved behind Quintus and placed an exposed tip of his sharp axe at the base of Quintus's neck. "You will not speak unless spoken to, Quintus Tullius, or I shall behead you right here. This is not about you, so just play along and we'll see that you don't come to any harm."

Silenced by the threat of the sharp metal, Quintus was forced to stand and listen to the lies concocted by the popolares. He was to be a scapegoat, he realized as he listened to the so-called witnesses tell vicious fictions about how he had met secretly with the elf king, how he had arranged for his legion to enter the pass last, and how before the ambush had triggered, he had climbed to the safety of hills. The accusations were submitted by affadavits signed by eyewitnesses from all three legions, forged, beyond any shadow of a doubt.

Their purpose, he realized as his fear mounted with every lie, each grander than the last, was to salvage the reputation of the late Lucius Varus. His allies might mourn his loss, but even more they must fear the repercussions of his failure. But why him? He was merely a tribune, and he could produce hundreds of witnesses to attest to his innocence!

Because Flavius Mamercus was dead, he realized, as his blood ran cold. The accusations grew ever more absurd, and despite his fear, Quintus almost began to get bored. At this rate, before nightfall they'd be accusing him of fathering himself by raping his mother.

The theory, garbled as it was, appeared to be that Quintus practiced sorcery in secret and hoped that the evil elves would install him as a puppet Amorran sorcerer-king. It was wildly ridiculous, but when the long list of lies finally came to an end, the praetor had only two questions for him.

"Is it true, Quintus Tullius, that you are a sorcerer?"

"No!"

"Is it true, Quintus Tullius, that you can see auras of magic?"

Immaculatus, they knew! But how?

The praetor still refused to look at him, and Quintus realized that the man was avoiding his eyes because enough of a conscience remained to him that he dared not meet the gaze of one he was about to murder. Quintus's first instinct was to deny the charge, but he knew that they must have a witness in hand . . . yes, there, waiting in anticipation behind a fruitseller's stand was Nicander, one of the tribunes from the Seventh. He must have been one of Varus's spies, curse it, and if Quintus perjured himself now, his word would be worthless to defend himself against the other charges.

He took a deep breath and looked down at the crowd. "Yes, but—"

The crowd, larger now, audibly gasped. A buzzing of voices broke out just as the axe blade jabbed deeper into his skin and the voice in his ear snarled for silence. Alarmed, he complied, and that mistake sealed his doom, for no one could hear his explanations after the crowd erupted a moment later. It was responding to the praetor loudly banging the heel of his staff against the marble in indication of a verdict.

"Condemned out of his own mouth! I pronounce you guilty, Quintus Tullius, of sorcery, treachery, and blasphemy! You shall be gagged, bound, and thrown from the Rock of Tarvas! May the Immaculate One have mercy on your soul."

When Quintus opened his mouth to protest the outrage, the lictor behind him slipped in a gag and drew it tight. Despairingly, he thrashed away from the man, but four of the man's fellows were quick to seize him. Quintus could not believe it! Had he survived Aldus Wald only to be murdered by his fellow Amorrans? The crowd was going wild, some were jeering at him, others, more rational, were shouting at the praetor.

"To the rock!" the senator boomed in his deep, carrying voice, and Quintus knew that he was dead. Oh, the shame that this would bring his father! Immaculatus, why did You not let me die with honor at the pass? Did You bring me back here for this?

I did not scorn a criminal's death. The voice flickered through his panicked mind, sounding almost amused. *Be at peace.*

Be at peace? Are You mad? I'm being murdered here! Quintus would have shaken his fist at the sky again if he could have only gotten it free. The lictors were wrapping him with thick ceremonial cords, the sort executioners used to strangle their victims; he noticed that the praetor had already disappeared. Off to collect his thirty pieces of silver, no doubt. Quintus hoped that the craven man too would be dead with tomorrow's dawn.

But as the lictors carried him down the steps, he could hear some sort of commotion ahead of him. "Stop," he heard a commanding voice thunder over the crowd, and to his surprise, his would-be executioners stopped. He craned his neck around, trying to see what was happening, but as they were holding him barely above waist-level, he could see nothing but legs, togas, and the occasional sword.

"Put him down . . . on his feet," the voice ordered, qualifying the command just in time as Quintus felt the lictors' hold on him relax. When they rotated him about and stood him upright, Quintus was surprised to see that this potential rescuer wore the royal blue cape of the Lazuli, the princely cadre of sixty-six archpriests who stood below no living man save the Sanctiff himself. Better yet, it was Julius Albus, a man Quintus knew to be an acquaintance of his father's. "Get that out of his mouth."

Quintus retched and coughed so hard he doubled over. Still, he felt tremendously relieved, at least until he realized that Albus was not looking at him. Nor did the Lazulus show any signs of ordering him released. His heart sank again when he heard Albus tell Ahenobarbus and the head lictor that the verdict was void, not due to its irregularities, but because the Sanctiff was claiming prior right of trial.

"The civil authority is subject to the Church authority where matters of sorcery and blasphemy are involved. Crimes of treason and the like are of no account when compared with the greater danger posed by mortal crimes against Church law."

When one of the lictors seemed disposed to argue, Albus gestured, and twelve Redeemed, ex-gladiators all, silently flanked him, six to a side. They belonged to the Church's most fanatical order, and each of them was scarred and hard, for all that they now served the Lamb instead of the Wolf. The lictor quickly closed his mouth, and even the curator decided that he was not inclined to argue the issue. A second gesture, and Quintus was again swept up from the ground, no more gently than before.

As the Redeemed carried him off toward the great alabaster building that housed the White Throne, Quintus found himself wondering if perhaps it wouldn't have been better if they'd simply hurled him from the heights. From what he'd seen at the pass, a quick death on the rocks was likely rather better than a slow and painful one by earth, water, and fire.

But once around the corner and out of sight of the crowd, the Lazulus ordered Quintus unbound. An armed Redeemed remained on either side of him, each holding an arm, but in a manner that suggested that they were primarily intending to help him keep his balance after his rough treatment. The walk to the Sanctiff's palace was not far, and by the time they entered it, Quintus was starting to hope that he might even survive these bizarre machinations. The only thing that worried him was that Albus had not spoken so much as a single word to him.

The Lazulus stopped before a tall pair of arched doors, nodding to the guards posted there. Then he turned toward Quintus, and for the first time his expression showed familiarity. "I cannot say that you have nothing to fear, Quintus Tullius, for I do not know the truth of the matter. But I can tell you this; the Sanctiff takes little note of the Senate and its political intrigues. So there may be hope for you. But if you have entangled yourself in the black arts, rest assured that there will be no saving you."

Quintus nodded. "I understand. But if I may ask you for a favor?"

"You may ask . . . "

"Please tell my father that I am here. Otherwise, I fear he will think me dead. And please assure him that I have never soiled my soul with sorcery of any kind."

Albus nodded his acquiescence without expression. "I will do so."

"Thank you, Julius Albus," Quintus bowed deeply, and when the Lazulus departed, he allowed the waiting guards to escort him through the doors and down the long corridor to the cell that awaited him. He smiled upon entering it; for all that it was a prison, and a sparse one at that, it was the height of opulence compared to what he'd known of late.

Locked in his windowless cell, he might have lost track of the time were it not for the faint sound of the priests singing the evening Vespers every night. By his reckoning, it was five days before he was visited by anyone but the silent father who brought him a simple but healthy meal of bread, wine, and fruit three times a day. Lacking anything for entertaiment, Quintus found himself musing uncharacteristically on the utter point-lessness of Æmor's war with the wood elves. Even if Varus had been a wiser general, even if Everbright had not proved to be so cunning, what would have been the benefit?

Treasure? The Amorran treasury was full, at least as far as he knew. Fame? Æmor's legions had been victorious so many times that only the historians could count the number of tri-umphs that had been celebrated, let alone who had won the glory. Power? Quintus was no merchant, but he found it diffi-cult to see how possession of the Merithaim elvenwoods would bestow the city with any additional strategic advantage against her foes. The legions much preferred the more straightforward fighting that took place on the plains and hills than the chaos that so often prevailed in the wilder hinterlands.

About the time that he was expecting his last meal on the fifth day, he was surprised to see Julius Albus standing at the open door of his cell. But this time, his blue cloak was pinned with a gold broach and he was not accompanied by uncouth ex-gladiators, but six Sanctal Guards resplendent in silver and scarlet.

"Come with us, Quintus Tullius," he ordered. Something in his eyes warned Quintus to hold his tongue and reserve his questions for later. He obediently followed the Lazulus, and as he did so, the Guards fell into position on either side of him, though they did not lay hands on him or on their weapons.

At the end of a walk that took him through enough turns to leave him thoroughly confused, they came to a small wooden door, unmarked. Albus held up a hand and entered, then returned and bid him follow. It was, Quintus learned, a side entrance to the great chamber in which the Sanctiff was enthroned.

It was not, however, the sight of the small elderly man in a light blue robe that caught his attention and took his breath away. Nor was it the huge alabaster throne on which he sat, carved from a single piece of ivory that was purported to have once been the jawbone of Leviathan. No, it was the welcome, if unexpected, sight of six men standing in chains before that throne that caused his heart to leap within his breast.

Gaius Aufinius, the Urban Praetor, was there, and next to him was Ahenobarbus, the red-bearded cousin of the late general. Nicander too was there, along with another of his accusers and a broad-shouldered man that might have been one of the lictors. Aufinius seemed to shrink at the sight of him, though his eyes turned to the Sanctiff when the old priest raised his hand and pointed to a man standing near the back of the wall.

Quintus nearly fainted with relief at the sight of Brutus, still clad in his battered, battle-stained armor. Never had he seen a more welcome sight than the centurion's ugly, weathered face. And accompanying him were at least ten men of the legion, including two tribunes and several centurions.

"Publius Junius, we have already heard your testimony and that of your men. Now, is the man who has just been brought before us the man of whom you spoke?"

Brutus glanced over and met Quintus's eyes. He looked as determined and ready to fight as he had in the mountain pass, but he half-smiled and nodded his head briefly in acknowledgment of Quintus before answering.

"He is, your Holiness."

"What is his name?"

"Quintus Tullius Acerus, senior tribune of the Seventh Legion, your Holiness."

"Thank you, Publius Junius." The Sanctiff turned to the look at the six men, and for the first time, Quintus understood that it was not him who was on trial, but his former accusers. His would-be murderers. Then the Sanctiff cleared his throat, and in a loud voice that echoed through the chamber, pronounced his judgment.

"Let it be known that these men are oathbreakers, false witnesses, and are guilty of attempted murder under the color of Amorran law. They have offended not only the dignity of the city of Æmor and its citizens, but also that of its Holy and Most Immaculate Church. I hereby remand them to the justice of the Curia and may God have mercy on their souls, for they shall find none here in Æmor."

"It is written," said a clerk from the side of the room, scribbling furiously. He passed the parchment to a young man seated next to him, who added no more than a line with a quilled pen.

"It is signed," he said, passing it to the third man at the table. The last clerk dipped a great stamp in wax that was heated above a small brazier beside him and slammed it down upon the parchment.

"It is sealed."

Quintus looked at the doomed men. No influence would save them now, not even if all three Consuls spoke for them. Ahenobarbus had turned white under his beard, and a mixture of horror and fear filled the faces of the others, though they remained silent. Aufinius alone remained composed; he looked more thoughtful than afraid. Nicander looked as if he might be sick. As Quintus watched, he swayed on his feet and nearly fell.

It would be better if he held silent. And yet, how could he allow a man, a fellow soldier, to go to his grave for nothing more than speaking the truth. Oh, but the temptation was great indeed. Then he saw a tear roll down Nicander's cheek, and he knew he could not hold tongue, not if he wished to live with himself.

"Your Holiness!" He stepped forward, and in a flash, two swords were pointing at him, arresting his progress. "May I speak?"

The Sanctiff regarded him with an air of curiousity, then nodded.

"I do not believe Marcus Longinus, the tribune there, bears any guilt in the matter. He spoke truly when he told them that I could see the spellcasters, so he did not perjure himself, as did the others. He has committed no crime."

The white eyebrows of His Holiness, the Sanctified Castimonius II, seemed to rise of their own accord as a brief, disbelieving murmur swelled throughout the room, then hushed as quickly as it had arisen. The Sanctiff, staring hard at Quintus, pushed himself slowly from his throne, then made his way down the seven steps from the dais upon which it sat. He walked, somewhat stiffly, and approached Quintus; though his shoulders were hunched and his head barely came to Quintus's chest, the young officer could feel power radiating from the man like the heat of the mountain sun. His eyes burned like flaming emeralds, seeming to see right through to the depths of a man's soul.

"You are no sorcerer, my son?"

"No, your Holiness."

"And yet you could see the works of the evil ones?"

"Yes, your Holiness."

The Sanctiff peered into his face, but the green eyes no longer burned. Instead, they seemed to be unsettled. "You had only to keep your counsel, and yet you chose to speak to defend your fellow. Most interesting. Is it possible that you have an explanation for this . . . seeming dichotomy?"

"Yes, your Holiness." Quintus swallowed hard. "I believe I could see them because we were being slaughtered and I . . . called out to the Immaculate One. In . . . in anger, your Holiness. I am sorry."

He was surprised to see a flicker of amusement suddenly appear on the old man's face. It was gone in a moment, but it had unmistakably been there, if only for a moment.

"The best prayers come from the heart, my son. It seems that yours was answered."

Then the Sanctiff did the last thing that Quintus, or anyone else in the great chamber, expected. He clumsily kneeled down in front of the young officer and drew Quintus's hand to his forehead.

"Bless me, your Holiness. Bless you me, my son."

• • •

The young priest frowned as his elder finished the story he had been telling. "That's it? But I always thought Saint Oculatus was a mighty warrior?"

The older priest smiled. He was a big man, built like an oak, and his skin was nearly as wrinkled and sun-hardened as bark. "He was a mighty warrior, merely not in the sense that you are thinking. After Aldus Wald, Saint Oculatus never took the field again, Horatio. Nor did he join the priesthood, although his second son did join our order after it was founded by Gnaus Gallus with the blessing of His Holiness. And yet, are we not as surely his children as were those who sprang from his loins? Now, are you ready to try again?"

"Yes, brother."

The older man nodded to a small figure standing in the shadow of a tree. It was a goblin, and a small example of the type at that. But the young priest couldn't help trembling a little as he stepped out and advanced toward it, holding his shield as if he was hoping to hide his entire body behind it. For the goblin was no ordinary ahomus, but a battlemage, a captured prisoner given special dispensation to practice his unholy magic here so that the Michaeline warrior-priests might learn how to defeat it with their immaculate faith.

"Remember, we are not given a spirit of fear, lad," his instructor called, even as he raised a finger. The goblin pointed both hands at the armor-clad young man and said something in his guttural, inhuman tongue. They began to glow, and a moment later, two bolts of purple fire leaped from his hand toward his target.

As they did, the young man shouted something unintelligible, but there was a noticeable tremor in his voice. The bolts
slammed into the shield and sent it flying into the air as the lad
tumbled onto his back. His shield landed in front of the elder
Michaeline, showing two more scorch marks on the much
abused metal. The warrior-priest sighed, shook his head, and
went to help the shaken youth back to his feet.

"I don't know if you're watching, Quintus Tullius," he muttered to himself, "but if you are, I suspect this one may need
your help."

FINIS

Printed in the United States
126029LV00001B/3/P